From: Cory

Dellosso establishes himself as a tian horror. His books delve in yet come out blazing with the light of God's power and forgiveness. *Darlington Woods* is fast-paced, creepy, and sure to spur readers toward a deeper walk with Christ. I'm a certified Mike Dellosso fan!

—Eric Wilson
New York Times Best-selling Author
of *Fireproof* and *Haunt of Jackals*

Mike Dellosso's brilliant light shines into the dark places of the human heart and illuminates our most terrible fears. Don't look away, because the only way out of Darlington Woods is through it, and it's a journey you'll want to take.

—Erin Healy
Author of *Never Let You Go* and
Coauthor with Ted Dekker of *Kiss* and *Burn*

Taut, tense, and frightening. A high-speed ride that will keep you guessing until the end.

—Tosca Lee
Author of *Demon: A Memoir*

Terrifying and exhilarating, *Darlington Woods* is a heart-wrenching and soul-healing story of a father's—and the Father's—love. One of my favorite writers, Mike Dellosso delivers a book that readers will find almost impossible to put down. Action junkies, mystery lovers, and supernatural fans will be held captive by the dark journey through *Darlington Woods*. Keep the lights on—and be assured that the talented Dellosso will take you on a journey by the light that *always* shines in the darkness.

—Kathryn Mackel
Author of *Vanished*

Dellosso never disappoints, and *Darlington Woods* is no exception. With spine-tingling suspense and Dellosso's trademark spiritual message that lingers long after the last page, *Darlington Woods* joins *The Hunted* and *Scream* as must-read chillers.

—SUSAN SLEEMAN
THESUSPENSEZONE.COM

Once again Mike Dellosso manages to shine the light of God's grace into the darkest crevices of the human condition with amazing clarity. Just when I thought Mike had bested himself in *Scream*, he brings us face-to-face with monsters so vivid they can only be real. *Darlington Woods* is his best yet, though I am sure he has even darker corners yet to explore.

—TIM GEORGE
FICTIONADDICT.COM

Dellosso skillfully blends suspense, symbolism, and the supernatural into a compelling thriller in the vein of Dekker and Peretti. Gray isn't a color in Dellosso's moral palette, and *Darlington Woods* makes that clear. This is a powerful story you'll be thinking about long after closing the book.

—C. J. DARLINGTON
COFOUNDER OF TITLETRAKK.COM AND
AUTHOR OF *THICKER THAN BLOOD*

DARLINGTON
WOODS

DARLINGTON
WOODS

Mike Dellosso

REALMS
A STRANG COMPANY

Most STRANG COMMUNICATIONS BOOK GROUP products are available at special quantity discounts for bulk purchase for sales promotions, premiums, fund-raising, and educational needs. For details, write Strang Communications Book Group, 600 Rinehart Road, Lake Mary, Florida 32746, or telephone (407) 333-0600.

DARLINGTON WOODS by Mike Dellosso
Published by Realms
A Strang Company
600 Rinehart Road
Lake Mary, Florida 32746
www.strangbookgroup.com

The characters portrayed in this book are fictitious unless they are historical figures explicitly named. Otherwise, any resemblance to actual people, whether living or dead, is coincidental.

Cover design by Justin Evans
Design Director: Bill Johnson

Visit the author's Web site at www.MikeDellosso.com.

Library of Congress Cataloging-in-Publication Data:

Dellosso, Mike.
  Darlington Woods / by Mike Dellosso. -- 1st ed.
     p. cm.
  ISBN 978-1-59979-918-6
  1. Missing children--Fiction. 2. Psychological fiction. I. Title.
  PS3604.E446D37 2010
  813'.6--dc22
                                        2009048377
First Edition

10 11 12 13 14 — 9 8 7 6 5 4 3 2 1
Printed in the United States of America

To all those who have faced and fought
that monster called cancer—this one's for
you. Shine your light.

Acknowledgments

WELL, HERE WE ARE AGAIN, ANOTHER BOOK complete and many thanks to go around. I'm not one to waste time with copious words, so how about we get to it. Many thanks go out to:

- My wife, Jen, who nursed me, encouraged me, and loved me through our battle with cancer. She is the inspiration for all my writing, my never-tiring fan, and my partner in all I do.

- My three sweet little girls—Laura, Abby, and Caroline. You're not old enough to read Daddy's stories yet, but someday you will be…and I hope I make you proud.

- My parents, for always supporting me and reminding me to never give up.

- My agent, Les Stobbe, for navigating me through the murky waters of all the business stuff I hate dealing with.

- My editors—Debbie Marrie, Lori Vanden Bosch, and Deborah Moss—and my publicist, LeAnn Hamby, for rooting me on and making me feel special. I always know you're on my side. I don't thank you enough.

- The rest of the folks at the Strang Book Group, from the design team to the sales team to the marketing team and everyone in between. I couldn't have done this without you. That should go without saying... but it still needs to be said.

- To my readers, without you I'd just be writing stories, but you make this writing thing a ministry. You make it worth all the hard work. I love your comments. Keep 'em coming.

- And last but in no conceivable way least, to my Savior and Friend, Jesus, who brought me through the toughest journey of my life, carrying me all the way. I owe everything to You.

Foreword

Let's talk about monsters, shall we? Let's just sit down and spend a little time in conversation about things that go bump in the night and images that haunt us while we sleep peacefully in our beds in our own homes.

They're real, you know, those monsters—just as real as the book you're holding and the words you're reading. Yes, it's a secret I have. Please don't tell anyone. I believe in monsters. I've seen them, even battled them. And no, I assure you, I'm not crazy.

Oh, I'm not talking about the stuff of old movies or comic books or children's tales. Not even the stuff of grown-up stories like the one you're about to read, but monsters are monsters, and the fear they ignite is all the same and very real.

The monsters of which I speak are around us every day and come in varying forms. They are called cancer...Parkinson's...juvenile arthritis. Or they come in the form of a lousy drunk who can't keep his hands off his teenage daughter, a maniacal boss with an axe to grind, or a husband who has nothing kind to say to his wife and kids. These monsters are abuse and murder and neglect. And the web they spin, the wounds they carve, the hatchet they swing all go by the same name: fear.

It's funny how things work out in life. During the editing phase of my last novel, *Scream*, I was diagnosed with colon cancer, a formidable monster in its own right. *Scream* is all about life and death, and if there's one thing to get you thinking about that dichotomy it's cancer. Now, during the editing phase of *Darlington Woods*, the story you are about to read, my youngest daughter, just seven, was diagnosed with juvenile arthritis. *Darlington Woods* is all about the monsters in our life and the fear they instill. To be a parent watching your seven-year-old suffer with the joints of a seventy-year-old is a fearful thing.

From now on, I think I'll be very careful about the themes behind the stories I write.

But these are the monsters all of us encounter in life. They're real and scary, and they're not going away.

I get asked all the time why I write the kind of stories I write. Why am I fascinated with the scary and horrifying? My answer is always the same: Aren't we all fascinated with it? Whether real monsters or the ones of lore and legend, aren't we all fixated on things that afflict us with fear?

I told my oncologist this once, that people think I'm strange because of the places my imagination goes and the things I pull out of my head. His response was right on. He said (in his Irish accent), "Michael, the things in your head are the same things that are in all of our heads; it's just that you aren't afraid to explore them." Well said.

So why do I write stories of fright and horror? You ask the question assuming I have a choice. I write the stories that naturally blossom in my head and infuse them with themes that are heavy on my heart. I didn't put them there; they were there all along. I simply go with the natural flow of that river of imagination.

So how about you embark on a journey with me to a place where reality meets fantasy, a place of monsters that are just as real as the monsters in our own world, a place where fear has teeth and darkness is a thing unto itself. It's not so much different from our own world, you know. It's not so much different from our own hearts. And hopefully, if I've done my job well, you'll see a little of yourself there and discover a way to conquer your own fear and find your way out of the darkness.

Welcome to *Darlington Woods*.

—MIKE DELLOSSO
www.MikeDellosso.com

Prologue

1987
Darlington Woods, northern Maryland

T HE SCREAMS WERE EVERYWHERE, PIERCING THE darkness like spears. Surrounding him. Closing in. Mixing with the wails and torturous moans of the other men.

Asher Wiggins ran pell-mell through the woods, blindly rolling over saplings and crashing through clumps of honeysuckle. Thickets pulled at his clothes, left jagged trails of blood on his skin. His bandaged face throbbed in time with his quickened pulse.

And still the screams grew closer.

To his right, Jerry hollered then went down in a complicated crash of crunching leaves and breaking sticks. The sound that followed reminded Asher of a pack of rabid dogs in a feeding frenzy.

Only it wasn't dogs. Far from it.

He came to a ridge where the ground sloped downward at a sharp angle for thirty yards or so, bottomed out, then rose on the other side. Lungs working furiously to keep the oxygen coming, heart in his throat, Asher stole a quick look around. To his left, in the distance, he heard Abe trip on a fallen limb and hit the ground hard. He knew it was Abe by the sound of his wheezing. Within moments he heard them attack—he didn't even know what they were. The sound of Abe's piteous screams for help sent chills racing along Asher's nerves.

He turned and pushed himself down the slope. He stumbled mostly out of control but somehow was able to keep his feet under him. At the bottom he looked up and saw a dark pulsating shadow at the top of the ridge. It was them.

"God help me."

One of them let out a terrible scream, like a woman in great pain, and they all responded similarly.

Without thinking, Asher turned and started climbing the opposite slope. His legs burned and his lungs were on fire, but adrenaline kept him moving.

"God help me, God help me, God help me..." he said over and over as he climbed, finding purchase with both hands and feet, grabbing on to saplings and branches where he could.

The gauze covering half his face—a hastily assembled bandage—was soaked with blood and working loose. It dangled like a lame wing.

Behind him he heard the crash of the horde as it charged down the slope, screaming and hissing.

Faster he climbed, clawing at the ground, pulling himself forward and upward. Finally at the top, he ran a few feet and stopped. He could go no further. His legs felt boneless, and every blood vessel in his body beat in sync with his rapid breathing. His vision blurred, and his chest tightened.

Asher tried to breathe deep, but his diaphragm spasmed and refused to cooperate. The woods started to spin around him, and he collapsed onto his back. The bandage peeled away like an old scab and left his wounds open to the air.

He could hear the horde coming up the slope now. But there was nothing he could do. He looked up with his one working eye—past the limbs, past the leaves—and found the early morning sky. It was just beginning to lighten with the dawn of day. He'd been in the woods all night.

His last thought before closing his eyes and accepting what may come was a passage from Scripture he'd used in a sermon recently:

> *The Lord is my light and my salvation, whom shall I fear?*

PART ONE

It is a fearful thing to love what death can touch.

—UNKNOWN

One

Present day

Ａs he pressed his beat-up Ford down an uneven stretch of asphalt, Rob Shields had death on his mind. His own.

The void within him had grown to colossal proportions, opening its gaping black maw and swallowing any hope or happiness he once had. Lost forever. No chance of return. Death welcomed him, enticed him, drew him in with its easy ways and comfortable charm.

Oh, he knew he would never do it. Taking his own life had a certain appeal to it, held a certain freedom that his bleak outlook on life longed for, but it took a much braver—or dumber—man than he to actually pull it off. But still he wanted, maybe *needed*, to pretend he was as serious as murder. And that meant it was time to see the house. If he was to fantasize about putting an end to his journey, he at least wanted to see the place that had promised a better life. Just one visit, one look, would satisfy him.

He glanced over at the empty passenger seat then into the rearview mirror at the vacant spot in the backseat. Kelly would be jabbering about what beautiful country this was.

"Look at the wildflowers. Oh, I love wildflowers."

And little Jimmy would be singing away to his MP3 player, getting the lyrics all wrong.

Man, he missed them.

A familiar sadness overcame him, and he once again thought of his own death. He couldn't bear to live without them any longer...

Life had become a great burden, an endless source of sadness. Every day was lived in despair. Unhappiness and discontent had become his bedfellows. He would see the house, allow himself one evening of pleasant dreams about what could have been, then return to Massachusetts to live out the rest of his life in isolated misery. And in his mind, that in itself was a form of suicide. A living death.

Rob depressed the accelerator, and the odometer needle climbed nearer to seventy. On the horizon, heat devils performed an arrhythmic dance, and the sun-scorched blacktop appeared to be glossed with mercury. The road cut through pastureland like a hardened artery. To his right, a handful of horses stood motionless, their noses to the ground. To his left, the land stretched out like a green sea, undulating slowly to an even tempo.

Mayfield had to be no more than an hour away, but the fuel gauge said he needed gas now. Up ahead, an elderly man in a ball cap was on both knees working his garden. Rob slowed the car and stopped beside him. The older gent turned his body slowly, revealing a patch over one eye.

Rob leaned across the center console and spoke loudly. "Where's the nearest gas station?"

The old man cupped one hand around his ear and raised his eyebrows.

Rob said it louder. "Where's the nearest gas station?"

The man nodded in the direction Rob had been traveling. "'Bout a mile down the road. Shell station on the left."

"Thanks," Rob said, and he pulled away. In the rearview

mirror he could see the man watch him for a moment then return to his garden.

Exactly one mile down the road Rob steered into a cracked-asphalt lot and up to an old-style analog gas pump, the kind with the rotating numbers. He didn't even know those kind still existed. The station had seen better days. From the sun-bleached Shell sign to the grime-coated plate-glass window of the little convenience store to the scarred and faded blacktop, everything spoke of neglect. This was one outpost time had forgotten.

Rob got out of the car and noticed the handwritten sign on the pump: *Pre-pay inside. Management.*

Walking across the lot, he could feel the day's heat radiating through the soles of his shoes. A little bell chimed when he opened the door. A thin, fair-skinned man with shoulder-length hair nodded at him from behind the counter.

"Thirty in gas," Rob said, reaching for his wallet.

The clerk punched some buttons on the register and said, "Thirty."

Rob paid him. "How far to Mayfield?"

The clerk looked up. "Where?"

"Mayfield."

After a quick shrug, "Fifty, sixty miles." He looked like he wanted to say more, so Rob waited. "Not much in Mayfield."

"A house," Rob said.

"Your house?"

"Should have been." Then he turned and left. The bell chimed again on his way out.

At the pump, Rob unscrewed the fuel cap and inserted the nozzle. Jimmy always loved to squeeze the trigger.

"Can I pull the trigger, Daddy?"

That's what he called it, a trigger. He'd pretend the nozzle was a cowboy gun. Thoughts of his son flooded Rob's mind, and he did nothing to stop them. Now was a time for remembering, for soaking up every good feeling and every fond image left to enjoy.

When the rolling numbers hit seventeen dollars, a quick movement caught Rob's attention. He jerked his head up and toward the side of the store where a stand of shrubs sat quiet and motionless. Then he heard it, a muffled giggle, and his breath caught in his throat. He knew that giggle. Knew it like the sound of his own voice. The movement was there again. An image ran from the shrubs to the rear of the store and out of sight. The nozzle snapped off and fell to the ground with a solid clunk. Rob knew that run too, the shortened stride, the slightly exaggerated pumping of the arms. He could feel his heart thudding all the way down to his fingertips.

It was Jimmy. His little buddy.

Crossing the lot in large walking strides at first, then a run, Rob rounded the building fully expecting to find his son, Jimmy, red-faced with brown hair matted to his forehead, waiting in a crouch to scare him.

"I got you, Daddy!"

Instead, all he found were a few rusted-out fifty-gallon drums, a stack of dry-rotted tires, and a haphazard pile of rebar. His breathing rate had quickened from the short sprint, and beads of sweat now popped out on his forehead and upper lip. He wiped them away with the sleeve of his T-shirt.

He walked the length of the building, scanning the field of knee-high grass behind it. "Jimmy?"

But no answer came. Not even a rustle of grass. And no giggle.

"Jimmy," Rob said in a normal volume, more to himself than the phantom of his son that had haunted him now for going on two months. The visions—the psychologist called them hallucinations—had come frequently at first, sometimes as much as once a day, then grew more sporadic. Until now, he hadn't had one for over two weeks. At first, Rob was convinced there was a purpose to them, a meaning. Maybe they even meant Jimmy was still alive, waiting for his daddy to find him and rescue him. Maybe. The psychologist disagreed. Rob thought he was a quack and stopped attending the weekly sessions.

Scolding himself for once again allowing his frazzled imagination to dupe him, Rob returned to his car like a man taking his final stroll down the long corridor to the electric chair. The sun's heat now seemed more intense, and his shirt clung to his back and chest.

He picked the nozzle up from the ground and balanced it in his hand.

"Can I pull the trigger, Daddy?"

Every time he pumped gas he'd think of Jimmy. It was one of those little things that would haunt him the rest of his life. But it was a haunting he welcomed. After squeezing out the rest of his thirty bucks, Rob returned the nozzle to the pump, opened the car door, and was hit by a breath of heat.

Sitting in his car was like hanging out in an oven, but Rob did not turn the ignition. The air outside was still and the heat sweltering. Sweat seeped from his pores, wetting the front of his shirt. He thought of the image of his son and that familiar gait and noticed his hands were trembling. Tears formed in his eyes, blurring his vision.

"Jimmy." He said the name again, as if it were some holy word that could cross the span of the finite and infinite and bring his little boy back. He wanted to hold him, bury his face in Jimmy's hair, and draw in the smell of sweat and cookies.

"I like how you smell, Daddy. You smell like a daddy."

Wiping the tears from his eyes, Rob started the car, pulled away from the pump, and headed east toward Mayfield.

As he drove, the empty seats beside and behind him burned like hot coals. As much as he tried, he could not dismiss the memory of Kelly reaching over and placing a graceful hand on his thigh, her hair rippling in the wind, a smile stretched across her face. Nor could he stop glancing in the rearview mirror, half hoping to see Jimmy bouncing against the back of the seat.

Rob slapped at the steering wheel. He knew he was going mad, that the solitude of the last three months had nearly driven him over the edge and blurred the line between reality and fantasy. And he was obsessing again. He had to think of something else, so he turned his mind to the house his great-aunt Wilda had left him. He'd never seen the place, had never even met Wilda. But when he found out he was the sole heir to the house, his mother raved about how much Kelly and Jimmy would love the place. That was six months ago.

Before his world got flipped on its head and everything went to pot.

Before he went insane and entertained thoughts of death.

The boy and his mommy walk back to the car to clean his hands. He's been working on a candy apple for some time, and it's creating quite the mess. Daddy told them he'd meet them at the lemonade stand. Lemonade is great for a warm day, he said. The grass in the parking area is brown and ground into the dry dirt from everyone walking and driving on it. His mommy is holding his clean hand and singing a Sunday school song about Joshua and the battle of Jericho. The boy is still thinking about the eagle the man behind the table was holding. He never knew eagles were so big. And when it looked at him, it seemed to see right past his skin and into his insides. They had other things at the stand too—an owl with big yellow eyes, a couple different kinds of snakes, and an aquarium full of toads—but the eagle was his favorite. He wondered what it would be like to be able to fly like an eagle, way up in the sky where no one could bother you, seeing the whole world at once.

"Here we are," Mommy says. Their car looks extra clean because Daddy washed it just before they left. The black paint looks like a dark mirror and makes him look funny, like one of those curvy mirrors at the carnival.

Mommy opens the trunk and leans over into it, looking for the napkins. It reminds him of a poem about a crocodile with a toothache. He wishes he could remember all the words. Something about the crocodile opening so wide and the dentist climbing inside, then SNAP! Mommy always claps her hands real hard at that part, and it always makes him jump.

A man comes up behind Mommy. He's wearing dirty old blue jeans and a tight black T-shirt. His face is big and round, and there are a lot of little scars on his cheeks. His eyes are placed real close together and pushed back into his head. With his shaggy hair and large face, the boy thinks he looks like a head of cabbage.

"Excuse me," the man says. He reaches out to touch Mommy's hip then looks at the boy.

Mommy jumps and stands up fast. She turns around and looks at the man, crossing her arms in front of her. She seems nervous. "Yes?"

Cabbage Head looks nervous too. He pushes his hand through his hair, and the boy notices the sweat on his forehead. It makes his hair wet where it comes out of the skin. "It's your husband—"

Now Mommy looks scared. "Wha—what's wrong?" Her voice shakes.

"I need you to come with me." He looks at the boy with those deep eyes then back at Mommy. "The boy can stay here at the car. We'll only be a minute."

Mommy bites her lower lip and looks around. She kneels beside the boy. She looks real scared and is breathing fast. Her hands are shaking, and she's still biting her lower lip. "Stay here, OK? Don't leave the car. I'll be right back. Don't leave the car."

She hugs the boy then kisses him on the cheek. Opening the back door of the car, she motions for the boy to get in. "Remember, stay here. Don't go anywhere. I'll be back for you soon." She closes the door, blows him a kiss, and leaves with Cabbage Head. The boy watches as they walk away and disappear behind a trailer.

It doesn't take long for it to get too hot to stay in the car. He opens the door and slides out, staying low to the ground so no one will see him. He leans against the car, but the black metal is too hot. So he sits Indian-style on the ground next to the back tire and picks at the grass. He wonders what could be wrong with Daddy. Did he have a heart attack or get cancer? Mr. Davies next door got cancer last year and died. This scares the boy. Maybe Daddy's just lost and the man needs Mommy to help find him. He thinks about the man and his deep eyes. They were like the eagle's eyes. Something about them didn't look right, though. The boy feels like if he looked at them long enough he'd see things that would give him nightmares for a very long time. And they would see things in him too.

It seems like a long time of sitting by the tire and picking at brown grass before the boy hears footsteps coming, the sound of dry grass crunching like stale potato chips. He stands and looks around, hoping it's Mommy. But Cabbage Head is coming toward him, alone. Where's Mommy? Is she with Daddy, and the man is coming to take him to them?

Cabbage Head comes close. He's sweating even worse now, and his hair looks like it has been messed up. He offers the boy his hand, a big meaty thing that looks like a bear's paw. "C'mon, son. You must come with me."

"Where's my mom?" the boy asks. He notices his own voice is shaking.

"She's fine. She wants me to bring you to her."

The boy can tell the man is lying. He wants to run away but is afraid he'll never find Mommy or Daddy on his own. "Where is she?"

Cabbage Head closes his hand and opens it again. His wide palm is all shiny with sweat. "Come. She's waiting for you."

There's no way the boy is going to hold the man's hand. He turns to run but the man catches him by the arm. "Oh, no, you don't. You're coming with me."

The boy tries to holler, but the man's sweaty hand is over his mouth, pressing so hard it hurts. The boy has never known what it is like to be so scared. He's sure Cabbage Head is going to kill him, or worse, keep him alive but never allow him to see his mommy or daddy again.

Two

MAYFIELD WAS NOT MUCH MORE THAN ONE STREET lined with well-painted homes and meticulously manicured lawns. A large white sign with bold black letters that read *Mayfield: Home of Maryland's Oldest Apple Festival* welcomed passers through. On the west end of town, the end Rob entered, there was a small grocery store, a barber shop, and a hardware store, all looking to be well managed and maintained. On the east end, which could be seen from the west end, stood a small brick school that housed elementary through high school. Midway up Main Street, on the left side of the road heading east, Mt. Zion Methodist Church sat like a keystone, holding the two ends of town together with its white siding, steeply pitched slate roof, and sharp high spire. Across the street from the church was the town's only eatery, Mary Jane's Diner.

As Rob entered Mayfield, he slowed his car to a comfortable speed and glanced at the address of Great-aunt Wilda's house. 310 Main Street. Following the even numbered houses on the left side of the street he counted up by tens until he reached the three-hundred block, which happened to be the final block before Mayfield ended and more rolling hills began.

Wilda's house was the last place on the left. And it was not what Rob had expected. Styled after a Mexican adobe, the stucco walls were coated with green mildew. One window was busted out, and the ceramic corrugated roof was cracked in some places, broken in others. A large half-dead hickory with bark that looked like peeling skin provided spotty shade in the front yard. The lawn, where there was grass left, was shin-high and waiting to be harvested.

Rob smiled. He could hear Kelly raving about how much potential the place had.

"It's exactly the way I imagined it. Think of the possibilities. Oh, I already have a million ideas."

She was always the positive one.

He pulled the car into the driveway, shut off the engine, and got out. Looking back up Main Street, he realized for the first time how quiet the town was for a Saturday evening. No one was strolling the sidewalks; no one was doing yard work or enjoying a moment's rest on their front porch. No cars drifted past. The town appeared lifeless, as if it was some movie prop and the cast and crew had wrapped up for the day and gone home. Maybe the heat had driven everyone indoors.

He circled the house, noting the overgrown garden beds, the rusted and bent gutters, and another broken window. The backyard was wide but shallow, bumping up against a sprawling field. A few more large hickories dotted the yard. By the house, not twenty feet from the back door, stood a mature dogwood with low twisted branches. A great tree for climbing. Jimmy would love this place.

"Cool, Daddy, look! A climbing tree!"

Standing in the breezeway between the side door and the one-car garage, Rob was suddenly overcome with a feeling of déjà vu, as if he'd been here before and stood in this very spot, eyeing the very same silver aluminum storm door. The feeling was so familiar, so common, that it was even accompanied by an emotion. He noticed again that his hands were trembling. For several seconds he remained there, in the cool shade of the breezeway, holding his hands, trying to calm himself. And for an instant, the briefest of moments, he had second thoughts about entering the house. But he'd never been here before; he knew that. He'd never met Wilda, and he'd never seen her house. He would remember a place like this. The memory and emotion were bogus, mere trickery of the mind.

Digging in his pocket, Rob found the key he had been given, turned the lock, and went inside. A large living room dominated most of the single-story dwelling. Two small bedrooms, separated by a full bath, opened off the main room, and a small kitchen and dining area were found at the end of a short hallway. With the exception of some cracked and water-stained plaster ceilings, the interior was in better shape than the outside. The family had left the house fully furnished, and everything was covered with heavy plastic sheeting. Boxes were stacked shoulder high along the walls of the living room and in each bedroom. In one of the bedrooms was a wooden door that opened to a steep staircase that led to the attic.

A rumble in Rob's stomach reminded him he hadn't stopped for lunch, making it twelve hours since his last meal.

Before leaving, he looked around the inside of the house one more time, and for some reason he thought of the attic. There was something about the wooden door leading to it that he didn't like. It reminded him of…something, but he had no recall.

"You're definitely going crazy," he said to the silence of the house.

And then he left the house and the attic and the strange feelings behind and headed out to fill his belly.

Mary Jane's was your typical small-town diner complete with an up-front cash register, vinyl-upholstered booths, a "Please Seat Yourself" sign, and a dozen or so seniors eager to dip into their Social Security checks. Rob found a booth in the corner, out of the locals' way. He could already feel their heavy stares. Mayfield may have appeared friendly at first glance, but under all that whitewash and landscaping it was like any other hick town—closed to strangers. He wanted to make it known he wasn't there to upset the rhythm of the town. He could make himself invisible.

Within seconds of seating himself a young lady no more than twenty-five years old appeared dressed in khaki pants and a maroon shirt with "Mary Jane's Diner" stenciled in the upper left corner. She was not attractive in the familiar way, but her dark hair and pale skin and blueberry eyes held a unique kind of beauty, the kind that gets mostly overlooked at school dances and church socials.

She smiled wide, revealing two rows of bone white, perfectly aligned teeth, and placed a laminated menu in front of Rob. "Welcome to Mary Jane's, Mayfield's number one diner. Get you something to drink?"

"Number one diner, huh?"

"Number one."

"How 'bout a Diet Coke."

"Diet Coke is something I can do. By the way, I'm Juli. I

always forget that part." She appeared confident in a cute, bouncy sort of way.

"You forget your name?"

"My name?"

"Juli. Remember?"

"Oh, no, I've had that my whole life. I forget to introduce myself. Most people who come by here already know me. How's about you look over the menu, and I'll be right back with that Diet Coke." She turned to leave then spun back around. "Oh, yeah, our special tonight is a fish and chips platter, and the soups of the day are cheddar broccoli and chicken noodle."

Rob smiled. "Thanks, Juli."

She headed toward the kitchen, and Rob turned his attention to the menu. Out of habit, he first flipped it over to check what was available for kids. They had a hot dog meal. Jimmy would be all over that.

"I want a dippy-dog. I want a dippy-dog."

Before he knew it, Juli was back, setting the soda in front of him with a paper-covered straw.

"Have you decided yet?"

He hadn't. "Would you recommend the fish and chips?"

Juli smiled wide. "Only if you're a fan of fish sticks and potato chips."

"Memories of school lunches. I'll take it."

"Good or bad?"

"Excuse me?"

"Memories of school lunches. Good or bad?"

"School lunch memories are always good. I still crave the grilled cheese."

"Nothing compared."

Juli retreated again, and Rob took in his surroundings

with a more careful, yet furtive, eye. There were four rows of booths, each able to seat four adults. One row over sat a man and his wife, ignoring each other while they worked their meals like cows apathetically chewing their cud. Across the aisle was an old woman, stooped over her plate, staring at it as if it revealed some secret message she was given to decipher. She glanced at Rob then quickly returned her attention to her plate.

From the kitchen, the sound of clanging metal and tinkling silverware mixed with the aroma of cooked grease and fried oil.

Then Juli was back, large brown tray held at shoulder height. She set down the tray and served Rob his meal, placing each plate before him as if she were serving a king. When she was finished, she stood with her shoulders back and tray under her arm and nodded. "Fish and chips."

"Thanks," Rob said.

Juli motioned toward the plate on the table and said, "Otto makes good fried flounder, but I wouldn't want it for my last meal."

Just then an elderly woman appeared behind Juli. Her graying hair was pulled into a tight bun, and she wore a gray skirt and maroon cardigan.

Juli dipped her head and smiled politely. "That's my cue. I'll check back in a bit."

She headed back for the kitchen, and the older lady with the sour-lipped face filled her void. The lines around her eyes and mouth were deep crevices and told a story of happiness and laughter a very long time ago.

"Is everything OK?" she asked. Her back was so rigid and straight Rob expected to find a rod sewed to her sweater when she left.

"It's great. Thanks."

She eyed him down her thin nose for a moment then said, "Well, then. You staying long in Mayfield?"

Rob shrugged. "We'll see how the wind blows."

The bells over the door jingled, and Rob turned to see a man dressed in a white shirt and black pants standing by the register. He looked to be about fifty or so, but his skin was so white and smooth he could easily pass for younger. His peppery hair, cropped close and thinning a little at the crown, gave away his age, though. His clothes were outdated but in fine condition. But it was his skin Rob came back to. There was something different about it, something odd. It was too smooth and had a subtle sheen to it. It almost looked waxy, like one of those figures in Madame Tussauds Wax Museum.

The man looked over and met Rob with coal-black eyes. Rob's heart stuttered, and a buzz ran along the crest of his scalp and down the back of his neck. The man's eyes were so piercing, like black sabers in the hands of an accomplished swordsman. Rob could have sworn they looked into his soul and found the fear and gloom that resided there.

Immediately, the woman turned and headed for the man. In her stride was the cadence of decisiveness and determination. She said something to him and pointed at the door. Rob couldn't make out what she was saying, but her body language was throwing him out. When she had finished, the man sported an easy grin that boasted the woman's words had no effect on him, then dipped his chin and left.

The woman stood there a few moments, taking deep breaths, then spun around and returned to Rob. Her face was flushed, and she was obviously shaken.

"You OK?" Rob said.

The woman's hand went to her throat, and she swallowed hard. "Yes. Yes, of course." She glanced around the restaurant. The other patrons quickly looked away.

Turning her attention back to Rob, she said, "I saw you at Wilda's. You kin?"

"Great-nephew," Rob said. "Not great as in fantastic but great as in once removed. Did you know her?"

"'Course I knew her," she said, as if it were the most ridiculous question she'd heard that night, maybe that week. "Everyone knew Wilda. You'll be planning to settle down here then?"

Rob noticed some of the locals trying not to let their eavesdropping look too obvious. He shook his head. "No. That's not in my plans."

"Very well," she said. "Enjoy your meal. If you need anything else, let Juli know."

The woman left, and Rob looked out the large front window of the diner. The man with the odd skin, the wax man, was standing in the parking lot. He was looking right at Rob. Smiling.

The sun was well into its downward slide by the time Rob left Mary Jane's. The air was cooling some as shadows grew longer and shade spread like oil across the yards and streets of Mayfield, Maryland. Still, no one was outside enjoying the relief evening brought. Porches were empty. Sidewalks abandoned. Yards vacant. No children laughed. No dogs barked. Again, Rob thought of a movie studio and its deserted set, and the idea gave him the creeps. Like something out of an old *Twilight Zone* episode: a quaint town wears a mask to hide the hideous creature that lies beneath.

When Rob arrived back at 310 Main Street, he stood at the base of the driveway and took in the old house. It appeared to have been built in the thirties or forties. He tried to imagine what it looked like new. The architecture was so odd and the house so out of place in Mayfield it must have been the talk of the town.

He started walking up the driveway when a movement in the tiny attic window caught his attention and stopped him dead. From where he stood, the window was at an odd angle, and he had to move over into the grass for a better look. But nothing was there, just empty darkness behind a grimy window. Maybe the glass had captured the reflection of a bird flying by. Rob stood there a moment watching the glass as one might watch the ocean for a glimpse of a whale surfacing for air. But the window only stared back with vacancy. He would have liked to just shrug the episode off as nothing more than his active imagination, but he couldn't. His mind kept going to Jimmy and the burning feeling that his little boy was still out there, somewhere.

Maybe here. In that attic.

Stop! Rob shook his head, trying to clear the thought. It was those kinds of thoughts that got people thinking he was going insane.

He entered the house and flipped the light switch. Nothing happened. Maybe a bad bulb. He moved across the room and into one of the bedrooms to try its switch. Still nothing. A bad feeling gripped his chest. Going to the next room he found the same thing. And in the kitchen the same.

The electricity had been turned off.

Rob checked his watch. Almost eight o'clock. Darkness

would settle over the town in less than an hour. His breathing grew shallow, and his heart rate picked up speed.

A knock on the storm door made him jump. He let out a little holler. An old man in blue coveralls stood there, peering in through the screen, hands cupped around his eyes.

"Hello," Rob said, crossing the living room.

The old man took a quick step back and shoved his hands in his pockets.

Rob opened the door and stood in the doorway. "Hi."

"Evenin' there," the man said. He was shorter than Rob and slightly hunched, balding and spattered with large wine spots. "You Wilda's boy?"

"Her nephew. Great-nephew."

"'Course you are." He stood staring at Rob as if they knew each other.

After a few uncomfortable seconds, Rob said, "Can I help you with something?"

"Nope. Just come by to be nosey is all."

Rob didn't quite know how to respond to that. Was everyone in this town odd? "Well, thanks then. Maybe I'll be seeing you around." He started to close the storm door and then, "Hey, got a question for you. The power's been turned off here. Do you have the number for the local power company so I can have it turned back on? Preferably this evening."

The old man with the wine spots smiled a mostly toothless grin and shook his head. "Ain't gonna happen tonight. But if you call first thing in the mornin' you might get it turned back on by tomorrow night."

A sinking feeling filled Rob's gut. He mumbled a "Thanks" and let the storm door shut. There were no motels in Mayfield, and the nearest one was probably an hour or more away.

He debated whether or not to try to find one, then scolded himself for acting like such a child. He was too old to still be scared of the dark. It was just an old house in a little town. There was nothing to be afraid of.

Overhead, in the attic, something clunked and a floorboard creaked. Then, a child's giggle.

The boy fights the hand that grips his arm too tightly. Digs his heels into the ground, twists his shoulders around. He tries to holler, but something has been stuffed in his mouth. It tastes like grass. That, along with the blindfold over his eyes and his hands tied behind his back, is very confusing. The hand continues to pull him along even though he tripped and almost fell a couple times already.

Tears wet the blindfold, and snot runs from his nose. He can't even wipe it. He tries to yank away again, and this time catches Cabbage Head off guard because he nearly gets loose. The man's hand slips but quickly finds the sleeve of the boy's shirt and yanks hard, dragging the boy to his knees. He hears his shirt tear too. The one his mommy and daddy gave him last year for his birthday. The one with G.I. Joe on it. It's his favorite shirt, not because of G.I. Joe, but because Mommy told him later that Daddy had picked it out himself. That means a lot to the boy.

He thinks of his parents. Are they looking for him? Do they even know he's gone? Will he ever see them again? He wonders again if anything was really wrong with Daddy. He wonders if Mommy is OK. She went away but never came back. More tears come. He wants to cry hard, but he can't because of the thing in his mouth.

He tugs his shoulders again and falls to his knees. He can feel hard ground and dry grass against his skin. The sun on his face.

Somewhere a ways off, a hawk is screeching. He knows it's a hawk because he heard one once in his backyard and his daddy told him it was a hawk.

Cabbage Head curses, then with two hands, one on each arm, yanks the boy from the ground and sets him back on his feet. Hot breath fills the boy's ear. It smells like onions. "Kid, one foot in front of the other, you hear? You keep tripping up like that and I'll tie your feet and drag you. How'd you like that?"

The boy has never been so scared in his life, and it gives him the feeling of drowning. Not that he's ever drowned to know what it feels like. But once, while at the beach, he saw a man drowning and waving his arms and gobbling like a turkey, and the lifeguards had to rescue him.

Something in Cabbage Head's voice says he's crazy.

A few more feet and the boy is walking on concrete.

"Steps," Cabbage Head says.

The boy stumbles up four or five steps; he can't tell how many. He feels the coolness of shade and for the first time smells the man's cologne over the odor of sweat and cigarettes and onion breath.

Then a woman's voice is there. "You said you'd bring him unharmed." She sounds scared but brave at the same time.

Cabbage Head grunts something and shoves the boy. Two smaller hands stop him from falling and hold him by his shoulders. Now he can smell a familiar flowery odor.

"You brought him here, now go," the woman says. "Please. Just go." There is no meanness in her voice, not like there is in Cabbage Head's.

"You know what to do?" he says.

"Yes. Please, go now."

The woman's smaller hand grips the boy behind the neck and squeezes but not so hard that it hurts. "Come on," she says. "Inside."

They must go inside a house because the outside noises become quieter and the smell of furniture polish and dust fills his nose.

"This way," she says, guiding him by the back of his neck. Her grip gets tighter, and he pulls his shoulders up. She lightens up right away. "I'm sorry. I didn't mean to hurt you."

He hears a door open, and then the woman says, "Up the steps." Her voice sounds shaky now, like Mommy's does when she and Daddy argue and she starts to cry.

Up he climbs, one step at a time, being careful not to trip or miss one. The higher he gets, the hotter the air becomes. With the thing in his mouth and the blindfold pressing against his nose he finds it very hard to breathe. The air feels thick, like trying to breathe through a straw. This has to be what it feels like to drown. But while he climbs and struggles with breathing, one thought circles around in his head over and over: he's going farther from his mommy and daddy. And the farther he gets, the harder it will be for them to find him. And the harder it is for them to find him . . . he'll never see them again.

He stops on a stair as fresh tears leak from his eyes and another deep cry catches in his throat.

"Keep going," the woman says. "You only have four more."

He counts the steps as he climbs, and yes, it's only four more. The room he's in smells musty and like old cardboard. It reminds him of the attic of his home. The woman leads him here and there, steering him by the back of his neck, then stops.

"Sit down here," she says.

He lowers himself to his butt, sitting Indian-style on rough boards.

"If I take the rag from your mouth, do you promise not to scream or holler?"

He nods.

"You can't even talk. Understand?"

He nods again.

"You make any noise at all, and I'll have to put it back in. Hear?"

Unlike Cabbage Head, he can tell the woman is telling the truth.

Suddenly, the rag is pulled from his mouth. At first, his jaw hurts so bad he can't breathe. He moves it slowly until it loosens, then sucks in a deep breath of the hot air. His mouth feels like it's lined with cotton, and he licks at his lips.

The woman's footsteps retreat, then go down the stairs. The boy listens but never hears the door close again. Maybe she left him. He works his way to his knees, balancing carefully so as not to fall over. But before he can make it to his feet, he hears her coming back up the stairs. Quickly he sits and crosses his legs again.

"Some water for you," the woman says. "Open your mouth."

He opens his mouth, and she pours warm water down his throat. He swallows in huge gulps, spilling the water down his chin and across his chest. It doesn't matter that it's warm; it's delicious.

The woman pulls the glass away and says, "You stay here and don't make a sound, and things will work out for you. For us." She takes his chin in her hand. "Don't make a sound."

Then she's gone, and he's alone with the darkness and his fear. He allows himself to fall to his left side and curls into a ball. Then he cries hard.

Instinctively, Rob glanced out the window toward the western sky. The sun was a swollen orange disk hovering just above the rooftops. Time was running out. In the waning light, the attic would be dark but not too dark. He had to do it now.

Crossing the living room in four large steps he reached the bedroom with the attic door. Then he was at the door, hand resting on the glass knob. A sudden surge of excitement raced through him, but it was tempered by a very real possibility that what he'd heard (and, he now realized, saw in the attic window) was not his Jimmy at all but rather just another cruel trick birthed by the synapses in his brain. As time went on, it was getting more and more difficult to distinguish between reality and hallucination. Either reality was growing foggier or his visions were getting more vivid. No matter the case, the line was becoming smudged, and it worried him.

Swallowing hard past a throat as dry as bark, he tightened his grip on the knob and turned. The knob clicked once, and the door opened on noisy hinges almost by itself. Before him was a staircase that ascended to a low-ceilinged room bathed in orange light. At the top of the steps two columns of cardboard boxes rose like pillars almost to the roof beams.

Rob heard the giggle again, and the hair on the back of his neck responded. Chills, like the flutter of butterfly wings, tickled behind his ears.

"Jimmy?" His voice sounded weak even to his own ears.

At first there was silence, then from somewhere deep in the attic came Jimmy's voice. "Daddy, look."

Rob wasted no time. He raced up the stairs, taking two at a time. At the top he was met by stacks of boxes, some closed tightly, some left open. In the open ones he could see collections of knickknacks, lamp bases, glassware, and piles of neatly folded linens. The boxes were piled high on either side, making an aisle that went maybe ten feet then made a ninety-degree turn to the right. He followed it.

"Jimmy?" he said, his voice gaining a little strength. "Where's my little man?"

"Daddy." Jimmy's voice came from just up ahead, behind those boxes.

Ten more feet and another turn, this one to the left.

"Jimmy. Talk to me, buddy."

Rob's heart was racing. Anticipation clawed at his insides like rats in a cage. He threw himself around the next corner, his son's name on his lips, only to find more boxes stacked to the rafters. But this is where they ended. There were no more aisles, no more mazes, just a wall of dented and discolored boxes full of dusty antiques.

"Jimmy!" He stood motionless, waiting, hoping for his son's little voice to respond. He had to be up here, maybe in another location, behind some other boxes. But there was only silence, so loud it was deafening.

"Jimmy? It's Daddy. Can you hear me?"

The silence laughed at him and his irrational anticipation. This settled it; he had gone over that edge that's reserved for only the clinically insane.

Rob sat down on the worn floorboards and cried. How long he sat there and how long he cried he didn't know, but when his head finally cleared, he noticed how little light was left in the attic, and suddenly his lungs felt the size of baseballs. He lifted himself onto unsteady legs and quickly found his way through the maze of boxes and down the stairs and into the bedroom, where he was met by more boxes and more, if only a little, light.

Back in the living room, he cleared the sofa and smacked the dust off the cushion. It didn't look like the most comfortable bed, but it would have to do. He lay down on it and shut his eyes, willing himself to fall asleep before total darkness fell.

When he opened his eyes again the room was awash in muted moonlight. The outside world was still and quiet, and the house was sleeping peacefully. Rob looked around the room without sitting up or moving his head. Furniture and boxes cast abstract shadows along the walls and ceiling. They took on all sorts of sinister shapes and outlines. Some even appeared to move soundlessly across the wall. Fear slowly crept into his chest, like a panther stalking its prey. He found it difficult to breathe.

He lifted his wrist and pressed the light button on his watch. Twelve twenty-five.

The sun would be rising in five hours or so.

He thought of Kelly and how her eyes crinkled when she smiled. He thought of the feel of her graceful hand in his. He pictured her in the kitchen, apron around her waist, making chocolate chip cookies with Jimmy, both of them covered in flour, laughing their heads off.

"We made you cookies, Daddy."

"Jimmy did most of it by himself."

Man, how she loved to bake, and she loved it even more when Jimmy helped.

Eventually, Rob's eyelids grew heavy, and he did drift back into sleep.

It was a moment of weakness and one for which she was gravely ashamed.

When she saw him, the man, after so many years, images flooded her memory like a broken dam, carrying with them the emotions—some hers, some his. She was overwhelmed. And with the pale one so close…part of her was shocked by his boldness, and part of her was not surprised at all.

It was a moment of weakness.

"Forgive me, Abba."

Looking into the man's eyes she saw his fear, his every weakness and vulnerability. He was so wounded and defeated. She was afraid for him and wanted to protect him. She wanted to grab him by the shoulders and shake him and tell him to run from this place and never, ever come back. Forget the house. Forget everything. Just run. After all, she was partly responsible for his pain. It was a guilt she'd carried for the past twenty-two years.

The pale one eyed the man like a hungry wolf and eyed her like a mortal enemy.

Fortunately, she didn't go so far as shaking and yelling. But what she did was enough. It was beyond her responsibility. She had been called upon to pray for him, to intercede, and that's all.

"Forgive me, Abba."

She was on her patio, studying the stars of Orion. Most people looked for the Big Dipper first, but she always located Orion. She wasn't sure why. Maybe it was the fact that he was a warrior, and in many ways she felt a lot like a warrior. And in many ways she felt like anything but a warrior. Her fingers ached and throbbed. Arthritis had bent them into crooked, malformed claws. Rubbing each one, she tried to stretch them out, spread her fingers wide. She remembered when her fingers were long and slender and how they could dance across a piano's keys. It had been years since she last played. Now, she has to be content to hum.

Even though the temperature was still in the eighties at eleven o'clock at night, the old woman shivered at the thought of the pale one. She hadn't seen him for so long, but one look when he walked through that door, and the memories and emotions—the anger—besieged her. He looked the same, that polished white skin and eyes like onyx. Those soulless eyes. She tried to avoid them, but it was impossible. It felt like she stood naked before him, all her vulnerabilities, fears, doubts, and worries exposed, laid out in the open for him to study and use to his advantage. She knew he had no real power over her, though; it was all a ruse, a game he liked to play. She remembered that much.

And the hunger she saw in those eyes. The hatred. The contempt. It made her blood feel like ice water.

Crossing her legs, she bowed her head and once again asked for forgiveness. Then she turned her attention to the man again. He was in Wilda's house now; she saw his car in the driveway when she got home. She stood, stretched her tight knees, and walked through her house to the front bay window. The lights were off, and the first floor was comfortably dark. The house was still and quiet. Sleepy.

From the window, she could see most of the houses on the opposite side of the street. She'd be the first to admit she'd been a nosy old lady, but sometimes being nosy had its benefits.

At the end of the street, just four houses up from hers and on the opposite side, was the house where the man now slept. It was a quaint little house, just a bungalow really. She'd spent many an evening in that house.

A sense of dread and worry overcame her then. The man wasn't ready, wasn't prepared. She feared he would fail and fall prey to the pale one. After all, the pale one was here for him.

"Prepare him, Abba. Please prepare him. He isn't ready."

My grace is sufficient.

It was His voice, speaking soft and gentle, speaking to her heart more than her ears. She inhaled deeply, wrapped herself in her arms, and hummed a familiar tune. She found the song comforting, an old Scottish hymn with a haunting melody. Something about the tune put her at ease, reminded her of God's goodness and provisions.

She leaned forward to get a better look at the house across and up the street. Wilda's house.

Her humming stopped.

What she saw put an eel in her stomach, writhing and turning.

"Abba, protect him. Watch over him." Her voice shook. Her words sounded hurried and panicked.

There, standing on the front lawn of the house, under the old hickory, silhouetted by the watery light of the moon, unmoving, was the pale one.

Stalking his prey.

And as if he felt her stare from a hundred feet away, he turned his head and looked directly at her.

"Abba!"

The voice came again. *My grace is sufficient.*

Shields was in there, in the house, alone and sleeping. The boy had returned. Sooner or later it was destined to happen. Twenty-two years had passed, twenty-two hard years of waiting for revenge, of planning for this moment. He had taken the opportunity time had given him to strengthen his resolve, fester his hatred, and dive deeper into the darkness that had become his religion, his life, his purpose.

He stood outside the house, feet spread, arms relaxed at his sides, but his eyes were inside, watching the sleeping man, working into his mind, dipping into his subconscious, stirring up fear and unrest and pouring in darkness. More and more darkness.

He loved the darkness. Fed on it. Lived in it.

As long as Shields was here, there was hope.

Seeing Shields in the diner had awakened his appetite, aroused his hunger. His jaw ached, his tongue lolled with anticipation. A cool sweat covered his body, and he began to tremble like a man in need of a fix. He wanted him so bad, right here, right now. He could take him, and it would all be over. Every cell in his body screamed for it.

But his curiosity wouldn't let him. He enjoyed watching fear have its place, watching it consume and devour. It thrilled him to witness the fall of man deeper and deeper into the pit of despair, to behold the destruction of a soul as it surrendered to the darkness. He wanted to drag this out as long as he could, toy with it like a cat with the almost-dead bloodied body of a mouse. The very thought of it excited him on so many levels, more than his desire to quench his hunger now. It was the same longing that drove a murderer to torture his victim first, the same pleasure that arose from watching the helpless suffer.

It was sick and demented and twisted...and he survived on it.

Soon enough Shields would be his, and then it could end.

Rob battled restless sleep. Dreams came and went like strangers soliciting miracle elixirs, selling empty promises. Here he was in the house, hitting light switches, frantically trying to find light but failing to succeed. Darkness crept into the room like a black specter slowly eating up the light, inch by inch, and creeping closer to him. Fear would paralyze him, and he would try to flee, but his feet felt like they were made of cement. Then he was in the diner, seated across from Kelly, but she wasn't paying attention to him. No matter how much he talked to her or begged her to look at him, her focus was elsewhere, somewhere behind him. He turned to find the stranger with the waxy skin and dark eyes smiling a wicked grin. His eyes were pools of death, like double gun barrels pointed at him.

Rob would awaken after each dream, cold and sweaty at the same time, still afraid of the dark. The dream would linger in his mind, sending signals to his nerves for a few seconds, then fade like an empty echo. Over and over he would remind himself it was just a nightmare. It was just a dream. Over and over. It was OK to sleep again. He'd lie there listening to the house breathe until eventually he would find sleep, only to slip back into the discombobulated circuit of broken imaginings again.

At some point during the early morning hours he found himself in another dream. This one fixated on Jimmy. His boy. His little man. They were in a crowd—he, Kelly, and Jimmy. People pressed in on every side, bumping shoulders, brushing arms, moving past, pushing through, talking, laughing, yelling. He looked down and made sure Kelly had Jimmy's hand.

Then they were at a booth, some kind of vendor. Kelly was saying how cute something was, and he was stretching to see over a heavyset woman with big hair.

Kelly was spinning around, searching the ground, the crowd, yelling Jimmy's name over and over. The panic in her eyes when she looked at Rob sent shivers through his muscles and immobilized his lungs.

Jimmy was gone.

Then the voices started. In his dream, Rob was standing in the middle of a frozen crowd. Jimmy was nowhere in sight. Kelly had disappeared too. It was just him in a sea of naked mannequins. Fear attacked him from all sides, binding him, freezing him. From somewhere outside the crowd, outside his dream even, a disjointed chorus of whispers like the drone of a thousand locusts increased in volume to an almost deafening level. They all seemed to be saying the same thing, but they were so out of harmony Rob could not make out what it was.

Slowly, like the piecing together of a jigsaw puzzle, the voices unified. He could almost make out what they were saying. Almost. Then, as if someone hit a mute button, the noise stopped. Seconds passed. Rob stood amidst the mannequins, anxiety and expectation chewing at his chest from the inside. Tension built in his muscles. More seconds.

Finally, every mannequin turned its head and faced Rob. At once, in a great whisper that sounded more like a rush of wind, they spoke.

Rob awoke in a sweat with one whispered word on his lips: "Darlington."

Three

THE RINGING PHONE WOKE JULI ADAMS OUT OF A deep sleep, a peaceful sleep in which she was busy dreaming of wild stallions and wide expanses of rolling plains and pristine, mirrorlike mountain lakes.

She rolled to her right side and pried open her eyes. The room was still dark, which meant it was still night, or early morning, depending on how you looked at it. The sun wasn't yet up; that was the point.

The phone on the bedside table rang again.

The digital clock numbers glowed green: two forty-four. Whoever was calling at this hour better have a good reason. She was just about to mount one of those wild stallions and ride like the wind across that plain.

The phone sounded again, and this time she caught it mid-ring.

"Hello?" Her voice sounded raspy even to her. She cleared her throat and tried again. "Hello?"

"He needs your help."

Juli recognized the voice right away, but the message was confusing. *He needs your help.* Who needs her help? And why at this hour?

"Lots of people need help," she said. "Who's *he*?"

"Robert Shields. You met him at the restaurant. He needs your help." The message was delivered in a slightly panicked voice. Not do-this-now-or-the-world-will-end panic but a strong sense-of-urgency panic. She quickly deduced who Robert Shields was—the stranger who'd ordered the fish and chips—but she hadn't a clue why he needed her help.

"Fish and chips. Sure. He needs my help."

"Your help, yes. You must go with him."

Juli reached over, clicked on the table lamp, and then sat in bed. She switched the phone from her left ear to her right. "Do I need to pack my suitcase?"

There was a pause of a few seconds during which Juli waited for the punch line. The caller wasn't the practical joke type, but hey, there was a first time for everything. "He's the one, Julianne. Remember, I told you?"

Of course she remembered. "Yes. Tough to forget something like that. So he's our guy. Wilda's nephew."

"Our guy, yes. He'll be leaving for Darlington in the morning. You have to go with him."

OK, first, it *was* morning. Second, just the mention of that town sent a chill through Juli's nerves that made her skin quiver. She didn't say anything.

The caller's voice was small on the other end. "I know how you feel about the place. But he needs you. He's not ready to do it alone. This is who you are. This is your calling."

Still, Juli said nothing.

"*He's* here too."

Juli's breath hitched. Her hand tightened around the phone, and with the other hand she gathered a fistful of sheets. "Who's *he*?" She knew full well who *he* was but felt she needed to ask the question anyway.

"You know."

"I can't do it. I can't face him again. It's been too long...and no way long enough."

"Child. Julianne. So much time has passed, and you've

grown so much. The counseling, you went so far in it. We both did. We've healed so much, haven't we?"

"I don't know if I'll ever really heal. I still have scars."

"We both do. But you're ready. You are. You're the only one who can face him. You have to. This is your calling."

She'd said it again. *This is your calling.* If it was her calling, why was she feeling so much hesitancy, so much apprehension? Shouldn't she be jumping up and down like a cheerleader at a pep rally, rejoicing that her time had finally come? But she knew it was true. She felt it. This *was* her calling. She'd been prepared for it, and now it was upon her.

Juli swung her legs over the edge of the bed and sat like that. "I know. But why does *this* have to be my calling? Why can't I be called to find good homes for mistreated kittens? Or knit prayer shawls for the homebound? Why can't I forget about *him* and rid my life of him?"

There was a sigh, then, "Child, each of us is given a job to do, and we're given gifts to enable us to do that job. It's not for us to pick our job or our gifts. It's for us to do what we're called to do. You know how important this is. He won't stop until it's over, and that means we can't either."

"Life and death stuff."

"Yes. It certainly is. And there's been enough of the death stuff. It's time to end it."

"Can't we just call the cops?"

"And tell them what?"

"Tell them he's here."

"He'd be gone by the time they got here. You know that."

"Then shouldn't we warn this Robert Shields? Tell him what he's up against?"

"You can try, but it will do no good. He'll keep looking

until it's over. That's why you have to go with him. It has to be you."

Juli slid off the bed and walked across the darkened bedroom. The hardwood floor felt cool under her feet. She reached the window, pulled back the curtain, and looked down the street at the adobe-style house. "OK. But how do I know he'll listen to me?"

"He will. He can't do it without you. He's not ready. Convince him of that."

"Sounds easy."

"It won't be."

"I know."

"Pray, child. Pray, and don't stop."

"It's the only thing I have."

"It's your gift."

"OK."

The caller disconnected, and Juli was left with a deadening silence that seemed to breathe. She suddenly felt all alone and very helpless.

This is your calling.

Her calling. Yes, it was. And if it was her calling, then she would succeed. Else why would it be her calling? Whether she truly believed that or had just convinced herself to say she believed it she wasn't sure, but what she was sure of was that she would not be alone.

She realized she was still holding the soundless phone to her ear and looking out the window. Clicking off the phone, she let the curtain drop back into place. It did so as quietly as rain falls. Just as silently, like a ghost gliding above the floor, she crossed the room and returned to her bed.

The clock read 3:02. She had a few hours of darkness left

before the sun made its daily appearance, but she wouldn't be using it to sleep.

Bowing her head, she prayed. It *was* her gift. And it was the strength she garnered from that simple act, the faith it imbued, that would enable her to fulfill her calling.

Rob had no idea how long he lay awake on that sofa in the middle of that living room, but eventually the birds started up, and minutes later the sun made its entrance and the darkness succumbed to light.

It was over.

And, Rob knew, it had just begun. He didn't know how he knew; he just did. Jimmy was alive, out there, somewhere, in a town called Darlington. It all made sense to him now. The visions, the dreams, even the nightmares. Maybe God was telling him not to give up, to keep pressing on, to keep looking. God only knew why, but maybe He was. Kelly would want that too. And Jimmy needed him.

With renewed purpose, Rob sat on the edge of the sofa and ran his fingers through his hair. His mind was running full speed downhill, barely in control, on the verge of wiping out. He needed to corral his thoughts or he would lose them.

First there was Jimmy. The detective had been wrong. The forensics team was wrong. The coroner was wrong. They were all wrong. His boy was alive. He thought about calling the police and starting the search again. Somewhere, maybe in his wallet, he still had the detective's card. What was his name? Sandusky. But he quickly discarded that option. They were sure about their findings. Sandusky even said himself, the science doesn't lie. If Rob went to them and tried to convince them Jimmy was still alive based on some dream he'd had, they would certainly have no choice but to institutionalize him. And where would that leave Jimmy? He'd have to find his boy by himself.

Then there was Darlington. The name had a strange familiarity to it. He didn't think he'd ever been there, and yet he knew it was a town in Maryland, like the knowledge had somehow been poured into his head while he slept. Again, had God told him? Or maybe it was just a common town name, like Springfield, and he'd seen it on some map somewhere.

Not wanting to waste even one second, Rob jumped up, ran to the car, and retrieved the atlas. Standing in the driveway in nothing but his boxers he flipped to the back index, found Maryland, and scanned the names of the towns. No Darlington. He ran his finger along the names again, thinking maybe he missed it in his haste, but got the same result. Something wasn't right. He knew beyond doubt that Darlington was a town in Maryland, knew it like it was common knowledge he'd known his whole life. He wasn't wrong about that. In frustration he threw the atlas to the ground and leaned against the car, arms crossed.

"Darlington." He said the word out loud, hoping the sound of it to his ears would trigger something in his brain. It had to be such a small village it wasn't included in the atlas. He'd have to ask around. Maybe someone at Mary Jane's would know.

Mary Jane's was not a popular place on Sunday morning. When Rob pushed through the glass doors he quickly counted a total of seven patrons. Taking a booth in the corner, he couldn't help the bouncing of his right leg as he waited for the server. One minute ticked by, then two. He was about to get up and find someone when Juli stepped through the swinging kitchen doors, two trays of food supported at each shoulder. Their eyes met briefly; she smiled then served a table of four old men.

Rob watched as Juli placed the plates in front of each man, endured their cheap humor, then turned and walked toward him.

"Mornin'," she said, reaching for her order pad. "I see you came back for more. School cafeteria thing got you hooked already?"

Rob pasted on a smile. His heart was fluttering. "Everything was great." His voice quavered slightly. "Do you know of a town called Darlington? Have you ever heard of it?"

As if he'd just told her that her mother died, the smile disappeared from Juli's face. She broke eye contact with him for the briefest of moments.

"Darlington." She said it the way a child says a cuss word for the first time.

"Darlington. Is it around here?"

The corner of Juli's mouth dipped into a subtle frown that quickly disappeared.

Rob tapped his finger on the table. "Juli? Where is Darlington? Do you—"

"Have you ordered yet?" It was the older woman with the straight back and long nose from last night.

"He was just about to decide," Juli said, not taking her eyes off Rob.

"Are you Mary Jane?" Rob asked the woman.

The woman tilted her head back so she could sight him down that beak of hers. "I am. What can we get you for breakfast?"

Rob looked from Mary Jane to Juli and back. "Directions to Darlington?"

Mary Jane snorted. "Darlington. What does anyone want with Darlington? It's barely a collection of dilapidated homes."

"Can you tell me where it is?"

The bell over the door chimed, and Rob noticed how Mary Jane's countenance darkened when she looked that way. Juli made a little grunting noise and shuffled her feet. Her hands twisted her apron. He turned to see Wax Man from last night standing just inside the doors, scanning the diner with those bored-out black eyes. His eyes met Rob's, held him for the briefest of moments, then he walked over and seated himself in a booth one aisle over from where Rob sat.

"What would you like, sir?" It was Mary Jane again. And again, she looked flustered by the sight of Wax Man.

Frustration quickly replaced whatever excitement Rob had felt. "Directions to Darlington." He noticed his voice had increased in volume. Looking around the diner, he had captured the attention of the other customers. Wax Man, however, pretended to be deep in thought, studying the menu.

"Sir, you don't want anything to do with Darlington. You

have no business going there. Now, would you like breakfast here or not?"

Rob noticed Mary Jane's hands were trembling. She quickly moved them behind her.

He took a deep breath and calmed himself. The last thing he wanted was to make a scene. If he was ever going to find Darlington, he'd need the help of anyone willing to give it. He swallowed hard. "Yes, please. I'm sorry. Two eggs, sunny side up, white toast, and bacon. And a large chocolate milk. Please."

Juli slipped away and headed for the kitchen. Mary Jane paused, glanced in the direction of Juli and then Wax Man, then said, "You really ought not pursue this. Nothing good happens in Darlington." Then she turned on her heels and headed to the front of the diner.

Juli was gone now, most likely in the kitchen getting the meals as they came off the hot grill. Several minutes later, she emerged carrying a plate and a mug of some steaming liquid. She crossed the diner and stopped at an old woman's table. Rob watched as the woman unfolded her napkin, placed it on her lap, then reached in her pocket and retrieved a small pillbox.

A commotion from the other side of the diner snatched his attention away from the old woman. Mary Jane was at Wax Man's table. Her voice rose and fell, and her hands moved about like a conductor's. Rob could only catch sporadic words and phrases. At one point he heard "not welcome here," at another "get out." Words like "disgrace" and "shame" were thrown at the man like knives.

Finally, Wax Man rose slowly and smoothed his shirt. He wore that placid smile again. Nodding at Mary Jane, then at the rest of the patrons, he left the diner by way of the aisle

Rob was in. Passing Rob's booth he leveled those dark eyes on him and dropped a folded piece of paper on the table. Then he was gone, out the front door like a phantom.

Rob unfolded the piece of paper and read the message scrawled on it: *Mt. Zion. 30 minutes.*

In the kitchen of Mary Jane's Diner, Juli Adams leaned on the counter and tried unsuccessfully to steady the shaking of her hands. This was ridiculous. Who did she think she was kidding? She couldn't even face him out there. She hadn't the nerve or the courage. She wasn't ready for this. There were too many memories that were still too raw, even after so many years and so many counseling sessions. The fact that she was only two at the time and had acquired most of her memories from other sources didn't matter. They were still memories she wished she could forget.

A sick feeling settled in her stomach like curdled milk. The temperature in the kitchen seemed to spike. Anger and disgust surged through her veins. For a moment she thought she'd vomit.

"Hey, Jules, you OK?"

It was Otto, leaning back from the grill, spatula in hand.

Juli swallowed and dragged a hand across her moist forehead. "Yeah. A-OK. Just felt a little…" She let her voice die out.

"You sure? You look like you just saw a ghost or somethin'."

"I'm fine, Otts. Just need a glass of water."

She grabbed a glass from the rack, filled it with ice, and

ran it under cold water. Her hands were still shaking, and the ice clinked in the glass like brittle bones in a bag.

A hand was on her back then, just below her neck. It was her. She'd followed Juli into the kitchen. "You're having second thoughts."

Juli took a swallow of the water. "And third and fourth and fifth. I can't do it. I can't go back to that place. I can't face him again."

"You can. You have to."

"*Have* to? That's kind of absolute, isn't it?"

"As absolute as life and death."

Juli shook her head. "I can't. Look at me." She held up a hand, and it trembled like a late October leaf still clinging to its branch.

The hand slid to her arm and squeezed. "You must. There's no one else. Find the courage within you, embrace your calling, and have faith. This is your time."

As before, after the phone call in the middle of the night (or morning, depending on how you look at it), she knew the woman was right. If she looked for it, courage was there. And with the courage came a peace that this *was* her time, and it *was* her calling.

The hand moved to her back and rubbed in slow circles. "Robert Shields needs you. He's going to Darlington, and he can't go alone."

Juli nodded. "I know. OK. But I'll need prayer and plenty of it."

"That's why I'm here. For you and Robert."

Juli drained the rest of her glass and placed it in the dishwasher.

"Food's up for table twelve," Otto said.

Juli smiled at the woman. "I can't do this alone."

A warm smile answered her. "You're never alone, child."

Grabbing the plate from the warmer, Juli said, "Thanks, Otts." Then to the woman, "You hold the rope."

"With my life."

Juli pushed through the swinging doors and headed for Rob's table. He looked so alone sitting there, so lost. She set the plate before him, shoved her hands in her pockets. "You're going to Darlington."

He looked up, a surprised look on his face. "Yes. I am."

"That wasn't a question."

Rob finished his breakfast in ten minutes, barely tasting the food before it hit his stomach. Kelly always scolded him for how fast he ate.

"You'll give yourself an ulcer the size of a dinner plate."

He never took her seriously, though, and that was a regret he'd tote with him the rest of his life, that he'd never taken her seriously, not just about stomach ulcers but about anything. But he'd been eating fast for twenty-seven years and hadn't gotten an ulcer yet.

It was early enough in the morning that the church crowd hadn't arrived at Mt. Zion yet. It was only seven thirty, and the sign outside said Sunday school didn't start until nine thirty. The doors were unlocked though, so Rob entered and sat in an unpadded pew in the back of the small sanctuary. Vaulted ceilings, high windows, and a color scheme of light grays and white gave the illusion that the room was much larger than it was.

Rob remembered attending a church very similar to this

as a child. A small Pentecostal church just outside Secretary, Maryland. Lots of hand waving and shouting and fainting every Sunday morning. His parents dragged him there for seventeen years, made him read his Bible stories and learn his verses. He remembered one hot Sunday in particular. He was seven or eight and standing next to Dad in the "big church." Everyone was singing loudly and swaying back and forth. Some were crying. Some falling over. Sweat glistened on every face. Suddenly, Dad's arms shot up and his head snapped back, and he started saying something Rob couldn't understand. But it wasn't really words he was speaking, more just broken noises and guttural sounds. Rob tried not to stare, but the scene was so odd it was scary. Then his dad's hand was on the back of Rob's neck.

"C'mon, son. Let's do this," Dad said, and he pulled him out into the aisle.

Stepping over and around bodies, they picked their way to the front of the sanctuary. Rob started shaking and sweating. His palms got real clammy. The preacher, a little man with thinning hair and a suit that was way too big for him, met them up front.

"My son needs a healing," Dad said, tears now streaming down both cheeks.

Rob looked at him, feeling very afraid now. "Dad?"

The preacher leaned in close to Dad, and the two exchanged a few words Rob couldn't understand over all the singing and shouting. The preacher looked at Rob then, and the room seemed to grow smaller and the air thinner. He was smiling, but it wasn't sincere. He took a step toward Rob, placed his sweaty palm on Rob's forehead—

The church door opened, shaking Rob from his memory. He turned in the pew and saw the silhouette of Wax Man in the door frame, backlit by the light of morning. Wax Man let the door shut and approached Rob. He sat in the pew on the opposite side of the aisle. Seconds passed, and he didn't say anything. He just stared at Rob with those eyes as if he were sizing him up, and not on a physical level.

"You're looking for Darlington," he finally said.

Rob swallowed. Something about this stranger was more than unusual, and it made him nervous. "You know where it is?"

The man nodded. "What's your business there?"

"*My* business," Rob said. "Do you know where it is or not?"

"I know where it is. Nice little town. Real friendly." He paused and held his eyes on Rob. For the first time, Rob noticed the blue veins, like rivers on a map, that crawled just under the surface of the skin on his face.

Something about those eyes and the way they dug into Rob made him look away for an instant.

"You looking for something there?" Wax Man asked.

"Are you gonna tell me how to get there, 'cause I don't have time—"

"People go to Darlington because they're looking for something."

What was that supposed to mean? "Look, what I'm looking for is none of your—"

Wax Man held up a hand. His palm was smooth and soft, and his fingers were long and slender, never marred by hard work. They were the fingers of a piano player. "*Who* are you looking for?"

A sliver of ice slid down Rob's spine. "What makes you think I'm looking for someone?"

Smiling like a phony fortune-teller at a carnival, Wax Man

leaned forward so his elbows were resting on his knees. If he would hold still like that, he could pass for a wax figure, Rob thought. How odd. "Listen close," he said, "because I'm only going to say this once. Take Route 1 south across the Conowingo. When you get off the dam, make an immediate right. At the fork go left. That'll take you to Darlington"— he stood and crossed the aisle to Rob, placed a hand on his shoulder—"and Jimmy. I'll see you there."

Before Rob could question him, Wax Man's grip tightened, and Rob felt a bolt of pain shoot up his neck.

Everything went black.

The feel of Shields's flesh under his hand stirred something in him he hadn't felt for such a long time. He allowed his hand to linger a little longer than needed, until his blood bubbled in his veins. He enjoyed enticing himself; it was a form of self-torture that aroused him, spiked all his senses.

He tightened his grip and imagined letting go of his inhibitions. He could do it too. So easily. Tear open Shields's throat and empty his sorry carcass of every last drop of blood. But where would the fun be in that? Yes, it would be satisfying. Very satisfying. But not fulfilling. There was much more fun to be had with Shields first. Much more misery to inflict. If there was one thing he'd learned over the last twenty-two years more than anything else, it was self-control.

And besides, he'd felt something in Shields. Something that caused him to pull back his hand and rub it, even smell it. A remnant of that poison from Shields's past. A pinpoint of light. He'd have to snuff out that first; then the time for blood would come.

He stood over the flaccid body of Shields and sneered. Such easy prey. Almost too easy. That's why he needed to prolong the whole thing, drag it out, make a game of it. He wondered how Shields would hold up. It would be fascinating to watch, like a scientist curiously studying the effects of radiation on a lab rat.

He squatted next to Shields, lowered his head so his nose was only inches from the exposed neck, and drew in a deep breath. The smell of blood, oil, and sweat—and underneath it all, the faint scent of fear—intoxicated him.

His tongue felt swollen with hunger.

PART TWO

*The oldest and strongest emotion of mankind is
fear, and the oldest and strongest kind of fear is
fear of the unknown.*

—H. P. LOVECRAFT

Four

ROB AWOKE ON THE SOFA IN WILDA'S HOUSE. WHEN he opened his eyes, the muted light was like knives. He shut them again, rubbed them, and opened them slowly, giving them time to adjust. The sunlight was not bright in the room, and at first Rob thought it was because it was still morning. He raised his arm to look at his watch and was scolded by pain along the left side of his neck. Clenching his jaw, he lifted his arm anyway. Seven oh five. In the evening.

Ignoring the shock of pain in his neck and shoulder and the throbbing headache he now had, Rob pushed himself to sitting and cradled his head in his hands. An image of Wax Man standing over him, that wolfish grin on his face, was stamped in his mind. Did he dream the whole thing? Had he slept the whole night and day on the sofa? Maybe he was coming down with the flu. He moved his left arm, trying to work out the pain and stiffness. No, it was real. The man was real, his wicked black eyes were real, and that Vulcan grip thing he did was real too. Then how did Rob wind up back here in Wilda's house? He had no recollection of walking or of being moved. Was that Wax Man's doing as well? Did he bring him here? The thought of that freak being in this house made Rob's skin itch.

And what about what he'd said…he knew Rob was looking for Jimmy. But how? Rob pushed his cloudy mind to remember the conversation. The man said the road would lead Rob to Darlington *and* Jimmy. And he said he'd meet him there. He knew where Jimmy was, which meant Rob was right; Jimmy *was* still alive. His boy was out there, fighting, surviving.

But what was the way to Darlington? He shut his eyes and brought the memory into focus. Route 1. Cross the dam, go right. At the fork, go left.

"Daddy's coming, buddy. Hang on."

He jumped up, grabbed the atlas, and headed for the car. There wasn't much daylight left. He'd have to hurry.

On the driveway, Rob opened the car door and was about to get in when—

"Wait." A woman's voice.

He looked over the roof of the car and saw Juli running up the driveway. She wore jeans and a plain green T-shirt, her hair pulled back in a ponytail. "Wait."

She arrived, breathless and flushed, and leaned one hand on the hood of the car. "I'm going with you."

"What? No. How do you even know—"

"You need me."

"Look, you were real nice at the diner, but—"

She straightened her back. "I've been there. I know the way."

"Been where?"

"Darlington. I know the way."

"So do I."

She shook her head. "No. He didn't tell you everything."

"How do you know what he told me?"

"How do you think you got back in the house, on the sofa?"

"You?" Rob gripped his head with both hands. His headache was getting worse. He had some Tylenol in his duffel bag. "You brought me back here?"

"You're heavier than you look."

"Thanks."

"We don't have a lot of time. The sun, it'll be down soon." She looked back at the setting sun. "We need to move. Quick like a bunny."

Rob paused. He hated this. The last thing he needed was some girl tagging along, asking a bunch of questions, getting in his way, slowing him down. But if she'd been to Darlington before, she could be of some value. "How old are you?"

Juli looked surprised by the question. She blinked. "Twenty-four."

"Really? You look younger."

"Thanks. You want to see my license?"

"No. Fine. Get in."

With each passing minute the sun slipped a little lower in the sky and inched closer to its union with the horizon. Darkness was looming, and Rob could already feel himself growing tenser, his skin getting clammy, breathing rate increasing. After crossing the Conowingo Dam, he'd turned right onto Jacknife Road, a winding, barely two-lane road with hills so steep and curvy he'd nearly lost control of the car a few times already. Thick woods overgrown with kudzu lined either side. No houses were in sight, not even driveways leading to houses. The woods seemed wholly uncivilized and totally wild.

"You sure this is the way?" Rob said to Juli, who'd remained mostly quiet.

"The way to Darlington?"

"Yes, Darlington. Where else?"

Juli looked out the side window, then back at Rob. "I can think of a few places I'd rather be going."

"So is this a shortcut or something?"

"Or something."

"What does that mean?"

"It means this is *the* way to Darlington."

The road dipped sharply and banked right ninety degrees. Rob leaned on the brake and steered the car around the bend. The tires slipped on some loose gravel but quickly found purchase again. "There's no other way? One that's easier on my brakes?"

"Only one way in to Darlington," she said. "And only one way out."

The clock on the dash said it was nearing eight o'clock. With clear skies, sunset would be around nine o'clock, but in woods this thick, darkness would fall sooner than that.

"So when were you here before?" Rob said.

Juli sighed. "To a teenager, a town like Darlington has a certain magnetic pull. I was fifteen and curious. I found my way there and was lucky to find my way out."

"That doesn't tell me much."

"It tells you as much as you need to know right now."

"And what is it I need to know?"

With her head turned toward the window and passing trees, Juli said, "Getting there is the easy part."

Rob and Juli fell into silence again. A few minutes later the road leveled and the trees thinned. They came around a gradual bend and found the fork in the road that Wax Man had mentioned. To the right, the paved road continued; to the left, a dirt lane divided by a thin grassy median curved around and reentered the heavily wooded area. Wax Man had said to go left.

Rob brought the car to a stop right before the fork. "You've got to be kidding me. We're supposed to go left?"

"Right."

"Right?"

"I mean, correct. Go left."

"But it looks like someone's driveway."

"The driveway to Darlington."

Rob sat still in the car, turning neither way and content to make no progress until he was satisfied going left was the correct way.

"Think Robert Frost," Juli said.

"Robert Frost?"

"You know, the fork-in-the-road guy."

"He took the one less traveled."

"And that made all the difference."

"The one less traveled," Rob said thoughtfully.

"All the difference."

Depressing the accelerator, Rob steered the car left. "And you've gone this way before?"

"There's only one way."

"Yeah, you said that before."

"And you keep asking."

The car bounced down the rough lane that took them back into the woods and the blankets of kudzu and growing light-lessness. "I hope you know what you're talking about."

"Me too."

"That's not very reassuring."

Like Jacknife Road, the dirt lane began to twist and turn

and dive and curve, rattling the car's frame like an old wooden roller coaster. Eventually it too leveled and widened some. The grass median faded, and the trees on either side became more sporadic. In front of them, the road straightened and stretched through a valley of meadowland splashed with goldenrod for at least a mile. In the distance, like the wall of a fortress, another tree line stood.

"We're almost there," Juli said.

"How do you know?"

"Just on the other side of those trees up ahead."

"Are you sure?"

"Pretty sure."

Finally the road met the tree line and pierced it like an arrow. Whatever sunlight was left was swallowed by the thick foliage, so Rob had to turn on the car's headlights. Immediately, that familiar fear was birthed inside him and began to grow. He gripped the steering wheel a little tighter.

As if she saw the fear on his face or simply sensed it from him, Juli said, "It's only a mile or so before we hit another clearing, then we'll be in Darlington."

Rob said nothing. The steering wheel was slick under his sweaty palms. That mile or so couldn't come soon enough.

Eventually the woods opened its mouth and let in the waning sunlight. Kicking up a rooster tail of dust, the car exited the trees and headed for a small clump of houses in the distance.

"Is that it?" Rob said.

"Darlington."

"Not much of a town. No wonder it wasn't on the map." It looked to be maybe ten or so homes and a couple other buildings. A church steeple rose like a dagger above the other structures.

"That's not the only reason."

Less than a minute later, the dirt road gave way to a strip of faded asphalt. By the side of the road stood a wooden sign, sunburnt and chipped, that read:

Welcome to Darlington

Then below that in smaller letters:

Shining Our Light

At the sight of that sign, a quiet feeling of dread washed through Juli, not like a tidal wave crashing over her but more like a slow infusion. It was that feeling again. Something was wrong. As a kid, while visiting her cousins outside Baltimore, she'd paid the three bucks to walk through a haunted house on Halloween. The first hallway was empty and dark, but a feeling accompanied it that was anything but peaceful or fun loving. It was fear mingled with the unknown yet expected. But that was a manufactured feeling, produced by fancy lighting and spooky sound effects. This, in Darlington, was real. As real as the hair standing up on the back of her neck.

Shining Our Light. She remembered that from the last time she visited too, when she was fifteen and stupid. The condition of the sign itself testified to the mockery of those words. There was no light in Darlington. Maybe there was at one time, but that time had long passed. Darkness ruled here now. All kinds of darkness.

Sitting in the car next to Rob, her right hand squeezing

the circulation out of her leg, Juli pushed back that feeling of dread. Regardless of what may or may not reside in Darlington, she would not be overcome by it. She would not be overcome by fear. She had to believe that, had to trust it to be true. Rob needed her. She knew that now more than ever. Her doubts about her ability to do this would have to take a backseat to the truth: that she *had* to do it.

She looked at Rob. He had no idea what was coming. Really, she had no idea either, only that it was coming. She could feel it like she could feel a major thunder boomer approaching by the change in barometric pressure. It was a weighty feeling, ominous and foreboding.

A sense of expectancy and tension was in the air all about her. All about Darlington.

Darlington appeared to be a town asleep except for the lighted windows in every home. The main street—and the only street—was lined with five homes on either side. A small grocer was positioned at the beginning of town and a church sat at the far end of the road.

At first glance it looked to be a quaint northern Maryland village, but as Rob advanced the car slowly down the street, he noticed the state of disrepair the homes were in. Roofs sagged, shutters clung to windows by single hinges, paint curled and peeled like dry skin, and uncut lawns stood knee high. If not for the glowing windows, he would have assumed the town had been abandoned long ago and left to decay. He could hear Kelly.

"This place gives me the major creeps."

And Jimmy.

"Is it a ghost town, Daddy? Like in the cowboy movies?"

The grocery store was empty and dark, its glass frontage marked with large duct-taped Xs. The sign that read *Darlington Shop 'n' Go* sat at an odd angle above the double doors. Weeds grew up along the sides of the building and through the cracks in the sidewalk.

Stopping the car in front of the church, a sad little clapboard building that had been left to suffer the abuse of weather by itself, Rob looked around the town. It sat in a clearing and was surrounded by trees on every side. In front of him the road stretched forward and disappeared into the woods a quarter mile away. No cars were parked along the street.

"Where's that road go?" he asked Juli.

"Nowhere."

"What do you mean? It has to go somewhere."

"Nope. It just fades away in the woods. I told you, there's only one way into Darlington and one way out."

Rob thought of Jimmy in this place. Was he in one of those homes? Did someone in this town know where his son was? He looked back at the church. In black snap-in-place letters, the sign in front announced:

WELCOM TO DARLINGTON METH CHURCH
WHERE GODS L GHT SHINES IN EV RYONES
HEART.
SUND Y APRIL 29 1987
SERMON WHAT S LOVE
PA TOR ASHER WIG INS

Something about the church was familiar. He had a cloudy feeling of déjà vu, but not quite. Not like back at Wilda's house. This was more like a distant memory or lingering dream feeling. "They haven't had a church service since eighty-seven?"

"Either that or their sign person's been asleep on the job."

"Not for that long. This place is—" Rob caught movement in his periphery. He snapped his head around toward the little single story across the street. A curtain fell into place. "Strange."

"Stranger than strange," Juli said. "You haven't seen anything yet."

Rob watched the windows of the house until the front door opened slowly and a thin man of around sixty stepped out. Wearing baggy khakis and a sweat-stained T-shirt, the man looked both ways, turned his head toward the setting sun, checked his watch, then headed across the street and straight toward Rob and Juli. He walked with a little hitch to his step and cocked his head sideways when he reached them, studying them like they'd just fallen from outer space. "You folks lost?" He appeared to be nervous, checking his watch then the position of the sun again.

Rob shook his head. "No. This is Darlington, right?"

"If you say so."

"The signs say so." Rob pointed back at the *Welcome to Darlington* sign, then at the church sign.

The man thought for a moment. Rubbed the patchy beard that covered most of the lower half of his face. "I s'pose they do."

Rob stuck out his hand for a shake. "I'm Rob, and this is Juli."

The man neither offered his hand nor introduced himself. Instead, he eyed the sun one more time then said, "Sun'll be disappearing soon, then the darkness'll come. You folks best be turning 'round and headin' back to where you come from. No good driving through them woods in the dark."

Rob had no time to argue with the guy. "I'm looking for my son. Jimmy. 'Bout four feet tall, five years old, brown hair. Looks a lot like me."

The man eyed him curiously but showed not even a hint of empathy. He glanced at his watch. "Mister, I'm gonna have to ask you to either get in that there car and drive outta here or"—he paused to steal a look at his house—"come inside with me."

Fact was, Rob wasn't excited about getting stuck here in the dark. Something about the single-street town (one way in, one way out) gave him the creeps and the urge to flee. But for Jimmy he'd stay. And for Kelly. He knew she would want him to do everything within his ability to find their son and bring him home again. And he couldn't disappoint her.

Rob looked at Juli, who looked at the man. "Leaving isn't an option," she said. She shot Rob a look that said *trust me*. "But getting indoors certainly is."

The man looked over his shoulder again and this time nodded. The first part of the sun touched the top of the trees and, surprisingly, didn't set them aflame. He met Rob's eyes, then Juli's. "Better get inside."

"Good idea," Juli said.

They crossed the street together, Rob sensing a need to stay close. When they reached the front stoop of the little home, the door opened and a woman greeted them in a blue housecoat and slippers.

Inside the house, the door was shut and the deadbolt set in place. The interior was bathed in the yellow glow of several well-placed oil lamps. The windows were shut and curtains pulled. The man turned and in a very serious tone said, "I'm

Norm Tuckey, and this here is my wife, Rose." Rose, a stout woman as wide was she was tall with a wide mouth and eyes that looked much too small for her face, made no sign of welcoming the strangers into her home. She stared at them with the most deadpan look Rob had ever seen.

As if on cue, a large man of about forty rounded the corner and stood in the doorway between the living room and kitchen. His shoulders were so wide they nearly touched the jamb on either side, and he had to duck his head slightly to avoid hitting the lintel. "And that there's Carl, our son. He ain't too bright but he's harmless."

Outside the light was fading quickly and darkness was moving in. In the distance, from somewhere deep in the woods surrounding the town of Darlington, a woman's scream raced across the meadow and pierced the walls of the house.

Five

THE OIL LAMP FLAMES FLICKERED AS IF THE SCREAM carried with it a breath. In the corner of the living room Carl started moaning. Rob looked at him and then at Norm. "What was that?"

Norm was a ball of frayed nerves. He looked at his watch, mumbled something about it not being time, then parted the curtains on the western side of the house and peeked out the window.

Rob's heart picked up its pace. "What was that scream?" He looked at Juli as if she had the answer. She stood by the closed and locked door, hands clasped in front of her, eyes closed like she was deep in prayer and hadn't even heard the scream.

Rose stood frozen in the kitchen; Carl continued his moaning in the corner.

Another scream ripped through the evening air, but this one was obviously from a different source. It had a different tonal quality about it than the first one.

"Are there people out there?" Rob asked. He was getting panicky. What if someone needed help? He headed for the door but was cut off by Norm. Juli stepped out of the way.

"You ain't goin' out there, son."

"Does someone need help?" Rob's voice was rising.

"Not yet, but you will if you go out there. Now, just have a seat on the sofa and let's talk about this."

More screams erupted from the outside world, some higher pitched than others, some sounding closer than others. It seemed they were on the move, maybe in the meadow by now.

Norm motioned to the sofa again. "Go on now, have a seat." He turned his head toward Rose. "Mommy, get our guests some blankets. They'll be staying the night."

Rob started to protest then stopped when Juli's hand found his arm. She was standing beside him. "Going out there isn't the best idea right now," she said.

"You know what that is?"

Juli looked at Norm then back at Rob. "Darklings."

More screams, this time close enough to be across the street. The sound made the hair on the back of Rob's neck stand on end. In the corner of the room Carl had stopped moaning.

When a pause in the screams came, the void was filled by a child's voice, hollering. Rob couldn't make out what was being said, but he recognized the voice—it was Jimmy's.

In one quick, fluid movement, Rob moved for the window and threw the curtain back. Across the street, between two houses, he caught the silhouette of a child running. He knew that run, so familiar it immediately put a knot in his throat. Jimmy.

Dashing for the door, he flipped the deadbolt and yanked on the knob. He heard Juli holler something, then Norm cursed. The door opened, and something grabbed at his pants leg until it took possession. A scream let loose and stung his ears. Then arms were around his torso, pulling him back into the house.

"No," he yelled. "Jimmy!" He fought to escape the doorway and find his son, fought to break the hold the arms had on him. Another hand groped at his pants, and something scratched at his leg. "Let me—"

He was suddenly yanked backward hard, losing his footing on the floor and falling on his butt. Norm leaned against the door and pushed it shut. But just before the door met the frame, a hand—small, bony, the gray-brown color of an earthworm, with elongated fingers—made one last attempt at Rob's sneaker, then pulled back and disappeared into the darkness.

A pitiful yell involuntarily escaped Rob's lungs.

The door closed with a solid *thunk*, and the deadbolt clicked into place.

The old woman was once again on her patio, standing tall, shoulders back, head tilted, studying the stars. They awed her. The power contained in just one of them was beyond comprehension, and yet they appeared so small, so insignificant, so…unnecessary. Just pinpoint lights. No common person would even notice if one went out. And yet to God, each one was precious and absolutely necessary.

So how much more precious and necessary are we?

These thoughts and more walked through her mind, and she took the time to stop and contemplate each one.

The air was cooler in the evening. A gentle breeze played with the loose strands of hair at her temples. She closed her eyes and breathed in the scent of roses. Against the backdrop of her eyelids, she could still see the pricks of starlight. Silently, she thanked her Father for the beauty of something so seemingly inconsequential.

Her eyes opened again; her thoughts went to the man. He was there, in Darlington now. She knew he would go. How could he resist? After all, it was part of the grand scheme. He had to go because in going he would become who he was meant to be.

And to think she was silly enough and faithless enough to try and stop him. It was the pale one who had caused her to stumble. Seeing him again. Speaking to him. Knowing what he was capable of. She had hoped the last twenty-two years would have cured her of all that, rid her soul of the guilt and wiped her mind clean of any memory of him. But she was wrong. Boy, was she wrong. It had all come back in a sudden rush, like a sandstorm sneaking up on a sleeping village in the desert.

But what frightened her more than anything was that they shared the same blood and were so much alike. As much as she loved God, he hated Him. As much as she was determined to stay faithful and do good, he was determined to oppose that and spread hate and fear.

For added assurance and to put her worrisome mind at ease even a little, she had sent the girl with the man. She wished she could go herself; after all, the battle with the pale one was her fight if no one else's, but her old bones would have none of it. The girl was young, but when the time came, she'd know what to do. She was fearful, and rightfully so, but her faith was strong, maybe even stronger than the woman's. She was the right one to accompany the man; she was the only one who could.

From her home, there were only two things the old woman could do: hope and pray.

"Lead them, Abba. Guide them with Your light."

The man's first test would come tonight. She could feel it

as if it were happening to her. Beads of sweat appeared on her forehead. Her palms went slick. Heart rate hastened, breathing quickened.

She was afraid, so afraid. For him.

He had to learn how to conquer that fear, but it had become such a part of his fabric it would take a miracle to separate the two.

"Abba, show him the way. Show him *Your* way."

She prayed for the girl too, the child. She was stronger than she appeared, a formidable foe for the pale one. But was she strong enough to keep the man from falling? That remained to be seen. The old woman could do nothing but stand by and pray and hope and keep her ears to the ground.

Lowering herself to her knees, slowly and with much pain, she placed her hands on the brick of the patio and lay prostrate. The bricks still held the heat from the day, and it felt good against her skin. In this position, she fell before the throne of her Father, helpless, powerless, humbled.

"Abba, guide them, strengthen them, place a wall around them. He is of so much value."

My grace is sufficient.

"Thank You, Abba. May You be glorified."

Suddenly, an image appeared in her mind, flashed through like a gunshot. Dark, lifeless eyes. Bony frames. Barbed teeth. Evil.

Her eyes flipped open like broken blinds, and she screamed.

Rob lay on his back on the floor, breathing hard, trying to wrap his senses around the image of that hand and the sound of those screams. Carl stood over him, slowly rocking side to side. He'd taken to moaning again. Juli was there too, kneeling beside him, her hand on his head, eyes closed. She was whispering something unintelligible, maybe praying.

Shutting his eyes, Rob drew in a deep breath and thought of Jimmy. Memories exploded in his mind like mortar shells. First Jimmy was running in the backyard, yelling for Daddy to watch him jump. Then he was building a house with Legos, concentration forcing his tongue out of his mouth. Here he was riding his two-wheeler for the first time, the wind in his hair, his face aglow with pride—"*Look, Daddy, I'm flyin'. Flyin' like the wind!*" Then, lying in bed, covers pulled to his little chin, puckering his lips.

Tears came to Rob's eyes and burned behind his closed lids. He reached a hand up to wipe at them, but Juli was there first, using her thumb to dash them away.

From the door Norm said, "Mommy, you got those blankets yet?"

Rob opened his eyes and saw Rose draw near, a pile of folded blankets tucked under her arms. Norm took the blankets and dropped them on the sofa. "You two can figure out the sleeping arrangements. One on the sofa, one on the floor. You decide. You're welcome here for the night, but first light you need to find your way outta here. You done brought enough trouble on this home—on this town—already."

Pushing himself up, Rob stood to his full height and

stretched his back. "I saw my son out there, with those things." His eyes were still wet with tears.

Norm placed one hand on his hip and pointed at Rob with the other one. "Mister, I don't know what you seen out there tonight, but I can tell you straight out you try that little stunt again and I'll lock ya in the basement."

Rob looked at Juli then at Norm. "What was that out there? The hand."

Juli said, "Darkling."

"Come again?"

"The screams, the hand. Darklings."

He turned his full attention to Juli. "And Jimmy."

She didn't say anything, but the way she broke eye contact with him made it apparent she wasn't in his corner when it came to Jimmy's whereabouts.

"I know what I saw," Rob said. "I heard him too. Didn't you?"

Norm had disappeared and now returned toting a shotgun. "Sorry I have to do this to you folks, but we really can't take no chances of you going for the door again and puttin' us all in danger." He sat at the kitchen table, gun propped between his thighs, Rose across from him.

Carl lumbered his frame to the recliner and eased into it with as much grace as a camel getting on its knees. Apparently he planned on spending the night in the chair.

"You can't keep us hostage," Rob said.

Juli started unfolding one of the blankets. "He's right." She looked over at Rob. "I'm sorry." And after a short pause, "You mind taking the floor?"

The floor was about as comfortable as a bed of screws. Rob had spread the blanket out for some padding, but the bare boards still dug into his hips and shoulder blades. He couldn't sleep anyway. His mind was churning like a steam locomotive going full tilt. He knew the figure he saw was Jimmy. It felt nothing like a hallucination. But then again, the last vision didn't either, and he had questioned whether he was officially losing his mind, whether that sacred line between reality and fantasy was being blurred beyond distinguishing. And if it really was Jimmy—which he was now convinced it was—how had he gotten here? What was he doing out there with those *things*?

And what was out there? Juli called them darklings. Rob's first thought was that they were some form of mutants suffering from some horrible deformity. Maybe the product of inbreeding or incest. Things like that weren't unheard of in remote hick towns like this. It would explain the seclusion and secrecy of the town. An image of that hand, childlike in size but with that tight earthworm-colored skin and those elongated fingers, played in his mind. It was anything but childlike.

Lifting his arm, Rob pushed the light button on his watch. It was a little after ten. He could hear Norm and Rose at the kitchen table whispering softly, the hiss of their words making it sound like they were speaking a foreign language, one not of this world. The recliner squeaked and moaned as Carl shifted his weight in it. On the sofa, Juli's breathing had already deepened and slowed. Sleep had come easy for her.

He'd wait until the house was quiet to make his escape. He didn't care what was out there; he had to get to his son.

He wished Kelly were there. She was always the voice of reason. She would know what to make of all this. He knew what she would do first, though; it was always what she suggested to do before anything else: pray. That was her thing. Rob remembered a day when he prayed regularly. As a kid he'd pray every night before bed, sincere prayers too, the kind children pray innocently and out of untested faith.

Then something happened, he couldn't remember what, but his faith was tested and found to be wanting. Fear moved in and pushed faith out. That's when the praying stopped. Not that he never prayed. When Kelly and Jimmy first went missing, he prayed all the time, nonstop. Begged God, pleaded with Him, bargained, made promises, wept and screamed and sometimes lay totally exhausted and spent and not knowing what to say. First came the news about Kelly. Then Jimmy. And again, his faith had proven to be frail, and fear had taken hold of him.

But they were wrong about Jimmy. He was still alive. And he was in Darlington.

Fighting heavy eyelids, Rob held his breath and listened. The kitchen was quiet. Carl was motionless and snoring softly. Rob was just about to make a move for the door when the sound of a chair scraping along the kitchen floor froze him. Someone walked across the kitchen, paused, then back to the chair. He'd have to wait longer. His eyelids were leaden, though. Sleep was fighting to overcome him; his body begged for it. And he wanted so badly to give in and drift off. But he couldn't. He had to stay awake. Scolding himself for even thinking about sleep, he opened his eyes wide and pumped his fists to get some circulation going. But still his eyelids were tugged down, and eventually, no matter how hard he fought, he gave in and succumbed to sleep.

He stood just outside the house, close enough to rest his hand on the clapboard and feel Shields's heart beating through the wood. It was slowing down. He was falling asleep. He imagined the muscle pumping rhythmically, the left side stronger than the right, top half, then bottom half. He visualized his hands wrapping around it, feeling the slipperiness, the firmness, the strength, then squeezing until it pumped no more.

Soon Shields would be no more. He would be driven to insanity and then devoured savagely. And he deserved every bit of it.

The bitter taste of the past two decades of torment and suffering still burned in his mouth. Yes, he had found ways to use the time to his advantage and had exacted revenge on so many during that time, but it was all practice, practice for this moment, for Shields.

A smile parted his lips at the thought of the consummation of all this. His thirst for vengeance would finally be satisfied, and his allies, the evil ones he'd summoned from the pit all those years ago, would be more than pleased. When the time came, they could have the girl. She meant nothing to him, never had. All he wanted was Shields.

Still on the outside of the house, he shut his eyes and dipped into Shields's dreams. This time he conjured images of Kelly. Dear Kelly. Such a beautiful creature and so full of life and vigor. The evil ones wanted her, but he refused and kept her for himself. He had fun with her too.

Shields would be different, though. He was already halfway to insane. He needed only a push or two to fall over the edge and right into the hands of death. But the push had to be perfectly timed, like the different notes of a musical score. Each one has its place and plays a role in the whole.

With his hand still on the clapboard, he began to hum a tune, an old Ukrainian folk song, concentrating on each note, the ebb and flow of the melody. It was a haunting sound, and it stirred something inside him that made him feel so alive.

Soon, when Shields was finally out of the way and the girl was begging for death, he would be unshackled and given the power he deserved, the power he'd been waiting for.

As during the previous night, dreams came and went like traveling salesmen selling their wares with a pocketful of promises. Catching and holding on to sleep was as futile as chasing down a greased pig. Images from the past raced through his dream vision, taunting him, luring, baiting, teasing. Kelly was there, smiling, laughing, crying. Within reach but always just beyond his grasp. In his dream he needed to catch her and hold her for sleep to come, but over and over his attempts proved fruitless.

Jimmy was there too. Running here, running there, always giggling. He was so happy, throwing his head back as he ran, spreading his arms wide. Giggling and laughing wildly. Rob hollered for him to come, but Jimmy couldn't hear him. He was only feet away, but Rob's voice seemed to drop dead after leaving his mouth. Oblivious to his daddy's pleading, Jimmy continued to run and laugh.

Then Rob was in the backseat of a car. Something was over his eyes, blacking out the world. The smell of cigarettes was all around him. He could tell by the muted sound of the tires on the road that the windows were closed. Sunlight warmed the right side of his body. The seat on which he sat was upholstered with textured vinyl. In the front, a man spoke softly. He strained to hear what he was saying, but his voice was too low and mumbled. Nobody responded, so he assumed the man was alone and merely talking to himself.

His arms were behind him, so he nearly had to sit on his hands. His shoulders throbbed like a toothache.

Fear gripped his heart and squeezed. It felt like his rib cage was shrinking and tightening until it was hard to draw in a deep breath. Strange thoughts entered his mind and ratcheted the fear up level after level. Would he ever see his parents again? Was this man going to kill him? Would he torture him first? Maybe his plans were to sell him.

Then he realized what was happening. He was Jimmy. He was seeing the world through his son's eyes. Feeling what he felt. He was in the backseat of a car, blindfolded, hands bound behind him.

By looking down, he noticed a line of light highlighting his cheeks. The blindfold wasn't tight enough.

The car slowed, and the man up front said something again.

Rob tilted his head back and found he was able to see out the gap between the blindfold and his cheeks. The world was blurry at best, but he could make out some things. Out the side window they were surrounded by open field. When he shifted to see out the windshield, he saw they were approaching a stand of houses. A sign was up ahead, on the right. White with bold black lettering. As they passed, he shifted again to see out the side window. The sign went by in a blur, but he caught the boldest words: *Welcome to Darlington.*

Rob awoke with a start. He was breathing hard and was wet with sweat. The house was darker than it had been. He checked his watch: three forty-five. The feeling of helplessness and fear that had gripped him so tightly in the car lingered. Involuntarily, tears came to his eyes. He still had residual images flickering through his mind, like sporadic surges of energy. Kelly. Jimmy. What the world looked like moving by from the backseat of that car.

Rob shut his eyes tight and sobbed quietly. The dream was too real. Too vivid. Too emotional. He wanted to scream, holler, anything to let out this pent-up frustration, anger, and fear. And grief.

Collecting himself and wiping at his eyes, he listened to the sounds around him. Juli breathed evenly and quietly; Carl in the recliner snored lightly but did not move. On the other side of the sofa, in the kitchen, there was no noise, no sound of movement, no talking, no rustle of clothing or paper. Norm and Rose must be asleep.

Slowly and carefully, Rob sat up and pulled his knees to his chest. From there he rolled to his side and went to kneeling, then standing. The kitchen was to his left. At the table, Norm sat slumped in his chair, arms hanging limp at his sides, chin on his chest. Rose was nowhere in sight. The house was lit by only one oil lamp on the hutch in the kitchen, and the soft light was so diffused it was almost pointless. The sofa was to his left, the door directly in front of him.

For a moment Rob stood still, calming his trembling, tingling hands and listening, telling himself how childish it was to be afraid of the dark. The outside world was quiet too. No birds, no squirrels…no screaming. He'd move slowly across the floor, then quickly throw the deadbolt, turn the knob, and be outside before anyone could awaken and realize what happened. There was no use attempting to sneak out. The click of the deadbolt would stir everyone from sleep. He would just have to make a run for it.

He thought of the darklings and the long-fingered hand and shuddered. His chest tightened; his breathing grew shallow. He almost sat back down on the blanket but forced himself to move forward, to put one foot in front of the other. He could do this for Jimmy. He could do it for Kelly. He had to.

Stepping carefully, as if he were walking on shards of glass, he made his way to the door without a sound. He hesitated, having second thoughts about what he was going to do. He still had time to give it up and return to the blanket and wait for daylight. But what if Jimmy couldn't wait? What if he needed his daddy now? What if two hours was two hours too late? He knew he was being irrational, but he also knew everything about this experience was irrational. The hallucinations that didn't feel like hallucinations. The dreams. The déjà vu. The darklings, whatever they were. Did any of it make sense?

He looked back at the sofa. Juli was still asleep on it. She was an odd one too and seemed to know more than she was letting on. He'd come back for her, of course. But right now he needed to look for Jimmy. And for some reason, beyond reason, he felt it had to be now.

Resolving himself to face whatever was out there, be it darkness or darkling, for his son, Rob reached for the deadbolt.

A voice out of the obscurity of the kitchen stopped him. Norm. "You really don't want to be doin' that."

Six

Rob's hands fell to his sides. A slow, hitched breath escaped his lungs.

A flame sprang to life in another oil lamp.

Norm stood, the shotgun hanging easily at his waist. On the recliner, Carl stirred, grunted, stirred again. Rose appeared at Norm's side, her sleep-stained eyes still half-closed, hair a teased tangle of gray wire. She wore a well-broken-in baby blue housecoat and matching slippers and carried an oil-lit lantern.

From the sofa, Juli said, "I was dreaming of one wallop of a tip, enough for a cruise to Iceland."

Rob looked at her then at Norm. "I'm leaving. You can shoot me if you want." Back to Juli: "You coming with me?"

She sat on the edge of the sofa, her eyes still clouded with dreams of big tippers and escapes to Iceland. "Am I welcome?"

Rob gave her the best smile he could, though he knew it must have looked terribly feeble in the dim light. "I wouldn't leave you with Clint Eastwood here." Then to Norm: "Now you'll have to shoot the both of us."

Carl climbed out of the recliner and positioned himself between Rob and the door. Rob eyed him from top to bottom, sizing up his mass and quickly deciding how best to use the larger man's center of gravity against him. He didn't want an altercation, but nothing, neither gun nor giant, was keeping him from finding his Jimmy.

"Outta the way, big guy," he said to Carl. "I don't want to fight you, but I will."

Carl looked at Norm as if seeking instructions.

This wasn't part of the plan. Had Juli known she was going to wind up on the barrel end of a shotgun toted by a most inhospitable host, she might have stayed home, might have never gotten out of bed this morning. Stepping past Rob, she stood next to Carl, lifted a shaky hand, and placed it on his shoulder. "It's not always wise to stand between a father and his child. Once he's started, he won't stop till he's out that door or dead."

Carl bowed his head low and stepped out of the way. Rob looked over at Norm, who was standing in the same spot, still leveling the shotgun on him. "You don't want to shoot me."

"Be an awful mess to clean up," Juli said.

"Shut up!" Norm said. "Sit down. I ain't gonna let you endanger this house, my family, by goin' out there and playin' hero or sumptin'."

Rose looked from Norm to Rob. She was holding the lantern chest high, and the light shone up on her face at such an angle that her cheeks appeared as round as apples, her eyes as dark as peach pits. "Maybe if they slip out real fast it'll be OK."

"Can't take that chance, Mommy," Norm said. "Now keep quiet."

Juli looked at Rob. There was an intensity in his eyes that said he wasn't backing down, not from Norm, not from Carl, not from Mr. Shotgun. Whether walking, running, or dodging buckshot, he was leaving this house.

"You coming?" he said.

She nodded. "Can't get to Iceland from here."

He turned toward the door and said to Norm, "You'll have to shoot both of us, you know. You ready to do that?"

Norm's eyes were hot as embers, but there was no malice in them. Juli could see he had no intent to greet a new day with two murders on his hands. Slowly, as if it pained him to do so but also brought great relief, he lowered the gun so the barrel pointed at the floor. "Make it quick, but know this; I ain't responsible for what happens to you out there. Your fate ain't gonna be on my conscience."

"Any words of advice?" Juli said.

Carl took one step toward them. His shoulders were slumped, and there was a look of great sadness in his eyes. "Darklings," he said with a shudder.

Juli touched his arm. "We'll be sure not to make friends with them."

"Light up the darkness," Norm said. "They hate the light."

Rob nodded to him and Rose. "Folks." Then to Carl: "Big guy."

"One more thing," Norm said. "You open that door, you ain't never welcome here again. They'll know we helped you and…can't have that."

"Good enough," Rob said and opened the door to the still dark morning.

A tremor ran through Juli as if a cold wind had passed over her, but the air outside was quiet and no breeze entered the doorway. Rob stepped from the safety of the house to the front stoop. With a little hesitation and a ton of apprehension, Juli followed.

Morning was at its deepest point in Darlington and the waning moon at its highest. It looked down on the town like a cataract-clouded eyeball. A static buzz coursed through Rob's body as he shut the door behind him and Juli. The click of the deadbolt being engaged from the other side sounded like gunfire in the quietness of the morning. Neither breeze nor animal stirred. The outside world was a photograph not fully developed. The greenish light of the moon cast muted, odd-shaped shadows across lawns and street.

The familiar heaviness sneaked into Rob's chest, but he pushed back, fighting to resist the urge to turn and pound on the door, begging entrance...and light.

Juli's hand found Rob's elbow. "Think we should head for the car?"

"You read my mind," he said, scanning the town for any shadow that moved. He pointed to his left where some light glinted off the car's chrome. "Over there."

Crossing the street, he felt dangerously exposed. He wondered how many darklings there were and just what exactly it was they were capable of. Why did Norm fear them so much?

At first glance, it appeared every other house along the street was darkened, but at closer inspection Rob noticed a pencil-thin line of weak light around each window where blind or curtain met the frame. Every home was lit on the inside, their way of warding off the darklings.

"They hate the light."

Sudden panic gripped Rob, and he picked up the pace across the asphalt. Stored heat from the previous day radiated from it. Juli was right behind him. The sound of their sneakers, though soft, sounded like drumbeats, the kind you hear in the jungle right before the cannibals strike and pierce their captives through with a spear.

When they finally reached the car Juli sighed loudly. "Looks like somebody enjoys our company."

She was standing on the passenger side, looking at the front tire. Rob looked at the driver's side tire. "This one's flat too. And the rear."

"Same here."

"All four sitting on the rims and only one spare. That won't get us very far."

"Not nearly far enough."

Rob looked across the car at Juli. "Any ideas?"

"Lots, but none that will put air back into these tires."

Rob went around to the rear of the car and popped the trunk. "I got a flashlight in here somewhere. One of those Maglites. Thing will cut a swath of light the size of a basketball court."

"I knew those middle-school years sitting on the bench would come in handy sometime," Juli said.

He rooted around in the trunk, moving blankets, boxes, and lawn chairs until his hand found what he was looking for. He turned it on and shone it at Juli's feet then down the street. The black road stretched out before them maybe fifty or sixty yards, then disappeared behind a curtain of darkness.

"Want to sit in the car and collect your thoughts?" Juli said.

"I'm still going after Jimmy," Rob said.

"That's why we're here. But since we're talking sports, a game plan wouldn't hurt."

"All right, a game plan it is then."

They both opened the car's doors at the same time, but just before they climbed in, the sound of women screaming originated in the woods and tore across the meadow.

Rob and Juli shut the doors simultaneously. Like inky water, darkness permeated the cabin of the car and carried with it the sounds of the darklings. Rob could see the whites of Juli's eyes all around her irises.

"I don't think that's the welcoming committee," she said.

For the first time in his life, Rob felt like the prey. Fear paralyzed him in his seat. A thought occurred to him that they might have time to make a dash for one of the houses and knock like crazy until some sleepy homeowner gave them safe harbor. But he couldn't move even if he wanted to. It was as if someone had sewn the seat of his pants to the car's upholstery.

The wails outside drew closer, not rapidly but at a steady pace. The darklings weren't running; they were stalking. The screams then spread right and left, encircling the car. The sound the darklings made was the stuff of nightmares, like a woman in full agony, and spread goose bumps over Rob's arms and neck.

Looking out the windows, side to side, Juli said, "The lights."

"What?"

"The headlights, turn them on. Turn every light on."

Rob flipped on the headlights, and both he and Juli gasped. Not fifty yards away a handful of darklings scattered like rats. The size of ten-year-old children, their thin, bony, naked frames covered with that taut earthworm skin moved quickly and with a fair amount of agility. Just before escaping the light, one of them turned its head and looked directly into the beam. Its black eyes glistened like polished obsidian.

The sight of the darklings so repelled Rob he almost shut off the lights.

"How about some high beams?" Juli said. She was pushed so far back in her seat that if the backrest wasn't there, she'd be in the rear of the car.

Rob turned the knob for the high beams, and the headlights got even brighter. Light spread a wider swath and pushed the darkness back farther. More darklings dispersed, their long, spindly legs scissoring against the black backdrop.

The screaming increased in volume as if the intrusion of light into their world of lightlessness was a severe insult to the darklings. It also inched closer. At the edges of the high beam's light, black eyes reflected back at Rob and Juli—so many it looked as though pairs were stacked on top of each other and just thrown together haphazardly. Upon closer inspection, it also appeared they moved in a subtle, rhythmic gyration of sorts, as one unit.

"I think we upset them," Rob said.

"You want to apologize?" Juli asked.

"Not really."

"Me neither."

Something hit the car, on the left side of the hood, with a loud thud. Then again, this time closer to the grille.

"I think we've just become target practice," Juli said.

Again, something *thunked* off the car, this time near the right headlight. Sweat beaded on Rob's forehead, and a metallic taste flooded his mouth. "Rocks," he said. "They're trying to bust out the headlights."

Juli slid down a little lower in the seat. "Let's hope there's no Nolan Ryan on the roster."

Now a stone hit the back window, leaving a nick the size of a dime. Then one clunked off the passenger side door. Then another, along the driver's side rear quarter panel. It appeared the stones they were hurling were no larger than golf balls, but even at that, enough of them, well placed, could do major damage...like take out a headlight.

"Monkey see, monkey do," Juli said. "They're copycatting each other."

"A sign of intelligence," Rob said. He looked at his watch: four twenty. "Sun'll be up in about an hour."

"Even if their aim is terrible, the battery won't last that long. You have the keys?"

Rob lifted his rear out of the seat and dug into the pocket of his jeans. Retrieving his keychain, he found the car's key and jammed it into the ignition. As he turned the key, the engine sprang to life and the lights brightened a bit.

A stone struck the driver's side window level with Rob's face and left a crack ten inches long. Rob flinched and ducked, reflexively covering his face with his hands.

"The flashlight," Juli said. "Take 'em out along the sides."

A thought occurred to Rob, and he swore for not thinking of it sooner. He grabbed the Maglite and clicked it on. "In the back," he said, aiming the light's beam out the window and finding a darkling, who shielded its eyes and scurried away, "on the floor is a spotlight my wife got me last year for spotting deer. It should still be in the box."

Juli climbed over the seat and into the back of the car. In a situation like this, you could never have enough light. She found the box right where Rob said it would be. "Got it," she said, and returned to the front.

A popping crack sounded, and the right headlight went out. Some darkling had hit its mark. A round of screams erupted from the darkness. Rob swept the beam of the Maglite across the front of the car. "Anytime you can get that thing hooked up will be great."

But the box was being stubborn—one of those taped-up jobs meant to ruin a shoplifter's day. It didn't help any, either, that her fingers felt as nimble as Twinkies. Oddly, it reminded her of Christmas mornings with her grandmother. She would wrap presents so thoroughly and use so much tape you needed a chain saw and some small explosives to open the boxes. Ripping at the cardboard, Juli said, "They made the box panic proof. Says right on it, not to be opened under extreme duress."

Still sweeping the light, scattering darklings like cockroaches, Rob said, "It's almost four thirty. C'mon, sun. Hurry it up today."

Juli suddenly stopped groping at the box and its labyrinth of taped edges and did the one thing that came naturally to her: pray.

"What? What's wrong?" Rob's voice sounded panicked.

Deep in prayer, her hands resting quietly on the box, head bowed, she said nothing.

"What're you doing?"

"Praying."

Another stone hit the rear window, and another right after it clunked off the grille.

"You think you could find a better time for that?"

Juli looked up at him. "There's a better time than now?"

Calmly and methodically, she found the edges of the tape and dismantled the box. She removed the spotlight, plugged the cord into the cigarette lighter, and, while flipping the switch, said, "Light the darkness."

A beam the size of a car cut through the darkness, igniting a fury of screams and shrieks. Darklings fell and scurried, their bony bodies fighting each other for traction, lashing out and clawing for relief from the light.

"You man the spot," Rob said, "and I'll handle the flash-light here. Keep sweeping the perimeter."

"Aye, aye, skipper."

Out of nowhere, something big landed on the roof of the car.

Seven

Rob looked up, then at Juli. Her eyes were wide and white.

"I'm really hoping that was just a big rock," she said.

Something moved on the roof, first to the left then right. The metal of the roof popped under the weight. They both knew what it was: a darkling had charged the car and jumped on top. Then, as if to confirm what they knew, a gruesome scream punctured the roof and filled the cabin.

Both Rob and Juli looked at the car's gear stick between them then at each other.

"We're thinking alike," Juli said.

Putting his foot on the brake, Rob shifted the car into drive then stomped on the gas. The engine growled, and the car lurched forward on four flat tires. Rubber flapped loudly as it was shredded by the metal rims. The darkling above them wailed again and began pounding on the roof. Rob watched the speedometer. When it reached ten miles an hour he slammed on the brakes, but no darkling sailed through the air as expected.

Juli continued spraying the light of the spotter around the perimeter, warding off any more ambitious darklings.

They were almost out of town now.

The clock on the dash glowed four forty-three.

"C'mon," Rob said through clenched teeth. He shifted into reverse and hit the gas again. The engine revved, and the car bucked backward, rims grinding into the asphalt. Again, he punched the brake, and the car jolted to a stop.

The darkling hung on and howled in defiance.

"One more try," Rob said. "Keep that light moving."

By now, Juli had grabbed the flashlight too and was holding it in one hand and the spotter in the other, wielding them like two battle swords.

Rob threw the car into drive again, stepped on the gas, and yanked the steering wheel hard to the left. The car lunged forward and swung around in a tight circle. Darklings appeared and scattered in the arc of light the solo headlight was slicing through the darkness. Rob kept the wheel turned as the car accelerated in a circle. Centrifugal force pulled him away from the door. The rims cut into the road, making an awful grinding sound. The darklings screamed their disapproval.

But above them, the darkling on the roof remained.

"Hang on," Rob said, and hit the brake hard. The car stopped like it had hit a wall, and the darkling on the roof finally lost its grip, wailed wildly, and landed on the asphalt in front of them, rolling a couple times. It writhed on the ground for a moment, a tangle of bony arms and legs, then jumped to its feet and stumbled away.

"Keep the light on it," Rob hollered.

Juli trained the spotter on the darkling as it staggered off the road. When it reached the grass, it stopped and stood upright, its back to the car.

"Keep the light on it," Rob said again.

The darkling stood motionless, arms hanging loosely at its sides, breathing heavily, its rib cage expanding and contracting rapidly. It was maybe thirty feet away but close enough that Rob could see it was hairless from head to toe.

Its arms and legs were disproportionately long, and it had no buttocks to speak of. The legs just began where the back ended.

The darkling turned its head slightly to the right, toward the eastern sky.

Rob followed its gaze and noticed the first line of soft light glowing above the treetops.

The darkling drew in a deep breath, contracted its thoracic muscles, and let out a terrible scream; it then bounded away out of the spotter's reach and disappeared into the darkness.

Within seconds, the area was void of darklings. At the first sign of dawn they'd vacated the town and went back to whatever dark cave they hid in during daylight hours. Rob slouched in the seat and tried to settle his breathing. He could feel his heart in his throat. Next to him, Juli continued scanning the perimeter with the spotlight, back and forth in wide sweeps. No darklings were to be found, though. The town of Darlington was once again quiet and still.

Several thoughts skipped through Rob's mind. One, he hadn't seen Jimmy among the darklings. But that didn't mean his son wasn't there, and it didn't mean he wasn't in Darlington. It just meant Rob hadn't seen him. Two, all that screaming and wailing and the racket the car made cutting up the asphalt had to awaken the whole town, yet no one had come to their aid. The darklings instilled such fear in the townsfolk that they'd rather let two of their own fall into those bony hands (Rob didn't even want to think about what that would entail) than take on the little devils as a town.

Fear could be a powerful thing. And three, he couldn't stop thinking how easily Juli had fallen into prayer in the midst of such pressure. There was a time, he supposed, when he would have considered prayer, but not anymore. He'd given God a chance with Kelly and Jimmy, and it just didn't work out. If Juli wanted to pray, that was fine with him. But leave him out of it.

With each passing minute the sky above the trees became lighter, showing off an array of colors from deep pink to burnt orange to auburn. Rob slowly drove the car to the church's gravel parking lot, put it in park, and shut off the engine. The outside world was silent save for the arrhythmic ticking of cooling metal.

Juli clicked off the spotlight and ran her finger along the inside of the windshield where a rock had gouged the glass. "Good luck explaining this to your insurance company."

Rob laughed. It felt good to release some of the tension. "I have great comprehensive."

"You think they'll buy that an angry horde of little green men attacked your car with rocks?"

"I could just tell them it was hail."

Juli shook her head. "They'd definitely get you for fraud. Stick to the truth; it might just be more believable."

They sat in silence for a moment, each looking straight ahead, watching the sky turn from a shade of muted red to soft blue. Morning was upon them. In the homes around them, one by one, shades were raised and curious faces peeked out of closed windows.

Juli, who'd still been holding the spotlight on her lap, placed it on the floor of the car. "Did you see him?"

"No. But that doesn't mean he isn't here. He is. I know it. I can feel him."

"Feel him how?"

Rob opened his mouth to speak then shut it. Explaining how he could feel Jimmy's presence wasn't an easy thing to do. He paused then tried again. "Are you a mother?"

"Not yet. But I have high hopes of someday being one. I like the sound of it. And I hear the perks are great."

"There's a bond that forms between a parent and child, something…mystical or metaphysical. Maybe even spiritual. You feel what they feel, see what they see, all in a figurative way, of course." He paused again. "This place. This town. Even this church, all feel so familiar to me. It has to be because Jimmy is here and in a literal way I'm feeling what he feels and seeing what he sees. At times, I swear I can even hear him. I know that sounds crazy. But I did see him last night."

Juli looked out the window and remained there with her head turned away from Rob for so long he thought she had checked out. Finally she said, "What's your wife think of you turning all new-age starry-eyed?"

The mention of "your wife" sent a wave of remorse through Rob's body. What would Kelly think of his obsession with finding Jimmy? Would she encourage it or tell him what everyone else told him, that Jimmy was gone and he needed to deal with his grief in a healthy way and move on? He'd convinced himself that she wouldn't want him to stop looking for their little boy, but now he wasn't so sure. Verbalizing his beliefs to Juli made him sound like a front-runner for Screwball of the Year. But screwball or not, he knew what he knew, and he wasn't leaving this town without his son.

"Kelly's dead," he said to Juli.

Juli turned to face him, and there were tears in her eyes. "Dead but not gone. How did it happen?"

"Some other time." He opened the door and got out. Leaning down to see in the car, he said, "Right now I have to find my son."

The boy has no idea how long he has been in the attic. He does know, however, that it has gotten so hot he thinks he might faint. He sweats until his sweat leaves salt on his lips. A couple times he dozed off, only to wake up crying from the pain in his shoulders. With his arms pulled behind his back like they are, his shoulders ache like two toothaches.

He had one toothache a year ago. It made his whole mouth hurt all the way up to his eyes. Dr. Stein said a cavity the size of the Grand Canyon was to blame and that if they'd waited any longer to get it filled, he would have had to pull the tooth. That didn't sound like a good idea to the boy. Even when his teeth were loose he didn't like having them pulled. He usually just let them fall out on their own. Once he let Daddy pull a tooth. Daddy was so fast the boy didn't even know he'd pulled it until Daddy held it up and laughed.

Thinking about his daddy brings the tears again. Now he's sure he'll never see his parents again.

Footsteps on the stairs stop his crying. The boy holds still and listens. It sounds like the way the woman comes up the steps, kind of an odd rhythm: one-two, one-two, one-two. If his hands were untied he could clap to the rhythm like they did in music class at school. Will he ever go to school again? Will he ever see his friends again?

The footsteps make it to the top of the stairs and wind around the attic toward him, creaking boards along the way.

"Brought you some more water." It's the woman.

He opens his mouth, more than ready for water, even if it is warm like before. His mouth is so dry the inside of his cheeks feel like sandpaper, and his tongue feels like a never-used sponge. The woman pours warm water down his throat again. And just like last time, he swallows in huge gulps, spilling some down his chin. His mommy would have told him to slow down and take smaller sips, but she didn't know how thirsty he was.

Before he is satisfied, the woman pulls the glass away, and he hears it clunk as she sets it down on the hard floor. "Stand up now," she says.

He tries to stand but with his arms behind his back like they are he can't do it.

"Come on," the woman says. Her voice still sounds a little shaky. "Stand up."

He leans to his side to slide his legs under him but instead falls to the floor, landing hard on his left shoulder. Pain bites into his shoulder and runs up along the side of his neck, and he hollers out.

Just like that, the woman's hand is over his mouth. Her other hand has a hold on the back of his neck. "You can't make a sound," she says. Her mouth is so close to his ear he can feel the hotness of her breath. She lets go with the hand covering his mouth. "If they hear . . . now, open your mouth."

He doesn't do it. He knows what's coming if he does. The rag or whatever it is that tastes like grass.

"Open your mouth now," she says again.

Tears build in his eyes and wet the blindfold again. He keeps his mouth clamped shut and shakes his head.

The woman squeezes the back of his neck a little harder, not so much that it hurts but enough that it gets the boy's attention. "You have to open your mouth. It's for your own good. You don't want anyone to hear. Come on now. Open up."

Crying even harder, he opens his mouth.

"Wider." She says it like the word hurts coming out of her mouth.

Slowly, reluctantly, he opens wider. In goes the rag. She doesn't put it in that far, though, and he thinks that if he wants to he can easily push it out with his tongue. But he doesn't dare try it now or she'll stuff it in farther and then that would be it.

She lets go of his neck. "Now, let's stand you up." Grabbing him under the armpits, she hoists him up onto his feet and places a hand behind his neck again but doesn't squeeze this time. "Walk forward."

She leads him around the attic as before and down the steps. He can feel the temperature cooling with each step down. They walk some more, some on hardwood floor, some on rugs until she says, "Stop here."

He stops and waits.

For a few seconds everything is quiet, and he isn't sure if the woman is still there or not. He wants to try to push the rag from his mouth but fears if the woman is there she'll put it back in. So he does nothing but stand there, listening to the sound of his own breathing through his nose.

Suddenly, he can feel the woman close to him, not her body, but just her presence.

"Now," she says, "here's what we're going to do. I have a box here, big enough for you to lie down in. If I untie your hands, do you promise to get in like a good boy and lie down?"

For a moment, fear keeps the boy from moving. A box? She wants him to lie down in a box?

"Do you promise? You have to promise."

Without really thinking about it, he nods. He just wants his hands untied. His shoulders hurt so bad.

He feels a tugging at whatever it is that ties his hands together;

then they are free. His arms fall to his sides like they are dead, and pain shoots through his shoulders. More tears come.

"Now, in the box," the woman says. She guides him forward two steps and then says, "Step up and over the edge."

But the boy doesn't move. With his arms free now, he wants to rip the blindfold off, spit out the rag, and make a run for it. He's the fastest kid in the second grade and knows he can outrun the woman. She sounds at least as old as his grammy, and he always beats her in races.

The woman's hand finds the back of his neck again, and she gives a light squeeze. "Please, just do it. There's no use resisting. We have to do as they say."

Feeling like a pirate walking the plank, the boy lifts one leg high and steps into the box. He then brings the other leg in.

"Now lie down," the woman says.

The boy squats then falls to his butt. Reaching out only a little with each hand, he can feel the sides of the box on either side. It isn't made of cardboard but wood. He wonders what shape it is.

The woman nudges his shoulder. "Lie down now. It'll be OK."

He obeys and stretches out his legs and lies down in the box.

"I'm going to put the lid on now. If you want to stay alive, and if you ever want to see your parents again, you'll be quiet in there. If you make any noise at all, I'll have to tie your hands again. And I don't want to have to do that. Understand?"

The boy nods his head furiously and reaches for the rag in his mouth. The woman grabs his hand and holds it tight.

"Not yet." She pauses. Her hand feels soft but strong at the same time.

The boy hides his hands under his butt and struggles to pull in air through his nose.

"Good," the woman says. "We'll get you back out in no time."

The boy hears the lid go on and various snaps going together.

Quickly, he reaches up and pulls the rag from his mouth then slides the blindfold up and over his forehead. The inside of the box is black as the sky at night. He can't even see his hand in front of his face.

All he can think about is that the woman has just put him in a coffin, and he is going to be buried alive.

The early morning air was cool and fresh. A light breeze escaped the surrounding woods and pushed through the town of Darlington. Standing in the church's parking lot, face turned toward the rising sun, feeling the cool air comb his hair, Rob had that familiar feeling again. Déjà vu. Like he'd stood in this very spot before, facing that same sun, feeling the same breeze. Only he hadn't. Was he remembering something from a dream? Or was he feeling what Jimmy was feeling? Experiencing the morning *through* his son? Was Jimmy in some meadow or field on the other side of the trees, feeling exactly what Rob was feeling here?

Rob shut his eyes and tried to picture his little boy, in his favorite G.I. Joe T-shirt and camo shorts, standing in a grassy meadow, hair being tossed about by an easy current. Jimmy was there, in his mind, as real as ever. Smiling. Giggling. The wind increases; Jimmy raises his arms overhead and parts his lips in an open-mouth smile. A noise from the nearby woods distracts him. He turns his head. Fear freezes his face. There, from the tree line, breaks a horde of faceless darklings, running full throttle toward Jimmy, their bony legs chopping through the long grass. Screaming. That awful, bone-gnawing wail. Jimmy stands paralyzed where he is, arms still raised, mouth open in horror.

The closing car door startled Rob and snapped him out of his trance. Juli approached him in an arc.

"You OK?" she asked. "Memories can be hard."

"What makes you think I was remembering?"

"You had that remembering look on your face."

"I didn't know there was a remembering look."

"There is. You know it when you see it."

They both stood quietly for a few moments, looking across the goldenrod-dotted meadow, studying the border of the woods. Rob knew Jimmy was in there somewhere or on the other side. He also knew standing here, in this parking lot, wasn't doing anybody any good. "I'm going in." He looked at Juli. "Thanks for the company, but I think I should finish this alone. Maybe someone here can take you back to Mayfield."

Juli kept her face toward the woods and cocked her head to one side. "Bummer. I was kinda hoping for a real heart-pounding adventure."

"I think you better leave the adventure stuff to me. Doesn't Mary Jane need you back at the diner?"

"Nope."

"You off today?"

"I am now."

Rob turned his whole body to face her now. "You didn't quit."

Now Juli turned her head to look at him. Her blue eyes were startling in the morning light, like fresh Maine blueberries. "Never. I love it there, but you need some company."

"I can't let you go with me. It could get dangerous. I can't be responsible for that."

Juli looked at the woods then at Rob. "You're gonna need a compass in there."

"I'll manage." Even as he said the words, fear crawled into his chest and constricted its tentacles around his lungs. What if he got lost in there and night came and darkness fell and the darklings came hunting?

Juli faced the woods again. "It's called Darlington Woods, but there's a reason the townies call it Fear Forest."

"I'll manage."

"I'm coming."

"No. You're not."

"You need me."

"Why? Why do I need you?"

"Because I know the way out."

"What, there's only one way out of the woods too?"

Juli looked him right in the eyes. "One way out."

"And how do you know?"

"Experience can be a harsh teacher but a good one." With that she put one foot forward and started toward the edge of Darlington Woods. Fear Forest.

Rob let her get a good twenty feet ahead of him before he reached in the car for the flashlight and spotter then hurried up alongside her. "You've been in there before?"

"In so many words...and in so many ways."

"Here, hold this." He handed her the spotter. "And you know your way around?"

"No one knows their way around."

"Then how do you know the way out? That there's only one way?"

"I'm here, aren't I?"

She had a point. If she was telling the truth that she'd been in the woods before, then she'd obviously found the way out.

They reached the border of meadow and woods in just a

few minutes' time. Juli stopped before entering the woods. She faced Rob. "It's OK to be afraid. Everyone is. But don't let the fear overcome you. What happened last night...Darlington and these woods are one."

Rob wasn't sure he understood what she was talking about, but he didn't have time for questions and answers. They could talk as they walked. "Fine, let's just get to it."

But before they could cross the threshold from meadow to woods a voice stopped them. "Wait."

Rob turned and saw a small group of five people standing in the church parking lot. There were four men and one woman, all much older than Rob, standing at least an arm's length from each other. They looked like human bowling pins, evenly spaced and motionless. The woman, a tall thin thing wearing a brown dress that hung on her like a curtain, stood in the back and rocked side to side, looking about nervously. One of the men held a rifle in one hand. Another gripped a hatchet.

For a few long seconds Rob and the gaggle of Darlingtonians stared at each other. No one moved but the woman in the back swaying, swaying like a bowling pin knocked off balance but not ready to fall.

Juli said, "Maybe we should see what they want."

Keeping his eyes on the group across the meadow, Rob said, "Better not be trouble. I'm not in the mood to get any more guns pointed at me."

"I can second that."

Working their way back through the high grass and goldenrod, Rob managed a friendly wave at the small assembly. One of the men, a short, balding guy with little round glasses, lifted his hand weakly.

"Mornin', folks," the man with the rifle said when Rob and Juli were within twenty feet.

"Morning," Rob said.

The man cocked his head to one side and rocked the rifle in his hand. "What brings you to this part of the woods?"

The woman in the back now had both hands partially covering her face as if hiding behind them. Her swaying grew more enthusiastic.

Rob thought it was odd that no one mentioned what happened last night and early this morning. They had to have been awakened by all the commotion, the screams of the darklings and grind of the car's wheels against the asphalt. And if they didn't, the deep scars in the road now would surely have clued them that something odd had happened here recently.

"Looking for someone," Rob said.

The man with the gun looked at the man to his right, a tall, lean fellow with a protruding Adam's apple and hooked nose. In a gravelly baritone voice that in no way fit his appearance, the tall man said, "Your son."

"Have you seen him?"

"Nope," the rifle-toting man said. "Ain't seen no one 'round here 'cept us."

"And we'd like to keep it that way," the man carrying the hatchet said. He looked at the tall man as if embarrassed by his directness.

"The woods aren't safe," the tall man said.

The woman moved her hands from her mouth and took a step forward. "The devil's in there," she said. Her eyes burned like coals, and her face twisted in fear.

"Shush, Nana," the man with the rifle said. Then to Rob, "The woods, they ain't safe."

106

The woman mumbled something unintelligible and beat her fist into the other hand. Her face had turned a deep shade of red, and she looked about ready to burst into tears.

"Not too safe here in town, either," Juli said.

An awkward silence loomed for seconds on seconds.

"How did you know about my son?" Rob asked.

"Word spreads fast in a small town," the rifle man said. "I doubt your son is in there." He tipped his head toward the woods.

"I need to find that out myself," Rob said.

"You'll get 'em angry," the woman said, her voice almost a moan.

Rob leaned to his right so he could get a good look at her. "Who?"

"Nana!"

"Them. All—"

"Nana."

"—three of 'em. Like a trinity."

The tall man turned to face the woman. "Go back to your house, Nana," he said. He didn't take his eyes off her until she reluctantly stepped back, turned, and walked away.

"She's talking about the darklings, isn't she?"

The rifle man looked at the tall man beside him. The other two exchanged nervous glances too. Rifle man finally said, "Son, you best be on your way now."

"You're afraid of them, aren't you? That if you help us they'll be back."

"Time to go, son."

"That we'll make them mad and they'll take it out on you."

The man adjusted his grip on the rifle. "That's enough now. Time for you and your friend—"

"That's what Norm was afraid of."

In a series of quick jerky movements, the man raised the rifle to his shoulder and aimed it at Rob.

"Whoa," Rob said, raising both hands to shoulder height. "Hang on there."

The rifle shook in the man's hands. The other men shifted about uneasily.

Juli stepped toward the man with the rifle.

He glanced at her then back at Rob. "You two just leave now. That's all we're askin'."

"Hasn't there been enough death in Darlington?" Juli said.

Beads of sweat broke out on the man's brow. The rifle shook more. It had to be getting heavy.

With a shaky hand of her own, Juli reached for the barrel and wrapped her fingers around it. "Hasn't there been enough death?"

The man finally lowered the rifle and let the barrel drop to the ground. His shoulders slumped, and he wiped at the sweat on his face. "Go on then. But you'll get no help from us." He raised his head and looked past Juli at Rob. "You go in there, and you're on your own."

Leaving the group of men behind, Rob and Juli crossed the meadow for a second time that morning. Juli's heart was still thumping furiously, and her hands were still unsteady.

When they arrived at the edge of the woods, Rob stopped and said, "What was that back there about enough death in Darlington?"

Juli looked back at the town. The four men were still standing there, motionless, watching. Beyond them, and at this distance, the town of Darlington looked as friendly and peaceful as any small town in northern Maryland. No one would suspect the horrors that had occurred there over the past twenty-two years and the fear they had spawned. "Those people have had their fair share. Enough for several towns combined."

"Care to elaborate?"

"Some other time. It's a lot to bite off in one sitting."

"I'll hold you to that," Rob said. He looked up at a towering oak and squinted. "You ready?"

"Lead the way."

They stepped through a low-lying clump of kudzu and into the woods. Immediately the temperature dropped a handful of degrees and the light muted. The ground was covered with underbrush and decomposing leaves and moss-covered rocks. Barren tree trunks rose from the leafy floor and shot into the sky, spreading their branches fifty, sixty, seventy feet above. Looking up at the canopy with only pin-sized holes of light poking through, Juli suddenly became very disoriented. She had to right her head and shut her eyes to adjust her sense of equilibrium. That's when she noticed the queer silence. The forest was void of the familiar sounds of birds, squirrels, chipmunks, and cicada. It was as quiet as a cemetery on a weekday morning. No breeze moved through the trees as it had so easily blown across the meadow.

Juli looked around. It all looked the same. Trees. Underbrush. Kudzu. "Where to?"

"Let's just walk and see what happens." Rob looked at his watch. "It's almost six. That means we have, what, at most fourteen hours of daylight left, less here in the woods."

They walked on, stepping over fallen limbs and around clumps of thickets and wild raspberry bushes. The air in the woods was cool but still, bringing out a sweat on Juli's forehead.

After some time of comfortable silence, Rob said, "So why Iceland?"

"Iceland?"

"Back at the house you said you were dreaming of Iceland. Why Iceland?"

"I'm a fan of volcanoes and boiling mud lakes. Great material for interesting dreams."

"You'll have to explain that one."

Juli climbed over a fallen poplar. "Iceland has over a hundred volcanoes, and the whole island is full of thermal springs. The hot water beneath the surface bubbles up and creates boiling mud lakes. I hear it's great for your skin, except for the boiling part."

"Fascinating." He said it like he found Juli's knowledge of Icelandic geography as interesting as watching a game of bridge.

Juli caught the sarcasm in his tone but ignored it. "In fact, most of the homes in Iceland—"

To their right, a breaking branch and shuffle of leaves stopped them in their path.

PART THREE

Fear of monsters attracts monsters.

—Unknown

Eight

JULI STOPPED TALKING, AND THEY BOTH FROZE AND looked at each other. Rob lifted a finger and placed it against his lips. The sound had come from a stand of honeysuckle about forty feet to their right. In Rob's mind it could be only one of three things: an animal (which they'd neither seen nor heard since entering the forest), a darkling (but it was daytime and that would be inconsistent with the little trolls' MO), or Jimmy. Since the other two options seemed less likely, Rob could only assume it was his boy. He took one step toward the bush when the rustling sounded again, rattling a few of the thin branches.

In a quiet voice, almost a whisper, Rob said, "Jimmy?"

But only silence responded.

If it was Jimmy, why hadn't he jumped up and run into Rob's arms? Maybe he'd been so traumatized he feared anything that moved. He probably thought Rob was a darkling.

Rob took another step closer to the honeysuckle. His heart thumped. He realized he was holding his breath and blew it out. Looking back at Juli, he noticed she was maintaining a safe distance behind him and had the spotter raised chest high as if to use it as a weapon.

Rob turned back around and took a few more steps forward. "Jimmy? It's Daddy, little buddy. It's OK. I'm here."

Rob paused and heard Juli stop behind him. He remained

still, listening, watching the bush for any movement. He was within twenty feet now but still couldn't see past the tight tangle of branches. His son could be right there, just feet away, moments from being reunited, and still Rob felt a sense of fear. And it was that fear that kept him from running headlong into the honeysuckle.

"Jimmy, talk to me, buddy. Tell me it's you."

Still nothing. Then another broken branch and more rustling leaves.

Closer Rob crept with Juli on his heels, armed with her spotter. When he was about ten feet away, he could hear breathing coming from the bush, deep and even, the way Jimmy's breathing sounded when he slept with a stuffy nose.

Suddenly, the bush exploded with movement and sound. Branches broke, leaves flew, and the earth seemed to shake. Rob jumped back, tripped on a fallen limb, and landed on his butt next to Juli.

She took a few quick steps backward, and Rob scrambled back on heels and elbows. They both stared wide-eyed at the large dog that had emerged from the honeysuckle.

Mottled gray and brown, the dog was about the size of a coyote and lanky like one too. Its fur was matted and bloodstained in places and absent in others. It stood with its forelegs spread wide, head dipped, ears back, mouth slightly ajar, watching Rob and Juli from the tops of its eyes.

Rob made a move to stand but froze when the dog took two steps forward and lifted its lips in a nasty snarl. The fur on the back of its neck and all the way down its back bristled.

"Wild dog," Juli whispered.

Blood surged in Rob's ears. On his butt in the leaves he

was in such a vulnerable position. He needed to get to his feet, to a position of defense. He moved again to stand, but before he even heard their soft paw steps, three more dogs appeared, one to his right, two to his left.

Juli took another step back. Rob glanced around at the pack. All four were in the same posture of watchfulness: forelegs spread, head dipped, eyes...

Those eyes. A chill, like a thousand spider legs, ran down Rob's back. Each of the dogs had irises as solid black as a chunk of coal.

He stood behind a tree, watching the events before him unfold. It was like watching a circus act, the guy on the high wire with no safety net, and the suspense was killing him. A smile played across his face. Killing him. What a perfect use of words. Pun intended.

Shields and the girl were facing down the dogs. This could be fun to watch. He looked at Shields's face. The fear was evident. Scrawled across his mug in deep creases and furrows. And the shadow in his eyes, that same look they all shared.

He knew what fear looked like. In fact, he considered himself quite the student of it. Over the years he'd seen fear on so many faces, and it looked the same on everyone.

And he loved it. This is what he fed on, what charged him. If he had a camera, he'd capture that look every opportunity he had and cover the walls of his home with the pictures. Keep them in his pockets, his car, his desk. That way, every-where he went he could be surrounded by the look of fear;

everywhere he looked he could be reminded of the weakness of man.

The dogs were closing in. He held his breath as long as he could and let it out again, then drew in a deep, satisfying breath. The thick aroma of fear was in the air.

"Got any great ideas?" Rob asked Juli, not moving his eyes from the dogs.

"My idea well is dry at the moment."

Rob pushed backward, digging his heels into the soft ground. Juli followed his cue and backpedaled as well. But the dogs matched them step for step, keeping their heads low, drawing in the scent of their prey, tasting the air. And watching, always watching with those black orbs.

"This is one problem I don't think duct tape could solve," Juli said, "but the flashlight might come in handy."

So blinded by fear, Rob hadn't even thought of the flashlight in his hand. He pointed it at the lead dog, the first one he'd come across, and hit the switch. Bright light landed on the dog's face, and it immediately reversed a few steps, shook its head, and sneezed several times in succession, as if Rob had just sprayed lemon juice in its eyes. The other three looked on with curiosity.

Rob shifted the light so it fell on the dog to his right, nearest him, and got the same reaction.

"Direct light," he said. "They hate it. Use the spotter."

"Already tried. No power. I guess our fate is in the hands of your light saber, young Skywalker."

Rob trained the light on each of the dogs' faces as he got

to his feet, and he and Juli put distance between them and their new admirers.

"How far can that saber reach?" Juli asked.

They were about fifty feet from the dogs. "Not much further than this."

"Time to show how fast our new sneakers are."

"Now would be a good time for that prayer thing you do too."

"One step ahead of you there."

Still double-clutching the light and moving it from dog to dog, spending enough time on each to keep it at bay and retard the inevitable advance, Rob took a deep breath and tried to steady his shaking hands. Around them the trees were silent spectators, as if in awe of the confrontation unfolding before them.

"On three?" Juli said.

"Three's good."

"One…"

"Wait. *On* three or after three?"

"*On* three."

They were standing still. The flashlight beam was stretched as far as it could reach and still be potent to the dogs' light-allergic eyes.

"Which way are we running?" Rob said.

"The only way that makes sense, away from them."

If Rob's sense of direction was right, the edge of the woods, where tree line met meadow, was directly behind them and not far away. They hadn't walked that long before coming upon man's best friend here. He stole a quick glance behind him, expecting to see a wall of sunlight a ways off through the trees, but instead all he saw were more trees, more forest. Had they gotten turned around?

Quickly, alternating glances at the woods around them and at the dogs before them, he searched for any sunlight at all, any sign that would lead them along the right route out of the woods. But in every direction, trees and underbrush and kudzu as far as he could see. He felt a prick of panic touch his nerves.

The dogs were getting braver...and smarter. The lead one, the largest and mangiest of the four, took two steps forward, keeping his head turned to the side so as not to have to face the light.

"On three," Rob said.

Juli placed a hand on his shoulder. "One...two..."

On "three" they both turned and bolted in the same direction, away from the dogs. Behind them, the dogs yelped and barked, and leaves crunched under their paws.

Rob pumped his arms and legs as fast as he could. Low-hanging branches slapped at his chest, and his feet struggled to find sure purchase in the soft leaves. Trees—oak, hickory, poplar, loblolly pine—motionless and stalwart, stood by and watched, offering no help at all. Juli was to his right, just behind him. He could hear her lungs sucking air, and she made a little grunting noise with each step.

Jumping a fallen tree, Rob stole a quick look behind him. The dogs were still about twenty feet away, but they had gained ground. He could hear their heavy panting, hear the snarl under their breath, the hunger in their throats. If they didn't reach the edge of the woods and the safety of full midmorning sunlight soon, they'd be overcome by teeth and claws in a matter of seconds.

What unfolded next happened so fast Rob barely had time to process it. Ahead of him and to the left he saw a shadow moving, almost gliding, weaving in and out of forest things, coming fast. The shadow arced left and headed toward them. When their paths met, a man, all baggy clothes and hairy face, bowled over a sapling, screaming like a poltergeist. Suddenly, a light exploded from him, as bright as a star, and just before hitting the leaves, Rob heard the dogs whimper.

Rob rolled a couple times in the leaves and came up covering his face with his arms, fully expecting to be on the receiving end of four angry dogs. But instead he sat looking at the rear of the strange man, walking backward, holding some kind of high-powered light in front of him with both hands. The dogs, on the other end of the light, cowered and alternated between whimpers and snarls. The one on the far right pawed angrily at the ground.

"Move back," the man said. "Back."

Somewhat disoriented from his full-throttle run and spill in the leaves, Rob got his legs under him and stood. Juli was there, her hand gripping his arm. They both started taking steps backward.

As his head cleared, Rob got a better look at the back of the man. He was shorter than Rob by at least a few inches, thin, and had dark gray hair pulled back in a tight ponytail. His clothes were worn but not rags and hung on him like they were several sizes too big. In his hands he held some kind of battery-powered high-wattage floodlight that cast a swath of light twenty yards wide across the forest floor. It was remarkably useful for keeping the dogs at bay.

Juli's hand tightened on Rob's arm. "Who invited Rip van Winkle?"

"Looks like he woke up just in time," Rob said, then to the man, "Where are we going?"

Never taking his eyes off the dogs or letting the light stray from them, the man replied, "Just keep walking. You'll see." His voice was high-pitched and strained, dry sounding.

Rob looked at Juli and shrugged. They both kept walking.

The next time Rob looked at his watch it was nearing nine o'clock. They'd been stepping through the woods for nearly an hour, the man with the light keeping pace, the dogs staying a safe distance away but there, just out of reach of the light, silently stalking.

Finally the man stopped and said, "There, to your left, see the cabin?"

Rob looked to his left but saw nothing other than trees and underbrush and dappled shadows. "I don't see it," he said.

"Look again. Closer. It's there." The man stepped left.

Rob looked at Juli, who appeared just as bewildered as he was, then back into the depths of the woods. This time he saw it. Through the trees, about seventy yards off, he caught the angle of a roofline. "Yes, I see it," he said, pointing to where the cabin stood.

"Head for it," the man said, still sidestepping left.

The dogs pawed at the ground and growled and snarled, their pink tongues licking at the air, growing more agitated by the second. They realized their prey was getting away.

It took Rob and Juli only a minute or two to reach the cabin, a makeshift structure pieced together by plywood and two-by-fours. They both stood there looking at it when the man approached, holding the light at his side, panting heavily. "Get inside. Go. They're coming."

Looking over the man's shoulder, Rob saw the four dogs

in full run, ears flat against their heads, tongues lolling from open mouths, hunger in their empty black eyes.

"Go on. Inside," the man shouted. Panic trembled through his voice.

Rob threw the simple lever latch and swung the wooden plank door open. Juli entered the cabin first, and he followed close on her heels. Behind them, the man with the shaggy gray beard stumbled inside and dropped the light.

"Shut it," he yelled.

Rob pushed the door closed. The man was there in an instant, sliding a heavy two-by-six into place across the inside of the door.

On the outside, a dog collided with the door then let out a yelp of frustration. The others began pawing and scratching at the wood, snarling and barking.

From inside the small shelter, Rob noticed for the first time the absence of windows. A single oil lamp burned on a rough wood table that sat in the middle of the place. With the dogs outside, the cabin felt like a cave whose walls were inching closer every second.

Rob collapsed to the floor and sat on his butt, breathing hard. His hands shook involuntarily, and he grabbed them to stop it. Juli sat on a chair at the table, leaned forward, and put her head in her hands. Her back rose and fell to a quick but steady rhythm.

The dogs outside ceased their ranting, and all fell quiet again.

The man moved across the cabin floor with a confidence

that comes only from experience, slid a board about eye level on the wall to the right, and peered out a peephole the size of a soda can. He stood like that, on his toes, for about a minute before sliding the board back into place, turning, and saying, "They're leaving. It's OK now." He walked over to the table. "It's OK," he said again.

"It's not OK," Rob said, getting to his feet. "None of this is OK. The darklings, or whatever they are, the dogs, these weird woods, you, my son is out there somewhere. He's out there"—he jabbed a finger at the door—"with them."

The man leaned against the wall, and for the first time Rob got a good look at his face. Sunken cheeks were partially hid by a wiry beard; a thin, long nose ended in flared nostrils. Deep-set eyes were spaced wide, and the right one was badly scarred and floated lazily toward the ear.

Rob caught himself staring at the man's eye and quickly looked away.

"It's all right," the man said. He pointed at his eye. "My first encounter with the dogs."

He walked over to the table and sat in the other chair. With the deep crevices around his eyes and mouth, he appeared at least eighty, though he probably wasn't that old. His thin hands rested on the table. Blue veins wound around taut tendons and bones under gauzy, almost translucent skin. Rob noticed the man's hands were shaking too.

"I assume they're not housebroken," Juli said.

The man just looked at her with thoughtful, intelligent, but sad eyes.

Rob extended his hand across the table. "I'm Rob, and this is Juli. Thanks…for what you did out there. If you hadn't gotten there when you did—"

"But I did," the man said, taking Rob's hand. "Thank the

Lord for that. The dogs, they're not the friendliest sort. I'm Asher Wiggins. You know, Paul warned about this. He told the Corinthian church to be watchful for dogs that come to destroy." He lowered his eyes to his hands. "I wasn't watchful, and my flock got the worst of it."

"The pastor," Juli said, "of the church in town."

Asher's eyes drifted from his guests and found some spot on the wall. "Was. I wasn't ready, though, and lost my flock." His eyes found Juli's again. "But that's a long story best told around a fireplace with lots of coffee on hand. Lots of tears to be shed there."

Rob looked around the rest of the cabin. In one corner was a small metal cot with some blankets folded and piled high; in another corner were a dry sink and a clumsy-looking hutch filled with plates and glasses.

"It's not often I get visitors," Asher said. "Welcome."

"It's not often we get chased by flesh-hungry dogs and then saved by a mountain man wielding a million-candle spotlight," Juli replied.

Rob wiped sweat from his brow and leaned both elbows on the table. "What happened out there? The dogs, the light, the effect it had on them?"

Asher pushed away from the table and stood, taking his time to stretch his back. He smoothed his beard with one hand. "You're asking me to explain something I don't fully understand myself. It started back in eighty-seven, with the boy. The fear came then and, shortly after that, the darklings."

He paused and appeared to lose himself in thought for a few moments, like a soldier remembering when life was simpler and innocent before the war. Smoothing his beard again, he returned to the present, and his eyes darkened a tinge. "Things have changed a lot since then. Everything's changed."

"April twenty-ninth?" Juli said.

Asher shook his head. "No, the twenty-eighth. That was the day they brought the boy here, the day fear showed up and everything changed."

Nine

SOMEONE LIFTS THE LID FROM THE BOX, AND THE BOY squints and raises both hands to his face to shield himself from the bright light. He hears voices in the distance, but there is someone standing over him. When his eyes adjust, he sees that it is a man.

"Sit up," the man says. His voice is not mean and in any other setting would have sounded kind.

The boy sits up and starts to say something, but the man holds a finger to his mouth. The man's face is young and smooth and white. A kind face. And his eyes are so dark they look like black marbles. When he looks at the boy, it feels like he can see right through his skin and into his guts. It makes the boy shiver.

The man smiles at him, but it isn't the smile of a friend. It reminds the boy of the way a wolf looks on those nature shows he watched with Daddy. That hungry look right before they pounce on a rabbit and bite its throat.

"Come," the man says, offering his hand. "Step out and let me see you."

Something about the man scares the boy, scares him more than being in the box and the dark. But what scares him even more is what will happen if he doesn't do what the man says. So he gives the man his hand and stands up.

"Easy now. Watch your step."

The boy steps out of the box and stands as straight as he can, trying to look taller than he is.

"My, aren't you a fine-looking boy. Turn around."

Slowly, feeling very uncomfortable, the boy turns in a clumsy circle. All around him are trees and grass. They are in some kind of park. He thinks maybe he can run away from the man, but he doesn't know where they are. Even if he does get away and hide, he'd still be lost. He doesn't know how long he was in the box, but it had to be over an hour. Maybe a couple hours.

There are two other men standing a good ways off, standing close to each other, talking. One man is bigger than the other, and louder. At one point, they both stop talking and look over at the boy, then go back to their conversation.

After making a full circle, he faces the man again.

"Wonderful. Now"—the man pulls a black handkerchief from his pocket—"I have to put this on you again and tie your hands." He bends his mouth down in a goofy frown. "I know. I'm sorry. But it's all part of the game."

Game? The boy swallows. "Where...where are we going? To see my mom and dad?"

"Sure thing," the man says. "Of course. This was all a game, and now there's just one more part. How fun."

He folds the handkerchief into a blindfold and places it over the boy's eyes, tying it behind his head. It isn't as tight as before, and a little light sneaks through along the bottom edge. The boy then feels his hands being tugged together behind his back and something soft being wrapped around his wrists.

"OK, now, I'll lead and you follow, like follow the leader, all right?"

Hesitantly, the boy nods. The man leads him across a stretch of grass then onto some gravel. The men in the distance have stopped talking, and the only noise the boy hears now is the sound of his sneakers grinding in the stones. The boy is still scared but makes himself think about his mom and dad and how excited they will be to see him. He isn't sure if the man with the dark eyes is telling the truth about the game or not, but he chooses to believe it because it makes him not quite as scared.

The man stops him by putting a hand on his chest. "There's a car here. We're going to go for ride to meet your parents, to see Mommy and Daddy."

The boy feels in front of him for the car, runs his hand along the open doorway, and gets in. The seats are hot against the backs of his legs, and it hurts his shoulders again to lean against them.

The man shuts the door behind him, and then the front door opens, the car rocks a little, and the door shuts.

"Ready?"

The boy nods. "Yes."

They drive for what seems like a long time. At first the road is smooth but curvy. Without the use of his arms, the boy has a hard time balancing himself on the seat. Then the road straightens but gets real rough. He bounces around on the seat like a doll. Normally, if Daddy was driving on a road like this they'd both be laughing and having a good time with it. But nothing about this game is fun so far.

There is no air moving in the car, and it's getting real hot.

The man clears his throat. "Won't Mommy and Daddy be so glad to see their little boy again. I bet they're having all kinds of fun, though. And we're having fun too."

Finally, the road smooths again, and a little while after that they drive onto some gravel and stop. "Almost there," the man says. He opens his door and gets out.

With the windows rolled up, the boy can't hear exactly what's going on, but it sounds like the man is arguing with another man.

The boy sits real still and strains to listen. The other man's voice is not his dad's. He hears the other man say something about cursing the town, and then he tells the dark-eyed man to get out, to leave. More voices join in, deep ones, hollering and cursing. Then the boy hears dogs barking and growling.

A man hollers then screams like he's hurt bad.

In the car, the boy begins to cry, and outside the car, he can hear a man crying. Other voices are there then, women hollering something about getting help and men telling them to shut up. The dogs are barking, women start screaming, men are cursing.

The boy slouches down in the seat and prays to God the car door would stay shut. He doesn't want any part of what's going on outside.

Finally, things quiet down, and the only noises he can hear are the muffled crying of women and a man moaning like he's in pain.

The car door opens, and a hand finds his arm. "It's time." It's the dark-eyed man. "Time to meet up with Mommy and Daddy."

"The dogs," Juli said. "You were telling us about the dogs and your lack of preparation."

Asher paced back and forth along the plywood flooring. He held his hands to his chest and rubbed them as if trying to keep them warm. "He appeared early Saturday morning, the man did, saying he and his friends had some business to take care of in the woods and they wouldn't be a bother to no one." Asher's gaze found a spot on the wall again, and he absently stroked his beard. "Had the darkest eyes I've ever seen. At the time I would have sworn he could see right into my heart with them. Now...well, experience has taught me a thing or two."

Rob looked at Juli then at Asher. "Did he have a real fair, smooth complexion, almost white like an albino?"

Asher's eyes snapped to Rob. "That's him. If it wasn't for

those eyes, I'd a'said he seemed like a right nice fellow. But those eyes…"

"What about a boy?" Rob asked, wondering where all this was leading, if there was a point to it. And what it had to do with Jimmy.

"Yes, the boy. The man and some of his friends—a bunch of thugs is what they looked like—left saying they'd be back later and we were to pay them no mind. I didn't think anything of it, so I did just that."

"Paid them no mind," Juli said.

"Paid them no mind." Asher was on the other side of the cabin now, arms folded over his chest. "Some of the men stayed. They had dogs with them. Four German shepherds. Big, mean-looking things."

"The men or the dogs?" Juli said.

"Both, but the men were uglier than the dogs. And that's the truth. They walked around town, holding those dogs at the end of short leashes, cursing and making a scene. Being real belligerent. The townspeople, *my* people, my flock, were scared and stayed in their homes."

Rob shifted in his chair. He was getting impatient. Jimmy was still out there. He wanted to hear what the old man had to say, though. Information was like gold right now. The more he had, the better chance he had of finding Jimmy. "So when's the boy get in the picture?"

"Later that afternoon the man with the eyes got back. As the town's shepherd I went out to meet him. I was going to tell him to do whatever it was he had to do and then leave town. His friends were disturbing the peace."

Juli wiped at her mouth. "So you were playing lawman too."

Asher looked at both of them. "Oh, my, look at me. I have

guests and haven't even offered you a drink." He crossed the room to the hutch and retrieved three stoneware mugs. Then he reached in the bottom and pulled out a plastic jug of bottled water. "Water?"

"Sure."

"Yes, please."

Asher unscrewed the cap and poured the water. "I'll have to apologize for it being tepid. No ice."

"Wet is what we're looking for," Juli said.

Asher handed them each a mug, and Rob took a long gulp. "Go ahead. He returned and you confronted him."

"Let me back up here. While they were gone, Marj Emswiler, I think that's who it was, got a call from her sister, who lived over in Mayfield, saying a young boy went missing at the apple festival. So when I reached the car and noticed a boy in the backseat, blindfolded and hands tied behind his back, I told the man to let the boy go, and I was calling the police. What little I could see of the poor boy I could tell he was terribly afraid." He paused and ran a hand over his eyes. "That's when things went bad."

Juli ran her finger over the raised grain of the wood tabletop. "Bad guys usually don't like being told what to do."

"And this one fit the mold," Asher said. "We exchanged some words, voices raised, and all the while the dogs barked and barked and tugged at their leashes." He blinked again and found something interesting to look at on the far wall.

The oil lamp flame undulated slowly behind the glass globe. Rob stared at it and imagined what it was like to face down the dark-eyed man and his cronies with their dogs. "Your eye. The dogs did it, didn't they?"

Asher winced and snapped out of his faraway thought. "The dogs. The German shepherds, they kept pulling at those leashes, straining hard. They'd tug so hard then start coughing in fits. I can still see the coldness in their eyes. The evil. Finally, the men let them go."

Rob pictured it in his head, big, meaty hands releasing the leashes. The dogs lunging forward, backs arched, muscles tensed, fur bristled, teeth flashing white, saliva swinging from snarled lips.

"Were you the only one? The only victim?" Rob asked.

Asher's eyes fell to the floor, and he lost some of his posture. "Maybelle Finfold died that day. She was ninety-two and had come out of her house to see what was going on. One of the dogs...May never bothered no one. She was standing there on her front stoop with her walker and...one of the dogs. They left her body in the street for the dogs to finish off. And there were plenty of others too. I lost a lot of sheep."

He looked up, and tears were running down his cheeks in long stripes, getting lost in his beard.

"Darlington's seen its fair share of death," Juli said.

"I didn't see any cemetery in town," Rob said.

Asher wiped at more tears. "You won't. They stopped burying people after the first night." He must have seen the question on Rob's face because he quickly continued. "The darklings. That day we buried twelve of our own. For a town of only a hundred and three—no, four, Anna Caldwell was pregnant at the time—that's devastating. The next morning the graves were all dug up and the bodies gone. The darklings had taken them."

"The dark-eyed man," Rob said. "Who is he?"

Asher's eyes turned cold, and he set his jaw. "As far as I'm concerned, he's the devil."

"And what happened to the boy?"

After swallowing hard and wiping at his cheeks with the sleeve of his shirt, Asher sniffed then said, "They took him into these woods, and that was the last of it."

"The last time you saw the men again?" Juli asked.

Asher shook his head. "No. Some of the thugs stayed behind and"—he put his fist to his mouth—"hurt some of our women. Then they told me if anyone called the police, they'd be back and do worse."

Rob couldn't believe what he was hearing. It was incredible and pathetic at the same time. Darlington was a town captive to their own fear. But Asher hadn't answered all his questions. "What about the darklings? And the dogs out there now? They can't be the same dogs."

Asher paced some more, arms crossed at his chest. "Their evil offspring is what they are."

"And the darklings?" Juli asked. "Please don't tell me they're the dogs' evil offspring too."

"What are they?" Rob asked.

"That evening, after we'd done our best to patch our wounds, some menfolk and me set out to search the woods for the boy. We were a peaceful town, so only a few had any weapons to speak of. A few hunting rifles and knives was about all. Others brought gardening tools, some kitchen knives, some hammers and screwdrivers. We never thought we'd need to use them but felt more secure with something in our hands, you know. We searched these woods until sundown. By the time darkness fell we were good and lost, which was odd because most of us grew up in Darlington and knew these woods like it was nobody's business. We played here, hiked here, and hunted here. But that night, every single one of us was lost as a blind man in a mirror maze. We wandered around, confused and disoriented for hours. I think it was Ed Bittinger who first heard the screams, away off. Naturally, we thought it was a woman at first, and we all started accounting for all our gals, all the Darlington women."

Rob felt a shiver run through his body. "But it wasn't a woman."

Asher walked over to the hutch, removed the jug of water, and poured himself some more. He held it up. "Any more?"

"No, thanks."

He took a long sip and wiped his mouth with the back of his hand. "We ran all night and into the morning through these woods, dropping one by one. I could hear them screaming all around me, hear their cries for help. What was I to do? I didn't hear one gunshot. They never even got a chance to pull the trigger. Eventually I was the only one left, and the darklings caught up to me. To this day I still don't understand what happened, but when morning came I was still alive. I went back to town, but it wasn't the same. The people—my people, *my* flock—had changed. They were so afraid."

"What are the darklings? Do you know?" Rob asked.

"Whatever they are, they were brought here by him. Conjured from the pits of hell, and now they do his bidding."

"The dark-eyed man."

Asher nodded. "Some say they're demons, other say aliens, and others, vampires."

"Maybe they're all of the above," Juli said. "Demon-possessed, blood-sucking aliens. Maybe they're from the IRS."

It all sounded so ridiculous. Every aspect of reason told

Rob this was all nonsense. Demons didn't ravage towns like Darlington and hide in the woods. There was no life on other planets. And vampires were the lore of old tales. None of it made sense. But the darklings were real; they were *something*. He'd heard them, seen them, and felt their grip on him. He'd have to suspend reason for now. If he was going to find Jimmy in these woods, he'd need to know more about what he was up against. "Are they very aggressive?"

"Only in the dark. In the presence of light, any kind of light, they're pretty docile and even act afraid, but in the dark they're vicious. Worse than the dogs."

"I think I'd rather be up against little green men," Juli said.

Rob sat back in chair. "Why do you live here in the woods? Wouldn't it be safer in town? Or somewhere else? Colorado? Hawaii?"

Asher returned to the table and sat in a chair. He turned his head so his lazy eye fixed on Rob. "After the massacre, that's what I call it because that's what it was, after that I was never welcomed in town again. My people were so afraid of the dark-eyed man and his thugs they ran me out. They were afraid if they were seen with me he'd punish them. Fear rules in their hearts now."

"So why didn't you just leave? Go somewhere else and start over?"

Now Asher turned his head so Rob could see his good eye. "They're my people, my flock. I could never leave them. I should have been prepared, but I wasn't, and I let dogs in. Paul warned about that. I pray for Darlington every day. And pray someday they'll have me back. In the meantime, I have my cabin here and my lights. I light up the darkness."

"That's what Norm said."

Asher leaned forward. "Norm Tuckey?"

"Yeah, he put us up last night. Odd fella. When we left this morning, he told us to light up the darkness."

Asher eased back, and Rob thought he saw the beginnings of a smile under his thick beard. "Did he now. Norm said that."

"How do you get your supplies?" Rob asked. "The nearest supermarket isn't exactly walking distance."

"Someone in town, I don't even know who it is, leaves me things at the edge of the woods. Whoever it is must feel guilty or sorry or both, but he won't enter the woods. Once a week he leaves batteries, food, water, and odds and ends."

"*He* is a she," Juli said. "Mary Jane."

Asher gave her a blank look.

"From Mayfield. The diner."

"Oh, yes. Mary Jane. It's been so long. I used to love her meat loaf."

"She does throw together a wicked meat loaf," Juli said. "Once a week she brings a carload of supplies to Darlington. Been doing it for twenty-two years."

Rob looked at her. "That's how you were here before."

Juli nodded. "I was never allowed to come with her. I didn't even know she did it until I was fifteen. Then I was so curious. Of course, as a kid you hear all kinds of stories about Darlington. How it's haunted, how people have gone there and never come back, how the woods surrounding the town are alive. Ripe stuff for a small-town teenager looking for adventure and danger."

"You followed her, didn't you?"

"Sure did. Rode my bike the whole way here."

"That's quite a hike."

"And a half. I was in great shape back then. By the time

I arrived, Mary Jane was already leaving. I hid in the woods and snuck up to the town. It looked like just a normal small town. The people were gathered in the church parking lot, rationing out the food and supplies. Before I knew it, though, the sun was setting and the sky was getting darker. I stuck to the road on the way back and never saw anything, but I could feel them. Hear them too. The screams. Footsteps. They were just on the other side of the trees. And under all the other noise I kept hearing someone whisper my name. Sounded like the wind was doing it, or the trees. Like the woods was alive and calling out to me. I pedaled so hard I thought my legs would fall off. Prayed the whole way home."

Rob stood, walked over to the wall, and slid the board away from the peephole. Outside, the woods looked peaceful and still. Huge poplars and oaks stood like sleeping giants. Even their leaves were motionless and quiet. A few pines were there too, their trunks straight as telephone poles. Rods of light reached from the canopy and touched the leaf-covered ground. But somewhere out there, just out of view, were the dogs. He knew it. They were there. He could almost feel them watching him with those dead black eyes.

"Why don't the townspeople leave?"

Asher sighed. "They're too afraid."

"Fear rules in their hearts," Juli said.

"The dark-eyed man," Asher said. "He told them if they ever tried to leave, they'd never make it out of the woods. And the town is surrounded by woods. There's no way out."

"If it wasn't for Mary Jane and her weekly trips, they'd all die, and Darlington would be no more," Juli said.

Rob continued to watch the undergrowth for any sign of life, any movement or glint of an eye. "The dogs are afraid of light but not daylight?"

"Only direct light. Daylight doesn't bother them in the woods. It would if they left the cover of trees."

"So there's the dark-eyed man, the darklings, and the dogs."

"Correct."

Nana's words were there: *Three of 'em. Like a trinity.*

"A trinity," Rob said. He looked at his watch. It was nearing noon. A sudden sense of urgency crashed over him like a wave. "So what now? I have to—"

His sentence was cut short by the sound of crying. The sound of a child crying.

Ten

T HE BOY," ASHER SAID, HIS EYES WIDE AND SHIFTING between Rob at the wall and Juli at the table.

Rob rushed for the door. "Jimmy."

"No," Asher yelled. He jumped up and threw himself between Rob and the door.

Rob stopped short. "Get out of my way, Asher."

Juli was there too, gripping Rob's arm. "This isn't the way, Rob."

Rob spun and returned to the peephole. He could still hear the crying. It was definitely Jimmy. He knew his own son's cry. Every parent does. It was coming from the far left of the cabin. Outside the cabin all was still motionless. The only sound was the soft cry of a child. *His* child.

Rob turned to Asher. "Do you have a gun or anything?"

"No. You can't go out there. It's a trap."

Rob felt anger and panic rise in his throat with the taste of bile. "A trap? I don't care. That's my son out there." He grabbed the light Asher was carrying when he rescued them. Flipped it on and off. "Get outta my way. I'm going out."

Asher must have seen the fierceness in Rob's eyes because he slowly backed away from the door.

Juli approached him. "Rob, I've heard of some pretty bizarre suicide attempts, but nothing like this."

"Get out of my way, Juli. Jimmy's out there. My boy. I need to go to him."

Reluctantly, Juli bowed her head and sidestepped. "You're not ready to face this alone."

Rob stopped short of the door and looked back at her. She was still facing the other way, head hung low. "What's that supposed to mean? Not ready. What does that mean, Juli?"

"Fear rules in your heart too." Her voice was low, somber. "You're not ready."

Rob had no time for her nonsense. His heart ached for Jimmy, to hold him again and wipe his tears like he used to. He gripped the light in one hand and lifted the two-by-six with the other. The door swung open...

...and the forest greeted him like an executioner.

When Rob was gone, Juli pushed the door closed and leaned against it. Her stomach growled like a grump.

"We have to go after him," Asher said, his face showing its age in the candlelight.

"We don't have to," Juli said. The words sounded thick and brusque. Worse than she intended, but her emotions were showing now. She was unable to stop him, and it hurt.

"Then we *should*. It's suicide. You said it yourself. The darklings..." His words trailed off as he stood staring at her.

They both knew what it was, and Juli knew she had to let Rob go. He wasn't ready, but he had to find that out for himself. The hard truth was, she could persuade and warn and even pray, but she couldn't stop him. Some things had to be experienced to be learned.

Juli shook her head and looked Asher right in the good eye. "We shouldn't. He has to face this alone."

Asher scurried to the peephole and pressed his eye against it. His hands were noticeably shaky. When he turned back around there was a wild expression on his face, the look of panic and terror. "He's gone. Out of view." He started pacing the floor. "We have to help him. His boy...it's a trap."

Asher made a move for the door, but Juli was there first, pressing her back against it, arms and legs spread like she was holding it shut against a torrent of wind and rain.

Armed with Rob's Maglite, Asher stood before Juli like a gladiator proud of the fact that he was about to die. "I have to help him. He doesn't know what's out there, what they're capable of."

Juli steeled herself. "You'll have to go through me, and you don't look like the type to hit a woman."

"I haven't yet."

"Then let's keep the streak alive."

Slowly, like the melting of butter, Asher's countenance changed. The lines of his face softened, the fierceness in his eyes dimmed, and his arm, once holding the flashlight high like a sword, lowered to his side. Sadness now colored his features, and he looked like he was about to cry. "I have to help him."

"You can," Juli said. "But not armed with an attitude and a flashlight."

Asher walked over to the table, placed the flashlight on it, and sat in one of the wooden chairs. His shoulders slumped, and his face looked like it would melt off his skull at any moment. "I have to *do* something. I have to go to him."

Still pressed against the door, Juli relaxed her muscles and took a step away. "That time will come, but not now."

"When?"

"It'll come."

Asher shook his head, ran his fingers through his hair. "I lost my flock once because I wasn't prepared; I wasn't watchful." He looked at her with that one eye; the other glared at the door. "I can't let it happen again."

"It won't, Asher. It won't."

"How do you know?"

"I don't. But faith is a powerful thing."

Asher nodded thoughtfully. "It is."

Juli approached the table and sat across from Asher. She thought of how much he'd suffered in these woods, both at the fangs of the dogs and the fangs of guilt. She reached for his hand and took it in hers. "There is something we can do to help him now."

"Pray."

"Yes. Pray like we've never prayed before."

Trees. Leaves. Thistles. Honeysuckle. Kudzu. The forest consisted of nothing more. Jimmy's cry sounded close and a mile away at the same time. To Rob's left.

He held the light with slippery palms, willing his hands to stop shaking. His legs felt weak, his feet heavy.

Jimmy's cry was not one of pain. It was the soft weep of sadness.

Looking around at the undergrowth, watching for any kind of movement and fully expecting an attack, Rob walked in the direction of the crying. "Jimmy?"

But no answer came, only the pitiful mew.

Rob moved closer, but the crying seemed to move as well,

keeping the distance between itself and him, a distance of what seemed like twenty yards or so.

Supporting the light with one hand, he used the other to push low-hanging limbs from his path and to support himself while stepping over fallen trees and branches. The terrain was uneven, and Rob tired quickly.

But the crying continued.

Rob imagined Jimmy wandering through the woods, lost, scared, weeping softly. He knew exactly how he would look too. His hair disheveled and hanging in his eyes, his eyes swollen and red, his chin dimpled. His little hands would be curled into fists and held close to his face.

Tired or not, Rob instinctively picked up speed, hopping a fallen oak and dodging a tangle of wild raspberry. His breathing had deepened and increased in rate, and now his lungs burned as they sucked in air. His legs were beginning to ache too. He was running at probably half his full speed, and still the crying kept pace and distance.

Deeper and deeper into the domain of the wild the weeping led him, farther from the cabin and the town of Darlington. Rob thought about this but didn't care. If the crying led him to Jimmy, it would all be worth it. He could find his way out afterward. Juli said there was only one way out, but she also said she knew the way. So when he found Jimmy and had his son safe in his arms again, he'd find the cabin, and Juli could lead them back to town where he would get help.

Juli's other words came back to him too.

"You're not ready yet. Fear rules in your heart."

He was afraid, sure, but who wouldn't be? The dogs could be hiding around any corner, behind any tree, any shrub. Waiting to pounce and tear at his flesh. And what if it was a trap? He held the light tighter. So what if it was? He had his light, and he'd find a way to get Jimmy out.

Occasionally Rob had to stop and rest his hands on his knees, his lungs drawing in huge breaths. His heart was thumping like a kettledrum, and sweat had nearly soaked his shirt front and back. When he stopped like this to rest, he would listen and find the crying, always ahead.

This time was no different. Jimmy was still a good twenty yards ahead. Rob wondered if the poor boy was so frightened that the sound of Rob's footfalls on the leaves scared him enough to run. Who knows what he had experienced or had been exposed to in the past three months? It was probably enough to make even a grown man cringe and run.

Rob straightened and listened for the crying. It had continued moving forward, but its progress had slowed. He cupped his hands around his mouth. "Jimmy. It's Daddy, buddy. It's Daddy. Don't go any farther."

Still no answer came, and still the weeping moved forward.

Rob looked around, making sure no dogs followed or crouched nearby, and set off again. He took about ten large steps before he stopped. He didn't hear the crying anymore, but what he did hear was the distant gurgle of water. The river they had passed on the way to Darlington. Maybe Jimmy was heading for the river, thinking that was the safest place and the most likely for someone to spot him.

Following the sound of the water as if it were a flute and he a rat, Rob traipsed through the woods, stopping occasionally to call for Jimmy and listen for any response. But none came. The only sound was the steady, comfortable rhythm of flowing water.

Finally, he came upon the river, a wide expanse of slow-moving water. Boulders broke the surface like warts, and a small island sat in the middle of the river, a few loblolly pines clinging to the rocks. Standing on the bank, Rob looked up and down the stretch of water. The ground was eroded into a steep embankment maybe ten feet high. Fallen trees lined the water's edge, piled up in some places like broken bones.

"Jimmy," he called, raising his voice above the burble of water. But again, no response came.

Downriver, maybe a hundred yards or so, Rob noticed the edge of a building jutting from the forest's edge. It looked large, like an old warehouse. He stepped back into the woods and picked his way toward the structure.

Sure enough, there sat an abandoned building, probably a shipping warehouse at one time. Rust stains streaked the exterior, and just about every other window was busted. Shards of glass littered the ground around the base. Weeds had taken over what once was the yard, and the building's façade was partially overrun by Virginia creeper and kudzu. Three pairs of double doors, each with a large window—or broken window—sat at equal intervals along one side of the building.

One was half open.

The chain that at one time bound the two doors together swayed slowly from one handle. Someone had just opened the door.

Jimmy. It had to be. He was heading for the building for shelter and protection. Maybe that was where he'd been hiding to avoid the darklings and dogs.

Rob's throat constricted, and tears pressed on the back of his eyes.

He approached the door and opened it a little more. Sticking his head in the cavernous warehouse, he listened. At first there was nothing; then he heard it, the sound of footsteps, a quick, light cadence, like that of a child running. Jimmy running.

He stepped inside, leaving the door open. The interior was dark but not totally; enough light filtered in through the windows to give the place the appearance of dusk. Rob thought about turning on the floodlight in his hand but didn't. He wanted to conserve the battery in case he really needed it. He thought of what Asher had said—*"It's a trap"*—but didn't care. Jimmy was in here, and he was going to get his boy out.

The warehouse was empty save for a few stacks of old skids and piles of scrap lumber. Oddly, there was no glass on the floor, indicating all the windows had been broken from the inside out.

He could still hear the movement of water outside, but it was muted, distant. He listened again for the footsteps and found them to his right. At the end of the yawning room, a pair of doors with crash bars led to another part of the building. Rob went that way.

At the doors he paused and listened, but he heard nothing. Pushing one open, he called in a soft voice, "Jimmy? You there, buddy?"

But, as usual, no answer came.

Behind the doors were a small room and, on the other side of the room, a staircase that led down. There were no windows in the room, and only a little light made it in through the open door. Rob's palms began to sweat, and his lungs felt like they were filled with sand. If he let the door close, he'd be consumed by darkness.

Then he heard it again, the crying, Jimmy's crying, coming from down the stairs. How far down, he couldn't tell. The sound echoed up the concrete stairwell and bounced around in the room. That settled it for him; fear or no fear, nyctophobia or not, he was going down those steps.

Flipping the floodlight on and letting the door shut behind him, Rob approached the top of the stairwell. He drew in a deep breath of the dry air and blew it out. The light shook in his hands. He aimed it down the stairs and found nothing more than a flight of concrete steps ending on a concrete floor.

"Jimmy? It's me, son. Daddy. Come into the light."

The question entered Rob's mind—of course it did: Why would Jimmy descend into the bowels of this warehouse, into utter darkness? But if this was where he'd found safety, if this was where he'd found asylum from whoever had taken him, wouldn't he feel comfortable here? He might have even spent a good portion of the last three months hiding out here.

And of course Rob thought of the darklings and their love of the darkness. But why would Jimmy be here if the darklings hung out in this basement? He must have felt safe here or he would never have come...and led Rob here.

Again, Asher's words whispered in his head...

"It's a trap."

No. It wasn't. Jimmy had led him here. It was time to rescue his son and take him home. Time to get back to living again.

Summoning what little courage he had, Rob swallowed hard, wiped each palm on his pants, and descended the stairs. The light cut a path through the darkness like a surgeon's scalpel. At the bottom of the stairs, Rob swung the light back and forth and found another empty room about the size of a basketball court. To his left the room took a turn and wound back around and under the staircase. The light could not reach that area from where he stood.

Rob tried to move, but his feet refused to cooperate. He hated the fact that everywhere but where the light fell was total darkness. He kept expecting something wild and ferocious to explode from the gloom and tear into him. Maybe a darkling, maybe a wild dog, maybe something much worse. Maybe Jimmy.

Stop that! He scolded himself for allowing his imagination to toy with him.

From around the corner, under the staircase, Rob heard the crying.

Jimmy was there, hiding in the darkness.

"Jimmy." Rob pointed the light at the darkened area and forced his feet to move. When he was almost there, about to round the corner, he heard a shuffle of running feet to his right. He swung the light around and caught a glimpse of a small form dash behind a leaning piece of plywood.

Rob's blood turned cold. He'd seen that form before, sinuous, naked. A darkling. Panic clutched at his throat. Before he could pivot back around and toward where he'd heard Jimmy, something hit him from behind and clung to his back. He lifted the light and shoved it hard over his right shoulder. It connected with something and produced a sickening wet thud. A yelp, then his back was free.

Rob spun in a circle, found the staircase, and jumped up three steps at once. Hands found his pants leg and held on. He kept moving up the stairs, dragging the darkling along. At the top, Rob twisted at the waist and drilled the thing with the light. It released its hold and screeched like a bird of prey.

Rob lunged for the door, yanked it open, and jumped through, falling to his knees. The light clanged to the floor. Again, he was hit from behind, fell, and rolled to his back. Two darklings stood half concealed in the doorway; another was crouched, hiding its face but ready to spring. In one fluid motion, Rob reached to his right, found a two-by-four on one of those stacks of old lumber, and swung just as the darkling sprang. The board connected with the little devil's head, and Rob heard the crunch of bone.

Not waiting to see how the others would respond to his show of aggression, Rob rolled to his knees, grabbed the light, and whipped it around. The darklings ducked behind the door and screamed angrily. Doing the only thing that came to him, Rob ran for the double doors that led to the outside world and the light of day. His footsteps sounded like gunshots in the empty warehouse.

He hit the crash bar running and tumbled outside, rolling once in the dirt and coming to his feet again.

He thought about heading for the river, jumping in, and letting the easy current take him out of these cursed woods, but then he thought of Juli and Asher...and Jimmy. He still believed Jimmy was alive and in these woods. What just happened here had nothing to do with his son.

"It's a trap."

Instead, he ran for the woods and didn't stop until he was a safe distance from the warehouse. There, Rob found a fallen oak and sat. He let the light drop to the leafy ground and ran both hands through his hair. He had no idea what was going on here, but two things he did know. One, as crazy and unbelievable as it was, the darklings were real—and vicious. And two, Jimmy was still out there. He was convinced of it. How those two went together, *if* they went together, he had no idea, but he had to find his son. He had to.

He had to.

He realized then that he was lost; he hadn't a clue where he was or in what direction he should walk to get back to the cabin.

His watch said it was five forty. Rob remembered that while he was following the sound of Jimmy's cry, the sun, what little he could see of it through the thick canopy of leaves overhead, was over his right shoulder, behind him. Now, with the sun lower in the sky and harder to locate, he would walk with it at his left shoulder and in front of him.

As he walked, the light in the woods grew dimmer, and the sun all but disappeared. Six o'clock came and went; seven o'clock... seven-thirty... eight o'clock was approaching when he heard the first of the screams far off in the distance. The darklings were emerging from their lair, the warehouse.

With his heart pumping double time again, Rob picked up the pace and thought about saying a prayer. That's what Juli would do. That's what Kelly would do too.

"Maybe we should pray about this, Rob...I'll pray about it."

He felt a sudden sense of sadness come over him. Kelly would be so disappointed if she could see him now. Afraid, faithless, defeated.

He thought of Kelly then, of her bright smile and quick laugh, the way her lips felt against his and how comfortable she felt in his arms. He missed her so much; he hated being alone... and the way she died, the way that... stop it. Anger and remorse took hold of him then, and for a moment, a very brief moment, he entertained the thought of surrendering to the darklings and their dogs. Juli had suggested his adventure this afternoon was suicide anyway; why not prove her right?

Because Jimmy needed him.

"Daddy, are you comin'?"

His wife might be gone, but his son was still alive, out here somewhere, and Rob wouldn't stop looking until he found him.

He heard another scream, louder. They'd found his trail and were closing the distance. Rob dug his heels into the soft, leaf-covered soil and shifted gears. He was half running now, not wanting to go too fast for fear that he'd miss the cabin altogether. Sweat soaked his hair and shirt and stung his eyes.

The screams, multiple now, grew closer yet. And now they were joined by barking. The dogs.

Panic sent tingles through Rob's hands, up his arms, and over his chest and head. He kicked the light on and watched as the beam bounced in front of him as he ran, faster now. The screams were still more than a hundred yards off, but he could feel them as if they were right on his heels. He wanted to scream himself, holler for help. He had to be close to the cabin. Maybe Asher and Juli would hear him and find him.

He was just about ready to let out a holler when he saw a light flash up ahead. It blinked three times. Asher?

Daylight in the woods was almost gone, and the other light blinked brightly three more times. Rob headed for it.

"Rob, over here." It was Asher. He recognized the old preacher's voice.

Rob reached Asher and almost fell into his arms.

"This way, follow me. It's not far." With both their lights on now, Rob followed Asher back to the cabin.

Juli was there, waiting for them with the door open. They entered, and Rob fell into a chair, breathing hard. Juli shut the door behind them, and Asher locked it. Outside, the screams continued to close in, and the barking grew louder. At last, after a few more moments, everything fell silent outside.

"They'll go now," Asher said. "They have little patience."

Minutes passed, and they heard nothing.

Juli placed a hand on Rob's arm. "I'm sorry about Jimmy. Tomorrow's another day."

Rob looked at her. Sweat still leaked into his eyes, and he had to wipe at it to see her. "Another day for what? It's too big out there. He could be anywhere." He pounded the table with his fist, which made Juli jump and remove her hand from his arm.

She sat back in the chair, a hurt look in her eyes. "I prayed for you while you were gone." She glanced at Asher, who was sitting on his cot now, then back at Rob. "We both did. You weren't ready."

"The crying led me to a warehouse," Rob said. "On the river's edge."

"I know of it," Asher said. "It was used to stock materials when the dam was built. At the time, the back roads couldn't handle the heavy equipment and materials. They'd use a barge to float the stuff down to the site."

Juli said, "Were there…"

"Darklings. Yeah."

Asher stood. "It was a trap."

"Are you OK?" Juli said, reaching for Rob's arm again.

"I'm here and in one piece."

"One piece is good. Let's keep it that way."

"And the crying?" Asher said.

"It wasn't Jimmy. Not at all."

Eleven

ASHER MOVED ACROSS THE CABIN AND SAT AT THE table. He leveled his good eye on Rob. His other eye looked blankly at the wall. "Juli told me your son was abducted, just like that other boy."

Rob met his eye. "The other boy. Nineteen eighty-seven."

"The dark-eyed man took him."

"I saw him in Mayfield. He told me how to get to Darlington." He was remembering the conversation now. The one that took place in the church. "He told me the way would lead to Darlington *and* Jimmy and that he'd meet me there. He knew Jimmy was in Darlington."

"He's the Elvis Presley of creeps," Juli said.

Asher ran a hand over his beard and said, "History repeats itself. But what's the connection?"

"I don't care about connections. I just want my son back. I'm going out there—"

"No." Asher was quick on the draw this time. "No, sir. Not tonight. You'll never make it, even with a light. There's too many of 'em come out at night."

Juli said, "He's right. Hide and seek with the darklings would be pretty dumb. Advantage them, every time."

Asher tapped his finger on the table. "First light and I'll go with you."

"I'm on that bandwagon too," said Juli.

Rob thought about that. If he was so easily duped and

almost darkling food in broad daylight, there was no way he would find Jimmy at night with only a spotlight to light the forest and hordes of darklings on his tail. As much as he hated to admit it, Asher had a point. "Fine. First light and we're going. And *I'm* going, with or without you."

Juli pushed away from the table and stood. "With would be preferable." Then to Asher she said, "I know this isn't a diner, but since it's the only joint on the block, you have anything to eat? My stomach's been talking to me since this morning."

Asher unfolded his thin frame and walked over to the little kitchen area where the hutch and dry sink were. "I don't have much, but what I do have you're more than welcome to."

"You don't eat grubs and wild berries, do you?" Juli said.

Asher grinned. It was the first time Rob had seen him smile, and he liked it. The old guy had a warm and inviting smile that crinkled his eyes at the corners. "Berries, yes. Grubs, only in yogurt."

"You have yogurt?"

"Nope. No way to keep it cold. But I do have granola."

"It's not dried grubs, is it?"

"Not all of it," Asher said with a quick smile. He handed Juli a bag of granola and assorted nuts. "Help yourself. You too, Rob. Now, if you don't mind, I'll excuse myself to my cot over here and bed down for the night. These old muscles aren't what they used to be, and all the excitement today wore them out." He lifted a couple blankets from the cot and placed them on the empty chair by the table. "You can use these and sleep on the floor. It's not as hard as it looks."

"No mints on the pillows?" Juli said.

"If that bothers you, I can leave a few grubs. Maybe even dip them in chocolate first."

154

"I could go for some chocolate sans grubs right now."

Asher lay on his cot and pulled a blanket up to his waist. It wasn't particularly cool in the cabin, but the temperature had dropped more than a couple degrees since the setting of the sun. He rolled over to face the wall, his back to the rest of the cabin. "Night, all. Don't forget to say your prayers."

"Thanks, Gramps," Juli said.

She shoved a handful of granola in her mouth and offered the bag to Rob. He wasn't hungry but knew he should eat something. His body still needed food, and he'd need the energy for tomorrow. He accepted, scooped a palmful into his mouth, and chewed slowly. It wasn't the tastiest stuff, but it wasn't bad either.

With the oil lamp on the table the only source of light in the small cabin, everything took on odd shapes, and shadows dusted every corner. He looked at Juli, chewing away on her granola, and thought how much she reminded him of Kelly. Her wit and charming sarcasm were right out of Kelly's playbook. No doubt the two would get along just fine...if Kelly were there.

Juli finished chewing, washed the rest down with a gulp of water, then said, "You feel like talking about what happened?"

"What happened where?"

The light from the lamp softened the edges around Juli's face and highlighted her cheekbones and forehead. "Your heart. Where did the fear come from?"

Rob went quiet. Already he could hear Asher's low, even sleep breathing on the other side of the cabin. Juli had poked at a tender spot. Zeroed right in on his greatest weakness. For anyone else but Kelly, he would never open up, but there was something about Juli, something comfortable and innocent that told him it was OK to be vulnerable around her. He shrugged. "I really don't know. My whole life, or at least as much of it that I can remember, I've been afraid of something. I don't even know what it is. I do know I'm afraid of the dark. Nyctophobia, they call it. Always have been. Crazy, isn't it?"

"Everyone's afraid of something. There's no shame in that. There's whole books full of phobias."

"But when the fear rules you, when it calls the shots, tells you what you can and can't do, when it paralyzes you for days on end and robs you of the freedom others enjoy so carelessly, that's crazy."

"Sounds like there's more to your story."

"Some days, I'm so fearful, so afraid of something, I don't know what, I can't even leave the house. It used to drive Kelly nuts. Then it would subside, and I'd be OK again."

"Must really put a cramp on your work life."

Rob shook his head. "I'm self-employed. I create and maintain Web sites, so that's never been a problem."

"So you're a techno-geek."

"Something like that."

Juli filled her mouth with granola again, chewed, and chased it with another gulp of water. "And Kelly and Jimmy?"

He knew they'd get there sooner or later. It was never anything he liked talking about, but Juli deserved to know. She was in this now too, and she seemed to know things Rob didn't. Important things. He drew in a breath and braced himself for an onslaught of painful memories. "A little over three months ago we were at a festival back home in Massachusetts. Kelly was originally from there, so when we got married we decided to settle down there. With my business being home-based, we could live anywhere we wanted. And Massachusetts is so beautiful. It was an unusually warm day."

"April in New England can be unpredictable."

"Yeah, but this was weird. Eighty in April? We'd spent the morning walking around, checking out the handcrafts, playing some games, you know, festival kind of stuff."

"Crafts. Games. Food. They're all the same."

"Jimmy was eating a candy apple and got his hands completely sticky." The memory came back to him in a rush. Jimmy's little hands covered in red candy coating. Sticky red smeared from the corners of his mouth along his cheeks. He even had some up his nose. "Kelly said she was taking him back to the car to get a hand wipe and clean him up. I said I'd meet them at the corn dogs. Jimmy loves corn dogs."

"Who doesn't?"

Rob hitched in another breath. He'd waited so long for them, growing more and more worried by the minute. He shrugged. "They never came back." At first, he'd assumed they just got sidetracked by some interesting vendor, but thirty minutes later when he'd tried calling Kelly's cell phone and got nothing, he grew concerned. "At five, when the festival was winding down and people started leaving and they were still nowhere to be found, I called the police."

"Filed a missing person's report."

"Not then. That happened the next day. The cops, they thought maybe Kelly took off with him." He was so angry about that. Kelly would never do that. They had their problems like any other couple, but they were close. They had a good marriage, a good life together. "Then they looked at me."

"A matter of procedure. Mother and child disappear, the husband is always a person of interest."

"I know. I realize that now." At the time, though, he was livid and let Sandusky know—a move that didn't help his case any. But here they were barking in the wrong forest when his wife and son were missing and time was being wasted. "They never did show up. Leads were always dead ends. Days passed, and we heard nothing."

"But that day did come."

Rob's heart felt swollen, heavy in his chest. This was the first time he'd talked about that day, the day Sandusky told him they'd found Kelly. Unwelcome tears filled his eyes. He took a moment to compose himself. "Yeah, it came. Eight days after they went missing. It seemed like eight months. Two kids were goofing around in an abandoned warehouse in Salem and found Kelly. She was dead...it was awful. Jimmy was still missing."

When Sandusky told him, Rob couldn't stop the vomit. The thought of someone treating his wife, his love, that way ushered a hatred into his heart that roiled his stomach. His anger could not be contained. Fearing himself and not sure of what he was capable, he'd locked himself in his house for four days. When he finally emerged from his cave, Sandusky was there with news of Jimmy.

"You don't have to go on if it's too hard," Juli said.

Rob waved her off. He needed to say this, if not for her then for him. "A few days later they found what they thought was Jimmy's body in a saltwater pond near Newport."

"They *thought* it was his body?"

"It was..." Images of the photos taken at the scene flashed in Rob's mind. Fish had already done a number on the body. DNA tests were needed to confirm, and even they weren't a hundred percent. "...hard to tell. It'd been a week and a half or so."

"And mistakes happen."

"Yes, they do. At first I believed them and started grieving all over again. But as time passed, I became more and more convinced they'd been wrong. That the tests were wrong."

"That Jimmy was still alive."

Rob pointed a finger at her. "Exactly."

"Mistakes happen."

"Exactly."

Juli was quiet for a couple minutes, running her finger along the grain of the plank. Finally she stopped and held her finger on a knot in the middle of the board. "You lost your wife and son. When did you lose your faith?"

What awakened in Rob was not anger or contempt or even annoyance; what arose was a sense of loss, a great void that seemed to open its bottomless maw and suck him in. He'd done more than lost his faith; he'd abandoned it. He felt that in his greatest time of need God had deserted him, so what was the point?

He wiped at his eyes, smearing tears across his face. "Life was going well for us. We were a happy family. Loved spending time together. Loved laughing together. Kelly…" More tears leaked from his eyes and now flowed freely down his cheeks. He felt no shame crying in front of Juli. This was him, who he was now, broken, exposed, defeated, frightened. "…I loved her so much. I needed her. Jimmy was a surprise, we were young, but…oh, Jimmy. And then they were taken from me." The familiar anger was there again, gnawing in his gut, tightening around his heart. "Just like that, my life was ruined, turned inside out." He looked at Juli through blurry eyes. "God was nowhere."

Now Juli was wiping tears of her own. "I'm sorry." She went back to tracing wood grain. "Even when you can't see Him, when the lights are out and you can *feel* the darkness, God is still there."

That was it. Time to change the subject. "So what about you? You put on this laid-back, wisecracking persona, but I can tell you're scared too."

Juli thought a moment. "More uncertain than scared."

"So what's your story?"

She shrugged. "Average girl story, really. Dad was a psycho, abused me as an infant, murdered my mom when I was two, and I was raised by my grandmother. The record won't list the murder in there, but he drove Mom to suicide, and in my book that's murder."

"Average girl, huh? Did you ever doubt God?"

"Sure I did."

"Did. You don't anymore?"

Juli shook her head. "Nope. Now I only doubt myself."

"You never ask why God allowed all that stuff to happen to you? Why He allowed some sicko to abuse you as a helpless baby and drive your mom to suicide?"

"I asked the questions hundreds of times and never got an answer. I stopped asking years ago. Faith is my answer now. Just letting God be God and trusting Him to know what's best."

Rob could feel his sadness turning to frustration. This was all the same mumbo jumbo he used to listen to in church. The same stuff Kelly believed...and he used to believe. Until it happened to him and he was the one asking the questions and getting no answers. "What's best? You really think what happened to you, what happened to your mom, was for the best?"

Juli looked at her hands then laced her fingers. "It doesn't seem like it, does it? I won't pretend to have God figured out. I don't. But I know this: bad things happen in this world, darkness is all around us—that's a reality we live with. And when bad things happen, God is always there. Always. He never leaves us, Rob."

Rob had heard enough. Why torture himself any further? He grabbed a blanket, stood, and walked across the room.

"Rob," Juli said, not looking up from the table. "I'm sorry you felt abandoned. I'm sure He never intended that."

What God intended or not didn't matter to Rob. Fact was, he *was* abandoned, and not only him but Kelly and Jimmy too. Well, he wasn't going to abandon Jimmy. His son was out there, and he would find him if he had to crawl on his hands and knees over every square foot of this forest.

After spreading the blanket on the floor, Rob climbed between its folds, lay on his side, and used his arm for a pillow.

Unlike the previous two nights, sleep did not come slowly. He seemed to rush into it like the downward dive of a roller coaster, plunging deeper and deeper, faster, until he finally awoke in a dream...where he was suffocating.

Darkness was all around him, pressing down like a weight, slithering its tentacles down his throat and nostrils, robbing him of air. It was all he could do to accomplish one breath. The air was stale and thick and smelled of wet soil. He tried to scream, but his vocal cords were like taut bands, stretched to their breaking point. He tried to move, but something pressed in on him from both sides. Bringing his knees up, they bumped something above. His hands found it too. Hard like wood. To his right and left he found the same thing.

He was in a box.

Laying his hands flat against the board above, he pushed with all his strength, but it would not move, would not even give. He knocked, but the sound of his knuckles on the wood sounded dull and dead. On the side panels it was the same thing.

Panic set in then. His heart began to race; his skin started to crawl. Respiration doubled. The heat in the box was incredible and immediately brought beads of sweat out on his face.

He made fists and pounded on the board above. Thrust his knees upward and kicked at it. But his attempts to break free were futile. The wood felt like it was several feet thick.

Fear strangled him, and for a moment he lost his breath. His throat closed, and he had to swallow hard to get it open again. But it didn't last.

The darkness mocked him, laughed at him, tormented him. He was lost in it, forever a captive of the lightless ones.

Hands started groping him, tearing at his clothes and skin, pulling his hair, dragging him down, down, down. They prodded and pulled, their claws scratching and biting.

And still he fought the box, hammered the wood with his fists and feet, tried to yell, to scream, to wail.

It struck him then, like a shock of electricity, and he fell limp, sucking in the stale air.

He was Jimmy.

And he was buried alive.

PART FOUR

Fear defeats more people than any other one thing in the world.

—RALPH WALDO EMERSON

Twelve

ROB AWOKE IN A CLAMMY SWEAT GASPING FOR AIR. He could still feel the wood under his nails, the splinters in his flesh. It took a minute or so to reorient himself to reality. He was in the cabin, on the floor, wrapped in a blanket. The box wasn't real; he was on the up side of the earth.

But the darkness in the cabin was every bit as real as the subterranean gloom. The oil lamp had gone out, and no light from the moon-ruled night found its way between the four walls. Rob sucked in a few deep breaths. His mind wasn't exactly churning with well-greased gears. Instead, it skipped and sputtered like an old junker with a one-way ticket to the salvage yard. He'd dreamed he was Jimmy again, seeing life through his son's eyes, experiencing what Jimmy experienced.

And he'd been buried alive. Panic shot through Rob's veins at the implication. His boy, his little buddy, was buried alive somewhere in those woods.

He tried to move, but fear nailed him to the floor. It was too dark. His heart was a jackhammer in his chest. His lungs were doing double duty. Sweat seeped from his pores, and his hands jittered uncontrollably.

But Jimmy needed him.

Forcing his legs to lift him, Rob stood and stilled himself to listen. The last thing he wanted was to wake either Asher or Juli and have them try to stop him. He knew what he was doing was crazy, but he had to do it. And if it meant taking on every darkling out there, then he was willing to go that far. Nothing was going to keep him from saving his Jimmy.

To his right Juli slept soundly, the rhythm of her breathing slow and even. To his left, on the cot, Asher snored lightly and grunted something incoherent. Rob knew the door was to his left and in front at a forty-five-degree angle from where he now stood. He also knew he had a clear path to the door. But where was the light? Where had he put it when he returned from the woods earlier?

On the floor by the door. He remembered setting it there when he came in. Slowly and methodically, he slipped on his sneakers and crept across the floor, one step at a time, pausing between each stride to listen for the sound of sleep, and each time he found it.

Finally, he reached the door. Feeling along the wall, he located the jamb, followed it to the floor, and found the light. His only hope was that there was enough battery power left.

Leaving the light on the floor, he lifted the two-by-six with both hands. It scraped as only wood on wood can but wasn't loud enough to wake either of the sleepers. Quietly, soundlessly, he leaned it against the wall. Then, as slowly as he would add one wall to a house of cards, he raised the latch and pulled on the door. It opened on smooth hinges.

Reaching for the light, he took it in one hand and stepped outside, pulling the door closed behind him. The outside world greeted him with a loamy odor and was not near as dark as inside the cabin. Through the leafy canopy he could see a clear sky and a just-past-full moon. Dappled moonlight colored the forest floor, lighting his surroundings enough that he could see without the light. That was good. That meant he'd only need it in case of emergency, in case the darklings decided to come out to play.

At once, he felt a pull. Not anything physical like a hand in his or tugging at his shirt, but something unseen, something inward. It was as though he were tethered to Jimmy, and his son was reeling him in, drawing him with an invisible thread.

So without thinking or analyzing, Rob gave himself to the call and stepped away from the cabin.

Juli awoke with a start, breathing hard, sweaty. She'd had a dreamless sleep, but still she felt uneasy, frightened, nervous. That feeling was there, screaming at her. Something was wrong.

Something...was...wrong.

"Rob," she whispered, trying to keep her voice low. But there was no reply. "Rob."

Panic poked at her lungs; her rib cage seemed to shrink. She needed to calm herself and focus. Taking a couple deep breaths, she exhaled a silent prayer.

Then, "Rob. You awake?"

Still no response.

She leaned to her right and felt where Rob should have been...and felt only blanket. He was gone.

Something was wrong.

Juli rubbed her hands over her face, pulling off the sleep cobwebs still clinging there. Think about this. There were only two options. He was either in the cabin or not.

Again, she whispered, this time a little louder, "Rob. You there?"

Nothing but the steady half-snore of Rip van Wiggins.

Throwing off her blanket, Juli stood and padded softly across the floor to the door of the cabin. She felt for the two-by-six and found it gone as well.

So he was outside the cabin. Two more options: either he'd slipped outside to relieve himself, or he'd gone after Jimmy.

Lifting the latch as slowly as possible, she pulled open the door and stepped outside. The air was cool and still. Above the treetops a moon glowed somewhere in the sky. She couldn't see it, but she could see its soft light dusting the leaves. She listened for any sound of Rob or anything else.

But the forest was uniquely quiet. As noiseless as a sarcophagus. And, honestly, it creeped her out.

"Rob." Her voice seemed to echo in the stillness. And no answer came. A chill spread over her skin as if a cold gust of wind had blown through the forest, but as before, no leaves stirred. He was out there, alone, in the dark.

A sense of failure overcame her. She'd lost him. This wasn't part of the plan.

She remembered her words: *"I can't do it."*

And the response: *"You're ready... this is your calling."*

Her calling. Her calling wasn't to sleep while he snuck off in the middle of the night to face the darkness alone. What if she hadn't awakened? Where would he be then? *Was* she ready?

"God be with him," she said aloud. "And me."

Stepping back inside the cabin, she pushed the door closed without a sound. On her blanket again, she knelt and rested her elbows on the floor in front of her. There she prayed.

Sometime later—Juli was unaware of how much time had

elapsed—she rose, slipped on her sneakers, took the Maglite in her hand, and opened the cabin door again, this time with the full intent of not returning unless it was with Rob at her side.

Leaves crunch under the boy's feet. He tries to stop, but the man pulls him by his arm. Pulls him hard enough that it hurts, which only scares the boy more. He keeps thinking about the sound of the dogs barking and the other man screaming. It was such an awful sound.

The man stops him then and pulls off the blindfold. "There," he says. "Better, isn't it?"

It is better, but the boy neither says so nor nods his head. He looks around for the dogs, but they aren't there. He and the man are now in the woods. Tall trees surround him and block out most of the light. Only a few beams of sunshine peek through. They look like white light sabers stretching from the green leaves above to the brown leaves on the ground. Why would the man bring him to the woods to meet Mommy and Daddy?

The man takes him by the arm again and says, "Let's keep marching, little soldier. Mommy and Daddy are waiting. Let's pretend we're on a secret mission, and your daddy is the commander. We have to meet him to get our next orders. Sound like fun?"

Again, the boy doesn't do anything. The man squats down in front of him. His skin is so white it almost looks like the flour Mommy uses to bake cookies. And his eyes are so dark, like two black marbles set in his head. "Listen, little soldier. I need you to be brave. We have a difficult journey back to see the commander. We need to move fast, and I need you to keep up, OK?" He looks at the boy a few seconds. His marble eyes seem to grow wider. "OK?"

Finally, the boy nods. The man scares him, but if he's going to take him to Mommy and Daddy, he should probably do what he says.

"Great." The man stands tall and pushes his shoulders back. "Now then, let's begin. Follow me, soldier."

They set off through the woods, not following any kind of trail, just pushing past little skinny trees and stepping over fallen branches. Back home, the boy plays in the woods a lot but not like this. He always sticks to the trails. Mommy is always telling him to be careful of snakes and poison ivy. He knows the saying "Leaves of three, let it be" and watches carefully for leaves of three while he's walking behind the man.

The man turns his head and talks over his shoulder. "We're looking for headquarters, so keep your eyes peeled."

After a while, the boy begins to get tired of walking. His legs feel heavy, and his arms hang straight. He slows down, and the space between him and the man gets bigger.

The man turns his head and notices this. He stops and heads back toward the boy. He looks angry. "Soldier," he says. His lips are tight, like he's been sucking on a lemon. "We need to move fast. Our mission is waiting, and the commander is waiting too. And we both know who the commander is, right?"

The boy nods. The commander is Daddy. Or so the man says.

"We don't want to keep the commander waiting longer than he has to. Now march like a good soldier and keep up." He turns around and starts walking again.

The boy hurries to catch up and tries to stay right behind the man, but he's walking too fast and there are too many branches to step over and bushes to go around. Soon the boy gets tired again and slows down. He needs to sit and rest.

Again the man stops and comes back for him. This time he looks really angry, and it scares the boy. His white skin has turned red around his face and neck. He grabs the boy's arm and jerks him forward. "Let's go, soldier; no time for dawdling."

The boy falls and lands on his hands and knees. The man loses his grip but quickly finds it again. He yanks the boy to his feet, again hurting his shoulder. The boy starts to cry. He's afraid the man will really hurt him. He seems so angry all of a sudden.

The man stoops over so his face is real close to the boy's, close enough the boy can see blue veins running under the man's white-but-now-red skin. His face is all scrunched up like he's in pain. "If you don't keep up, do you know what they do to bad soldiers?"

The boy says nothing.

The man squeezes his arm harder and shakes him. "Do you?"

The boy shakes his head. He's still crying and wants to wipe his tears, but he's afraid to, so he just lets them run down his cheeks. They reach his lips and taste salty, then his chin and tickle it.

"They let the dogs have them. All I have to do is whistle real loud, and the dogs will come."

The boy believes he would do it too. He starts to shake and feels sick in his stomach.

The man starts walking and keeps his grip on the boy's arm. "Not much longer now," he says.

They walk a little ways more until the boy trips on a branch and falls again. The man curses and tugs on the boy's arm, but the boy can't get up and gets dragged along. He tries to get his feet under him, but with the man dragging him and cursing, he just can't do it. He starts to cry harder and louder.

The man stops and yanks him up hard. He grabs the boy's chin and squeezes until it hurts. His face gets real calm then, and he smiles a little. "Kid, I'd like watching the dogs eat you then pick their teeth with your bones, but I have more enjoyable things in mind for you."

He pulls the boy along by the arm another few minutes then stops. He's looking at something to the right. The boy looks too and, through the trees, sees an old cabin, falling apart and spooky. The roof sags in the middle, and the whole thing leans to one side, like a strong wind would blow it over. There are no windows and one door that looks about ready to fall off the hinges.

The man starts again and tugs the boy with him. When they reach the cabin, the man opens the door and pushes the boy inside. He falls and scrapes his knees. More tears run down his cheeks.

"Where's my mommy and daddy?" the boy says.

The man grins and tilts his head to one side. "I'm sorry, son. Mommy and Daddy won't be coming for you. They've got other plans." Then he closes the door, and the boy hears something heavy, like metal, bang up against it. Leaves crunch as the man walks away.

The boy goes to the door and pushes on it, but it won't move. It's locked tight. He looks around the cabin, but there is no way out. There's a hole in the roof, about the size of a TV, but it's too high for him to reach. He sits in the corner, hugs his knees, and begins to sob.

For the first time since awakening, Rob looked at his watch: two ten. Morning would not come for over three hours. He thought of the cabin and the sleepers inside. The door was unlocked now, and sleeping, they would be easy prey for the darklings and their demon dogs. What concerned him more, though, was Jimmy, underground, suffocating, scared, crying for help. Drawing his daddy in.

Asher and Juli would be safe. If the darklings were out for the night, they'd be after Rob anyway. That thought put ice in his veins, and he momentarily considered returning to the safety of the cabin. But the pull Jimmy had on him was too strong. He couldn't break it now. It was the bond only a daddy and son can share.

Around towering loblolly pines and thick-trunked oaks and through stands of honeysuckle and tangles of wild raspberry he walked, accompanied by only the sound of his own footfalls in the dry leaves. Occasionally, he thought he heard another pair of footsteps mimicking his, but when he stopped, there was only silence. No screams echoed in the distance. No barking broke the stillness. In fact, the quietness of the deep forest was so eerie it seemed to be a noise all its own.

Finally, he came to a clearing where the inner tug ceased. This was it, the site. The light in his hand suddenly felt like an anvil, so he set it down by a tree. He looked around the clearing, frantically searching for some disturbed ground, loose soil, anything that would mark a grave.

There, by a smooth-barked beech. The leaves had been pushed aside and the ground depressed, like a giant footprint. He rushed to it and dropped to his knees. The soil was moist and soft, recently loosened. Without even thinking, he began digging with his hands.

In a matter of moments sweat was dripping from his nose, and his breathing had become labored. His fingers began to ache, but still he dug, scooping handfuls of dirt and tossing them to the side. The smell of decaying leaves and wood was strong in his nostrils.

Whether it was reality or just a trick of his brain he wasn't sure—he could no longer tell the difference between the two—but he thought he heard Jimmy's voice calling to him from beneath the ground. He stopped digging and put his cheek to the dirt to listen. It was Jimmy. He was there, feet below Rob, calling to him, begging to be set free. Rob dug even more crazily now, throwing dirt this way and that. His chest heaved, saliva leaked from his mouth, and sweat ran a steady ribbon off his nose and chin.

"Jimmy. Hang on, buddy. Daddy's coming."

His arms worked like pistons, plunging his hands into the dark dirt then lifting them out again. Every muscle in his shoulders and back screamed with fatigue.

But still he dug, pushing himself to go faster and faster. The trees around him stood in stunned silence, unable or unwilling to lend aid.

"Ahhh, c'mon. Dig. Dig. Jimmy. I'm coming."

Jimmy's voice was steadily growing louder and clearer. He was calling to Rob, urging him on, begging him not to stop. He sounded so small and pitiful. So alone. So scared.

"Jimmy!"

Then the voice came from outside the hole. Jimmy's voice. From behind Rob. He stopped digging and spun around. Sweat dripped in his eye, stinging, and he rubbed it away. There, standing not twenty feet from him was his son, his little boy.

Jimmy.

Thirteen

IT WAS GOOD. ALMOST TOO GOOD. SHIELDS HAD TAKEN the bait and followed the scent of lies laid for him.

While crouching behind a tangle of thistles, blending beautifully with the darkness only the forest can offer, he watched with great curiosity as Shields dug feverishly in search of his son. The man's determination and passion intrigued him. And his fear excited him.

Again, he thought how easy it would be to step from his hiding place and pounce on the unsuspecting Shields. But his curiosity was not yet satisfied. He had more to do, further to push, deeper to go. Shields was not fully broken yet, but he would be soon. Then the time would come. His underlings would play a role, and he would let them have their way, but not until he'd taken the vengeance that was rightfully his first.

Showing Shields the boy was nothing less than an act of genius, like allowing the fish to taste the bait before digging the hook deep into its mouth. Shields was now hooked. There was no escape. The only thing left to do was to play him until it got boring and then dispose of him.

He was going to enjoy watching the fear grow in Shields's eyes and watching the life fade from them, two candles slowly burning out.

"A little longer, my friend," he whispered into the darkness that concealed him. "A little longer, and you'll get what you want. What you've been waiting for so patiently."

Occasionally a cloud would drift by the moon, partially veiling it and diffusing its light. The old woman tried to imagine it was the eye of God, watching her as it watches even the smallest sparrow, but instead she kept seeing the eye of the pale one, studying her, searching for any weakness, any vulnerability. With a shudder, she drew in a deep breath and lay prone on the bricks. They were damp from dew and cooler than last time, but she didn't care. She'd been awakened from a sound sleep by a voice in her head. *His* voice. Abba's. Urging her to pray for the man. He was at a crossroads.

Evil was all around him.

She knew the child would be praying too. That's why she'd compelled her to go.

She lay still, unmoving, quiet. Just listening for His voice, for direction, for comfort. The world was too busy; no one took time to listen to Him anymore.

Listening, focusing, meditating, she heard it again. This time, *This kind can only be defeated with prayer and fasting.*

Of course, prayer and fasting. She would pray more, every waking hour, every thought bathed in prayer. And she would fast.

"Abba, give me strength. Be my strength."

My grace is sufficient.

"Protect him now. He faces the evil. Rescue him from the

evil one." A thought occurred to her then. "Send the child. Lead her to him. Spur her to action."

Again, she felt as though she were one with the man, feeling his pain, his fear. And such pain it was. The pain of loss and regret and grief and great sadness. And fear. Oh, such fear. She trembled and shivered. How could he bear to live with such fear?

She cried out, "Abba, strengthen him." Tears flowed from her eyes and spilled onto the bricks. She didn't bother to wipe them away. "Strengthen him. Take him in Your arms and hold him. He needs a father. He needs You, Father."

The voice was silent. The outdoors were silent. The old woman rolled over onto her back, breathing hard, and looked up at the sky. The moon was silent too. But it watched, watched. Its glare pinned her to the patio and held her there. Studying her like an insect under a microscope. Dissecting her soul.

Finally she could take no more of it and rose and went inside. There she collapsed on her bed and let the sobs come.

Jimmy stood still, shoulders drooped, head slightly cocked to the right. He was wearing his G.I. Joe shirt and camouflage shorts. Both were crusted with dirt, as were Jimmy's bare knees.

Rob's heart felt like a brick in his chest. A knot the size of a baseball formed in his throat. Tears leaked freely from his eyes. Still on his knees, he faced his son and opened his arms. "Jimmy. Come here, buddy."

But Jimmy didn't move. He watched Rob through cautious eyes, holding his ground and not moving. His arms hung limp at his sides.

Rob stood and climbed out of the hole he had been digging and lowered himself to one knee. He had no idea what Jimmy had been through, so he didn't want to rush his son and scoop him up in his arms just yet. But he had to use every ounce of self-control in his body to refrain. Jimmy was no more than twenty feet away, and Rob could be there in six easy steps. He could hold his son close again. But he would take it slow.

"Jimmy," he said, stretching out his arms. "Come here, son. Come to Daddy."

Rob looked at his hands and saw how dirty they were, how dirty he was. He realized what he must look like, caked with dirt, climbing out of a grave. No wonder Jimmy was keeping his distance.

"It's OK, Jimmy. Really. I love you so much. Please come to me. You're OK now."

But Jimmy still said nothing and made no move toward Rob.

Rob moved a little closer, slowly so as not to appear threatening.

"We'll be all right now, buddy. You and me. Everything's gonna be fine. Come on, let's go home."

Jimmy's right hand twitched, and he lifted it to scratch his head. He winced and looked at his hand as if it pained him. He then held it palm up for Rob to see.

"What happened, pal? Hurt your hand?" He stood and took one step closer to Jimmy.

Jimmy responded not by running for his dad or advancing a step toward Rob but by taking a stride of equal length backward. He blinked, opened his mouth as if to say something, but then clamped it shut again.

Rob was tempted right then to run for Jimmy, take him in his arms, and hold him close. Yes, the boy might try to run, but Rob was faster. Yes, he may even struggle, but he'd be in his daddy's arms. Yes, Jimmy might be frightened, but being out here alone in these woods with those demon creatures had to be scarier.

Shifting his weight forward, setting his mind on what he had to do, Rob initiated the first step but was frozen by a familiar voice: "That's a step in the wrong direction, Rob."

Rob swung his head to the right and saw Juli standing not thirty feet away. She stood directly under a moonbeam as it parted the canopy and reached for the forest floor. It glistened around the crown of her head like a halo.

"Juli. What are you doing?" He glanced at Jimmy and noticed his son's eyes had widened and were shifting between Rob and Juli. There was something about Jimmy's eyes that didn't look quite right.

"Playing superhero. I left my cape at home, though."

Rob pointed at Jimmy. "Look, I found him."

Juli had Rob's flashlight in one hand. It was turned off, and she now pointed it at Jimmy. "Don't go over there, Rob. Please."

More tears flowed from Rob's eyes. "But Juli. Look, I found him. He's so scared."

Jimmy eyed Juli like he was afraid of her then looked at Rob. "Daddy?"

At the sound of that word Rob advanced two more steps and practically fell at Jimmy's feet.

"Rob, don't. Please." Juli said. There was an edge of panic to her voice. "Go back. C'mon."

"Why, Juli? It's Jimmy. My boy. He needs me."

Jimmy was standing in the same place. His feet hadn't moved, but now he reached his little arms toward Rob. The distance between them seemed only a matter of feet now. A span Rob could cover in less than a second. He reached for Jimmy, and their fingers almost touched.

"Tell me why I shouldn't, Juli," Rob said. His heart told him to close the gap between him and his son, wrap Jimmy in his arms, breathe in the familiar smell of sweat and tears, and end all this now. But something else urged him to heed Juli's warning. She hadn't lied to him once yet, nor had she been proven wrong about anything.

Juli hesitated, then turned on the light, keeping it directed at the ground. Jimmy flinched.

"Because," Juli said, "that's not your son."

Rob's mouth went as dry as Death Valley. A buzz spread out across his skin. *Not your son.* The words throbbed in his ears. He wanted to reject them, push them away, defiantly refuse to believe, but for some reason he couldn't. It was as if he'd known all along.

He took an almost imperceptible step backward.

Jimmy lifted his head, and Rob almost vomited right there in the woods. His son's eyes were as black and lifeless as oil.

Juli was saying something, but Rob wasn't paying attention. Suddenly his hands and feet burned hot, and fire spread across his scalp. He tried to swallow but couldn't. He tried to move but was paralyzed.

The Jimmy-thing turned its head and in an instant

morphed into a darkling. This was the first close look Rob had gotten of one. Its worm-colored skin was stretched tight over its entire body, like a burn victim's scarred flesh. It had no ears or nose, only holes where they should be, and its lips were thin and wide. Behind them were two rows of teeth like the teeth of a piranha. It stood only a little taller than Jimmy, not even five feet, but was mostly arms and legs with a short, sinewy torso. Its chest expanded and contracted with each rapid breath, the muscles beneath that tight skin moving like steel bands.

Suddenly the thing snapped its head up and drilled Rob with a piercing scream.

To his right, Juli let out a primal holler of her own and nailed the darkling with the light. It snorted angrily, spun around, and disappeared into the darkness of the forest.

"Definitely not your son," Juli said, keeping the light moving along the perimeter of the clearing.

Rob's legs felt like bags of sand, and he would have collapsed if Juli wasn't right there to support him.

She steadied him then let go. "You all right?"

"Yeah. No." He was in a fog. His mind seemed to be stuck like dry gears. "That wasn't Jimmy."

"Not unless your Jimmy is Eddie Munster's evil cousin." Juli retrieved Rob's light and handed it to him. "Here, light up the darkness."

Rob flipped the light on and pointed it at a tree. All was quiet again in the forest—as if the whole incident with the darkling had never taken place. He looked at the hole he'd been digging. It was about two feet deep. Suddenly he felt foolish and naïve.

Juli must have noticed because she came to stand beside him and put a hand on his shoulder. "Gonna have to start calling you shovelhands." She was quiet for a moment, moving her light back and forth. "Anyone else would have done the same thing. You love your son."

Rob pulled away from her hand and turned around, sweeping the light across trees and underbrush. They were out there, the darkling that mocked his son, along with his darkling friends; he could feel them, just on the other side of the light, watching, waiting. Panic seized him, and he had the urge to run screaming into the woods like some idiot on a warpath. He had the sudden feeling that he would never see Jimmy again. That all this looking and running around in the woods was nonsense, the manic obsession of a madman. But what if it wasn't nonsense? What if it wasn't madness? There was a seed of hope there, a pinpoint of light, and that was what would keep him looking. He realized he would never stop until he knew beyond a doubt that Jimmy was truly gone. And isn't that what a daddy should do?

Something behind him moved in the woods. Leaves crunched. He swung around. Juli was about ten feet away now, facing him. She mouthed the words, *Did you hear that?*

But before Rob had time to nod, several darklings exploded from the shadows, moving faster than Rob would have thought possible, and slammed Juli from behind, sending the flashlight sailing and her to the ground.

PART FIVE

Where light abides, fear cannot.
—THE BOOK OF LIGHT AND DARKNESS

Fourteen

JULI HIT THE GROUND HARD WITH A SOLID THUD, THREE darklings on her back.

Rob was frozen by fear and shock for an instant. One of the darklings on Juli's back reared its head, contracted its abdominals, and let loose with a piercing scream. The sound traveled right through Rob and knocked him back a step. He gathered himself and lunged forward.

Something charged from his left. He flinched and dodged right, but he was too slow. A darkling hit him from the side, pushing him off course but not off his feet.

Pain shot up his leg. Something was attached to it. He glanced down and saw a darkling clinging to his pants, its teeth buried in his calf. He shook his leg, lost his balance, and took a spill. Before he hit the ground, though, another darkling was on him, tearing at his shirt.

Rob rolled in the leaves, trying to dislodge the darklings. The one at his torso groped at his shirt. A hand landed on his head and grabbed a fistful of hair. Rob's head was yanked back. More darklings piled on top of him, immobilizing him and pressing the air out of his lungs. He turned his head and found Juli, on her stomach, arms stretched behind her back, face contorted in pain.

Rob tried to holler, tried to fight back, but any effort was futile. There were just too many darklings. They were coming out of the woods and into the clearing now in swarms, like bees from a hive. All of them with that same scarred skin and black eyes and piranha teeth.

Juli was still prone, but now only one darkling perched on her back like a gargoyle, its eyes shifting around the clearing, as if challenging any of the others to dismount him from his prize. She lay still, and at first Rob thought the worst, but then he noticed her back rising and falling with rapid respirations.

The burning in his calf was radiating up his leg like fire in his veins. With the darklings on him and his head still pulled back, it was difficult to breathe, and his neck was now throbbing.

Slowly, like the movement of the tide, the darklings began to congregate around the outside of the clearing, forming a circle around the perimeter. They moved about impatiently, shifting their weight from foot to foot, twitching uncontrollably, snapping their jaws, clenching their fists.

Four of the darklings held frayed ropes with a dog on the end of each, a makeshift leash. The dogs pulled and pawed at the ground, snarled and barked. Foam gathered at the corners of their mouth.

When a circle was finally formed, Rob and Juli in the center, still pinned down, one of the larger darklings stepped forward and approached Rob. Squatting on its haunches, it leaned forward so its face was only inches from his. Its black eyes were like bottomless pits, no life at all in them. They reminded Rob of a shark's eyes—emotionless, cold, dead, and full of hate. The thing opened its mouth, revealing those knifelike teeth, and snapped its jaws shut. It contracted its abdominals and thoracic muscles several times, like a dog does before it vomits, then released a howling scream that lasted several seconds and smelled of decayed meat.

Around them, the evil horde began to move about, and a rumble of whispery sounds spread through the gathering. The dogs had settled down some and now paced in front of their masters. The darkling in front of Rob snapped its jaws again at him, stood, and walked to the center of the clearing. There it arched its back, threw back its head, and screamed again.

On one end of the clearing the line of darklings separated, and the rumbling among them increased. Several of them let loose with involuntary outbursts of screaming. Beyond the reach of the moon's light, there was commotion in the woods, leaves rustling and branches breaking. A tree shook. Something was coming.

From the dark shadows, three darklings emerged, snapping their jaws and twitching reflexively. Behind them a larger figure followed, flanked by several more darklings on each side and several from behind. It was a man, staggering, struggling to stay on his feet.

When a ray of moonlight fell on the man, Rob's heart stilled in his chest. He looked at Juli, and their eyes met. He didn't know what she saw in his, but in hers there was obvious fear.

The man was Asher Wiggins.

The darklings pushed and pulled Asher into the center of the clearing. Their nimble movements were both graceful and grotesque.

Rob and Juli were on either side of Asher now, each about ten feet away. Asher's head was bowed, his shoulders slumped. When he came to a halt, his knees buckled, and he almost went down. He wobbled and swayed as if he were either extremely weak or extremely drunk. Rob doubted it was the latter.

Darklings danced around Asher, taunting him and nipping at him with their mouths. They were like sharks circling their prey, breathing in the scent of his blood, relishing their imminent feast.

The whole scene made Rob's stomach churn. The darkling on his back continued its grip on his hair, holding his head back. There was an evil electricity in the air, an anticipation of what was about to take place. Rob didn't know what it was, but he had a good idea and hoped to God he would be able to avoid watching.

Finally, the larger darkling broke from the crowd again and approached Asher. It breathed heavily and wasted no time getting to the center of the clearing. Circling Asher, it clenched its fists and snapped its jaw over and over again. Rob wanted to cry out; he was already sickened by this grisly scenario. The big darkling walked around behind Asher, reared back its right arm, and brought it down hard on the back of Asher's knees. Asher yelped, his legs buckled, and he dropped to the ground, kneeling.

Now he was on the same level as his captors.

The big darkling continued circling Asher, eyeing him hungrily.

Asher turned his head and made eye contact with Rob. Surprisingly, Rob found no fear in his eyes, only sadness and fatigue. He wanted to reach out to Asher and take the older man's hand, extend to him one last touch of hope and love.

At one point, the big darkling stopped in front of Asher, positioned its face so close to Asher's their noses almost touched, and let out a sound that sounded more like a hawk's screech than a woman's scream.

The horde of darklings around the perimeter grumbled and muttered their approval. The excitement in the circle was clearly building, racing from one darkling to the next.

The big one continued its circling and finally stopped directly behind Asher. It lifted its arm and, with those bony, elongated fingers, took hold of Asher's hair and jerked his head back so the soft skin of his neck below where the beard ended was exposed.

Asher winced and hollered in pain. He was breathing hard through clenched teeth now. He moved his good eye to the extreme right and found Rob. "Robert," he yelled, his voice strained and high-pitched. "You shine your light."

The circle fell silent. Not a darkling moved or snapped its jaws. Not a one twitched or shifted its weight. They were frozen with expectation, stilled by unholy eagerness.

Rob's nerves were overstretched bands ready to snap. He shut his eyes tight. When he opened them again, what he saw happened faster than his mind could register it. The big darkling threw its head forward and sunk its teeth into Asher's neck. As if the cue had been given, the rest of the darklings and their demon dogs came to life and rushed the chilling scene unfolding in the center of the clearing. They tackled Asher as one and engaged in a feeding frenzy matched only by a school of piranha.

The darkling on Rob's back released its grip on his hair and joined the vicious bash.

Rob let his head fall to the ground and promptly vomited.

Then, from across the clearing, he heard Juli scream.

The air was ripe with fear, saturated with it. Like a sponge fully waterlogged. And the odor was intoxicating. He had no need to join in the feeding. Let the underlings have their fill. His hunger was reserved for Shields.

It had to happen soon, though. He couldn't control his desire much longer. It was a wild lust, a craving that was almost at full maturity.

His body was now showing every sign of suffering withdrawal. His palms were slick with sweat and his brow wet. Tremors had overtaken his hands. His vision had even dulled.

This was why he'd endured the beatings, the violations, the humiliation. Why he'd allowed cowards to subdue him and inflict all kinds of pain on him: to ripen his hatred like a piece of deadly fruit and heighten his desire for retribution. In his way of thinking, Shields was the cause of so much suffering, so much lost time, and he needed to know, to experience, even a sliver of the anguish he was responsible for.

He needed to end this soon. Tonight. He needed to bring to completion the plot he'd been preparing for the past two decades.

Fifteen

ROB WAS TO HIS FEET IN A FLASH. HIS FIRST INCLI-nation was to run for it. Head into the woods and keep running until he found the way out. Asher...he still couldn't believe what his eyes had seen. Fear had such a hold on him now, he could only think of self-preservation. But then he thought of Juli. He couldn't leave her alone to face the same fate as Asher. He moved in a wide arc around the pack of feeding darklings to stay inconspicuous and get a look at Juli. The sounds coming from the center of the clearing brought the bile to his throat again.

When he came into view of Juli, his heart dropped into his stomach. She was lying facedown on the ground, head turned to one side, unmoving. The scream he'd heard must have been her last.

Rising tears put pressure behind his eyes, and he found he could not swallow the acid in his throat. Fight or flight was the decision of the moment, and there was no doubt about his choice. But as he turned to duck into the utter darkness of the woods, he saw Juli lift her head and turn it toward him.

Juli. She was still alive.

Keeping his arc wide and sticking close to the outer perim-eter of the clearing, Rob moved quickly to where Juli lay.

The darklings were still preoccupied with their victim and didn't notice his movements.

When Rob reached Juli, he crouched beside her. "You OK?"

"I'm still alive."

"Can you run?"

Juli gave one nod. "I got my running shoes on."

"OK, let's go."

Rob stood and helped Juli up. The front of her shirt and pants were covered with grass stains and dirt, and there was a nasty brush burn across her cheekbone, but she seemed not to notice.

"This way," Rob said, taking Juli by the wrist. He had no idea which way was back to the cabin, but he figured if they could stay out of the darklings' reach until sunup, they'd live to find a way out of these woods. Quickly, he looked at his watch: four forty-five. Another thirty, forty minutes, and it would be light enough to drive the darklings back into hiding. "Quickly," he said. "We need to get a good head start."

So off they went through the woods again, ducking branches, dodging limbs, weaving around stumps and underbrush.

When they'd been running for a minute or so, Rob tripped and landed on the ground. He was breathing heavily and noticed for the first time that his calf felt like it was on fire.

Juli, who'd kept running, came back and crouched beside him. "I don't think those guys are honoring time-outs."

Rob pushed himself up.

From the clearing, not three hundred yards away, a scream cut through the morning air.

"That's our cue," Juli said. "Ready or not, here they come."

A cacophony of angry screams erupted from the clearing and, soon after, the complex sound of breaking branches and shuffling leaves. The darklings were on the hunt again.

"Time to go," Juli said, tugging on Rob's arm.

Rob jumped up and got his feet under him again. His calf throbbed, and his leg felt like it was loaded with bricks.

"Go ahead," he said. "I'll be right behind you."

"Guess again. We fly this coop together or not at all. Now let's go. One foot in front of the other."

Rob willed his leg to move, and soon he was racing through the woods again, ignoring the pain that jolted his leg with each step. Behind them, a storm of screams and hatred and violence brewed and closed in.

Navigating the woods in the dark proved to be a difficult task, and again Rob went down. This time, though, he was back on his feet and moving before Juli even realized he had fallen.

When he caught up to her, she said, "You OK to keep going?" She was moving at a good clip but said the words almost effortlessly. Her stamina was incredible.

"I'm going," Rob said. His lungs were heaving, pulling in air double, maybe even triple, time now. His quads felt the size of tree trunks and ached like someone had tightened a clamp on them.

And still the darklings pursued, huffing and snorting and screaming through the woods.

Rob pushed on, in spite of the fire in his calf, in spite of the knives in his lungs, in spite of the vice around his quads, and in spite of the fear in his heart. Juli was only feet ahead of him, her ponytail swinging like a pendulum, keeping time to their steps.

Suddenly Juli disappeared. Rob slowed up but was too late. The ground beneath him sloped off, and he found himself tumbling down a steep embankment. He fell uncontrollably, legs flailing, knees and elbows thumping the ground with each revolution. Finally, at the bottom he was stopped by a fallen tree. He lay there for a few seconds, staring up at the silhouetted canopy, shaking things back into place in his head.

To his left, Juli moaned and pushed herself to her knees.

Above them, at the top of the embankment, a few darklings could be heard but not seen. It was still too dark.

"Are all your pieces still in place?" Juli said.

"I think so. How 'bout you?"

"Present and accounted for. Let's roll."

Rob stood and looked around. Even moonlight was minimal at the bottom of the embankment, but he could see they were in some kind of gorge with steep hills on either side.

The darklings had gathered their forces at the top of the embankment and grew louder with each passing moment.

Juli, now on her feet too, bent her arm at the elbow and winced. She looked up at the darklings. "If they're waiting for an invitation..."

"They're waiting to see what our next move is gonna be."

"Hopefully something unpredictable."

"I have a feeling this gorge leads to a streambed, which leads to the river."

"The mighty Susquehanna."

"You ready?"

"As ever, Freddy."

Leaving the darklings standing atop the gorge, Rob and Juli fled south, toward the river and hopefully a way out of the woods. Within seconds, though, the little devils were keeping pace with them along the gorge's ridge. And seconds later they disappeared into the darkness and fell silent.

"Keep going," Rob said. "We need to keep moving."

They both slowed a little to a pace they could keep up for longer than a few minutes. The sun wouldn't be lighting up the sky with its first rays for another twenty minutes or so. They had to get as far as they could in that time. And stay alive doing it.

While they ran, feet pounding the leaves, arms going like pistons, Rob's mind kept flashing back to that last image of Asher right before the big darkling planted its teeth in his neck. He tried to ignore it, wipe it off the slate of his mind, but it kept coming back, more vivid than the time before. He also thought of that darkling impersonating his son, and anger bubbled up in his chest. He clenched his fists and pumped his arms harder.

When his feet landed in water, Rob knew they were close to the river. The stream. Follow the water. He took one side, and Juli took the other. But before they could advance any further an inky shadow poured down the embankment ahead of them and gathered across the stream.

Both Rob and Juli stopped. Rob moaned, and Juli let out a defeated sigh. He looked behind them, thinking maybe that would be one last getaway, but there stood a shadow as well, covering most of the gorge.

The darklings were back.

And this time there was no escape.

In the gorge there was even less light to see by, and the shadows ahead of and behind them seemed to move as one. There was something different about the darklings this time, though. An eerie hush had overtaken them. There were no screams, no hisses, no snapping of jaws. Even the dogs were quiet. Instead, they undulated rhythmically as a unit, like the rise and fall of swells at sea.

Rob stole a glance at his watch. He knew it had to be time soon, time for the sun to make its daily appearance and push back the darkness. Time for salvation to come. Five ten. The first spears of daylight should be poking through the forest in the next thirty minutes.

He looked at Juli. She was eyeing the darklings behind them. When she turned her face to him, surprisingly, he found no fear in her eyes.

"In the movies, there's always a way out," she said.

"This isn't Hollywood."

"It's Darlington."

"And they"—Rob nodded toward the throbbing horde of darklings—"aren't CGI special effects."

They kept their eyes on the darklings and spoke low so as not to invite an early advancement of the enemy troops. Rob said, "Any suggestions?"

"There's always a way out. Movies or no movies."

"You said there was only one way out of these woods. Did you mean through them?"

"You should audition for *Jeopardy*."

"I always wanted to meet Alex Trebek."

The horde stopped moving, and all was quiet in the gorge.

From the shadowy mass in front of Rob and Juli, a single figure emerged, the big darkling.

Rob hitched a breath. This was the same scenario that had unfolded minutes ago with Asher.

The darkling approached with slow, even steps.

Keeping his eyes forward, Rob said to Juli, "Is there a way through them?"

From the corner of his eye, he saw Juli's head turn toward him. They were shoulder to shoulder, so her face was no more than a foot from his. "Asher's death wasn't in vain."

Asher? What did Asher's gruesome death have to do with Rob and Juli getting through the darklings and out of Darlington Woods? Whatever it was obviously didn't work for him.

The darkling was steadily closing the space between them, now less than thirty feet away.

Then it hit Rob. Asher's last words, right before the big darkling—the one not twenty feet from him now—took his life. *You shine your light.*

"Shine your light," Rob said aloud.

The darkling was there, standing before him. The other ones stood about as high as Rob's belly, but this one was almost to his chin. It was thicker too, more muscular. It stood inches from Rob, its face turned upward. Anger and hatred twisted its scarred skin, furrowed its brow, tightened its jaw. It breathed heavily, air wheezing in and out of its nostrils.

From the horde, a scream broke the silence. The big darkling looked over Rob's shoulder, eastward, and narrowed its eyes. It huffed in annoyance then looked at Rob again. Rob gazed into those dark orbs and was so overcome with fear his knees almost buckled. He wondered if Jimmy had looked into the same eyes and felt the same fear. But Juli was right there, taking his hand in hers. Her grip was firm and, oddly, dissipated the fear.

The darkling took a step back, not moving its eyes from Rob's, then turned to face the horde. It raised both arms into the air and let out a full-throated scream. At once the two hordes, the one in front and the one behind, advanced.

Rob squeezed Juli's hand harder. This was it. *Shine your light.* What did it mean? He didn't have the flashlight anymore.

Within seconds the hordes were there. The rest happened so quickly and in such a blur Rob had no time to think let alone shine a light even if he had one.

The darklings overcame both Rob and Juli, knocking them to the ground and swarming them like flies on roadkill. The weight of the horde on him was so great Rob could barely draw in a breath of air. Claws tore at his clothes; hands pulled at his hair. He tried to fight back, but his arms and legs were pinned to the ground. He heard the big darkling screaming from somewhere outside the horde. Something grasped the back of his neck and squeezed. Pain shot up into his head, and then everything went black.

Sixteen

ROB AWOKE IN A LIGHTLESS ROOM VIBRATED BY A low thrumming. He ran his hands along the walls and floor. Concrete. Somewhere in the room, he heard the hollow echo of dripping water too. And in the distance, under the thrum, was the sound of moving water.

He turned his head to listen better, and a sharp pain bit into his neck. His calf still throbbed too.

Triggered by the dark and pain, Rob's muscles tensed, and his lungs felt like they were filled with gravel. He quickly spiraled into that familiar panic. The darkness felt alive, like it was an evil unto itself, a malignant thing working its way inside him, possessing every cell in his body. His breathing became labored, and his heart rate spiked.

"Juli?"

There was no answer but the steady thrum, the rush of water, and the rhythmic drip, drip.

"Juli."

Still nothing. Rob feared the worst, that the darklings had, for some reason, only detained him in this room but had delegated a much more grisly fate to Juli.

"Juli." One more time.

Then, "Dam." It was Juli's voice.

"What?"

"The Conowingo Dam."

The sound of Juli's voice blew over Rob's nerves like a cool breeze. And of course it fit. The rushing water, the thrumming turbines, the dripping. They were inside the Conowingo Dam. They'd crossed it on the way to Darlington.

"Are you all right?" Rob said.

"Never better. I always wanted to tour this place, but they don't do tours for the public anymore. How 'bout you?"

"My neck is killing me, and my leg...but besides that, I can't complain. We're still alive."

"And alive is good."

Rob could see nothing. The room was totally void of light. But by the sound of her voice he could tell Juli was directly across from him. "Where are we?"

"Feels like a utility or storage room in the dam. Under the spillway." She paused for a few seconds. "That sound, the humming—"

"The turbines, I figured that."

"You're across the room. Come over here."

Rob started to stand but sat again. His mind conjured up images of darklings waiting in the darkness, waiting to pounce on him like hungry wolves and devour him like they did Asher. "I can't."

If she was disappointed or irritated, Juli's voice did not show it. "Yes, you can. Follow the wall around to where I am."

Rob put both hands on the concrete floor. It was cool and dry and vibrated. He wanted to stand and go to Juli, sit beside her, but he couldn't; his legs wouldn't move. "I–I can't."

He heard the rustle of Juli's clothes. Then a broken scraping sound—her sneakers sliding along the floor. Then she was next to him, sliding down the wall to sit. "Hey, mind if I drop in?"

Rob liked having her close. Already the panic was waning. "Why do you think they brought us here?"

"Um, it's dark."

"Seriously."

"They couldn't take us in the woods; there wasn't time. Just like you're afraid of the dark, they're afraid of the light."

"Saved by the sun."

"The glorious sun."

There was a moment of silence between them. Rob's stomach grumbled loudly. He pushed the button to light his watch. "It's eleven thirty-five a.m. ... and I'm starved."

"They'll be back at sundown."

Rob thought about that. And he thought about Jimmy. After all that happened last night—his encounter with the Jimmy-thing in the woods, the confrontation with the darklings, and Asher's grisly death—he now doubted more than ever that Jimmy was still alive, out there in Darlington Woods surviving among the darklings or having found a way to avoid them altogether. And if Jimmy really was gone, what point was there in living, in going through the motions? He'd already lost Kelly, an inconceivable tragedy that, by itself, would have caused him to give up all will to go on, and now, if he was admitting Jimmy was dead too, he had no purpose to live; he was a dead man already.

But he wasn't admitting it, wasn't admitting anything. Just because he doubted didn't mean Jimmy was dead. In spite of what his head told him, he had to press on. He had to unveil the truth. He needed to get out of this room and find Jimmy. He wasn't ready to accept a world, a life, without his little boy.

"But we won't be here," he declared.

Juli was quiet until Rob felt her hand lightly touch his. "Yes, we will."

Anger climbed into Rob's chest. "What's that supposed to mean?"

"You can't always run from your fears, Rob. Eventually you have to face them all."

Rob didn't like getting angry with Juli. They'd already been through some horrific things together, and he was feeling a bond with her. The kind of bond he imagined soldiers forged on the battlefield. "This has nothing to do with facing fears. This is about survival and finding my son. I'm not sticking around to face those things again and die like some kind of martyr, like Asher did. I'm not dying in the dark."

"This isn't about dying in the darkness. It's about living in the light. That's the only way out."

Rob pushed his fear aside and mustered up the courage to stand. "As I see it, the only way out is through a door. I'm getting out of here, and you're coming with me."

"I wouldn't have it any other way."

Feeling along the concrete wall, Rob inched his way around the room. There were a couple spots where metal cable casing ran up the wall like petrified vines. He found the leak and the drip, a metal cabinet that was empty, and a drainpipe in one corner. The room was small, maybe fifteen by fifteen. Just before he made it the whole way around, he felt what he was looking for—a metal door. Running his hand over the door he felt no knob or handle of any sort. No locks either. It was just a sheet of smooth metal.

"I found the door," he said. But Juli said nothing in return.

Rob pushed on the door, but it didn't budge. He knocked on it and found it to be solid, like knocking on the concrete wall. Running his hands along the edge, he located three hinges on one side. So it was indeed a door and opened inward. He knocked again, this time with his fist. Then again, harder. The door didn't budge, and his knocking sounded dead. Kicking the door in frustration, Rob followed the wall back and sat next to Juli.

Her hand found his again. It was warm and offered some comfort. "There's only one way out."

"Yeah, you keep saying that."

"Face your fears."

"And you're not scared?"

"It's not a matter of being scared or not. It's what you do with that fear."

"But are you scared?"

"Do birds fly?"

"Not all of them."

"Touché. Yes, I'm scared."

Rob paused to think about his own fear, his fear of the dark, which he knew was irrational, and his fear of the dark-lings and dying like Asher did, which seemed totally rational. "Are you afraid to die?"

"Dying isn't something to fear if you know what's waiting on the other side." She said it like she meant it.

"So you're saying the only way out of here is by dying. Like Asher. He's free now. I'm not ready to accept that. What happens to Jimmy then?"

"Actually, I had something else in mind. I'm not looking to emulate Asher either. No, thank you. Your fear has crippled you and held you captive. You have to break those chains and let your light shine. That's what Asher was saying."

"Asher was crazy." Even as he said the words, Rob knew they were not true. Asher was anything but crazy. His words—"*You shine your light*"—still echoed in Rob's ears.

"And you think I am too?"

Rob ran his fingers through his hair. His neck still hurt, and now his head did too. "I don't know. I don't know what you're talking about. I don't understand."

Juli sighed deeply. "You will."

Time passed slowly in the room. Rob's mind churned continuously, running through options, scenarios, situations, but nothing he thought of provided a way out before sundown. He'd circled the room several times, running his hands over the entirety of the space, looking for anything that might offer a way of escape, but he found nothing. He thought maybe there'd be a ventilation duct in the ceiling, but the ceiling was too high to reach. With each pass of the room and each reminder of their imminent meeting with the darklings, Rob grew more and more morose and slipped further into a dark hole of discouragement.

Juli had grown quiet too. Rob sat next to her on the concrete floor, lay his head against the wall, and listened to the thrum of the turbines and the steady movement of water over the spillway. Juli was whispering something. The low hiss of her voice sounded like wind moving through a willow tree. Rob tried to listen but couldn't make out what she was saying. She was praying, he knew.

Until now, he hadn't even thought of praying, and for some reason that bothered him. Kelly would have thought of it. Jimmy would have too. He tried to pass it off by reminding himself that his praying days were over, that he'd tried the whole prayer thing and it hadn't worked for him. But somehow that reasoning seemed hollow now. It didn't carry weight anymore. He needed to pray. He wanted to pray.

God, I don't want to die. Get us out of here. Please. Show me the way out.

That was it. It wasn't much, but it was something. It would have to do for now. He couldn't say he felt any different afterward, but why should he?

Closing his eyes, he let his mind drift to thoughts of Kelly and Jimmy, of times when life was happier and devils roaming the woods at night was the stuff of campfire stories.

Slowly he lost his footing in this world and slipped into the place of dreams.

Rob found himself strolling through the woods along a meandering trail. It was late evening, and the canopy glowed a deep orange. A cool breeze worked its way through the leaves and around the trunks, tousling his hair. Squirrels chattered and birds sang their late-day songs. Occasionally, a half-eaten walnut would drop from a tree, just missing him. Kelly was there too, walking with him, her hand in his. He felt happy and content. In the distance, just over a hill, Jimmy laughed excitedly. He'd gone chasing a squirrel.

Rob was fully aware of all that had taken place but felt no anxiety, no fear, no sorrow. He was with his family, and his spirits were high. He looked at Kelly. She was watching a chipmunk on a fallen limb. The chipmunk twitched, jumped to the leafy forest floor, ran a circle around itself, and disappeared under a fold of wet leaves.

Kelly laughed. Rob loved that laugh. Every day, no matter what was going on or how busy they were or what heavy matter was weighing them down, he'd find some way to pull that laugh out of her.

Rob and Kelly ascended a small hill, finding rocks in the trail for traction. Just out of sight on the other side, Jimmy continued his happy giggle.

Right before they came to the top of the hill, while Jimmy was still preoccupied with the squirrel, Rob stopped and faced Kelly. He touched her cheek, her ear. Let his fingers comb through the length of her hair. She was so beautiful, so tender, so real. He leaned forward and kissed her full on the lips, and the feelings stirred by that kiss were enough to bring tears to his eyes. He started to cry. Kelly smiled at him, wiped a tear from his cheek, and returned his kiss.

Suddenly, Rob pulled away. The woods had gone silent. He looked around and found no squirrels, no chipmunks, no birds. The canopy overhead was darkening, looming. He listened. No Jimmy either. Leaving Kelly, he ran five steps to the top of the hill and gasped in horror. Jimmy was gone. He turned back to Kelly, but she was gone now too. He was alone, and it was quickly getting darker.

Panic seized his chest, paralyzed his lungs, weakened his legs.

"Kelly!" But she did not answer. She wasn't going to answer.

Rob spun around and looked down the other side of the hill again. "Jimmy!" But no reply came.

He threw himself down the hill, running full speed along the trail, allowing gravity to pull him along faster and faster. At the bottom he stopped and breathed in, filling his lungs with air. Sweat touched his brow; his carotids throbbed. He tried again, "Jimmy!"

This time a tiny voice answered. It was Jimmy. "Daddy?" In the distance, to Rob's left.

He abandoned the trail and headed for the sound of his son's voice, pushing branches and thistles out of his way. Every several steps he'd stop and holler Jimmy's name again. And every time he'd be rewarded with a reply.

But it was getting darker in the woods and more difficult to see where he was going. Shadows were growing longer and deeper, more menacing.

He raced on, calling to his son and following the replies, until finally he came upon an old cabin, a shack now, just a bunch of sheets of pressboard nailed together with a tin roof.

From inside the shack he heard, "Daddy? Help me."

"I'm here, Jimmy. Daddy's here." Relief swept over him like a cool mist. He rushed for the door and grabbed the latch, but it wouldn't budge. He shook it, hit it, kicked at it with his foot, but the latch appeared welded in place.

From inside, Jimmy continued to call out for his daddy. Rob could hear the fear in his son's voice, and it made him angry that the door wouldn't open.

Around him, darkness crept in, stealing the last bit of light. But Rob didn't seem to notice. He continued working on the door, ramming it with his shoulder, kicking at it, pulling on the latch, but it proved unmovable.

Angry, frustrated, and scared, Rob began to cry. Tears stung his eyes and blurred his vision. His throat constricted.

"I'm still here, Jimmy," he said in a tight voice. "I won't leave you. I'll never leave you."

He leaned against the door and put his hand on it. A one-inch-thick piece of oak was all that separated him from his son. He imagined Jimmy on the other side, leaning against the door too. So close. So blessed close.

The silence was suddenly broken by the sound of a woman screaming.

Seventeen

THIS WAS IT. SHIELDS WAS IN THE ROOM, PINNED down by darkness and fear, vulnerable, helpless. There was no escape this time, nowhere to run. There was only one way out, and that was through the underlings. And that really wasn't an option.

Twenty-two years in the making, the time had finally come. Every nerve in his body pulsated with feverish excitement. Every hair was on end. Adrenaline-saturated blood coursed through his arteries. His muscles twitched with anticipation. Salivary glands worked overtime.

He stood in the corridor, pumping his fists, trying to calm himself before entering the room. This time, he would draw first blood. He would take the life from Shields and discard his body like a piece of garbage. It had to be that way. And when the deed was done, all debts will have been paid, vengeance will have been served, and he will have been vindicated.

At that thought a smile touched his lips. Free from this burden, the destruction he would bring forth, the mayhem, the death, oh, it was a beautiful thought. The fear he would instill in so many would be a show worthy of an audience.

The time had come. He sucked in a lungful of air and blew it out, then set off down the corridor, his horde of underlings following silently behind.

Locked in the lightless room with no way of escape, Juli had time to think and pray. To her right, Rob was asleep. His steady, deep breathing fell into rhythm with the low drone of the turbines. Several times, her eyelids got heavy too, but each time she was able to fend off the attack of sleep and get back to praying.

The end was coming; she knew it was. Not necessarily The End, but the end of this ordeal. The final showdown, if you will. She'd be lying if she said she wasn't nervous about it. She was. She wondered if Rob was ready and prayed he would be. She wondered if she'd have the strength to be there for him in every way he needed her to be and prayed she would be. She wondered if she'd have the courage to face *him* and stand her ground and prayed she would.

She knew he was coming, and the thought of being in this room with him, in such close quarters with someone so vile, made her nervous.

"This is your calling."

The familiar doubt was there, gnawing at her insides like a sewer rat.

Juli thought of Christ in the Garden of Gethsemane, Him knowing full well what horrors were to come. Fear and doubt and all kinds of trepidation must have been ripe in that garden. A constant onslaught by the enemy. Stress levels were maxed out. Sweat glands worked overtime. His heart pumped like a galloping horse. Capillaries burst.

And He battled it all with prayer.

"This is your calling."

Again, she prayed.

Sometime later—time was of no consequence here in the dark—from somewhere in the bowels of the dam, Juli heard a scream. The time was upon them. He was coming. Beads of sweat poked through her skin. Her palms were instantly clammy.

She filled her lungs with the stale air of the room, calming her jittery nerves.

"This is your calling."

Yes, it was. And she was ready to accept it. Come what may.

Another scream bounced around the concrete innards of the dam. It was impossible to tell from which direction it came.

Juli nudged the sleeper beside her. "Rob...Rob."

Rob started and opened his eyes. Juli was saying his name and nudging him.

"Bad dream?"

"The worst." He rubbed his eyes and forked his fingers through his hair. The room was still black; he was still sitting against the wall; Juli was still next to him. "What—" He took a look at his watch: nine fifty. "Man, I was really out."

"I didn't want to disturb your beauty sleep, but..."

From somewhere in the tunnels beneath the spillway a scream echoed off the concrete. Juli's hand found Rob's again.

Other screams joined the first one in a creepy chorus.

"We have to get out of here," Rob said. "I know where Jimmy is."

"All of a sudden?"

"Yeah. My dream. I know where he is." He was convinced now: Jimmy was out there, in that shack. The dream was so real, so palpable. Everything about it shouted authenticity. He had to go.

The screams grew louder, like a gaggle of wailing women in an empty basement.

Rob stood and wiped his palms on his pants. He felt the wall around to the door. "There has to be a way to open it." His hands slid along the smooth metal, searching for any kind of handle or lock or... "Come on!" But there was nothing. It was just a sheet of metal.

He hit the door hard, hurting his hand but ignoring the pain. Jimmy was out there in that shack, calling for him. His son needed him, and he was trapped in this blasted room. He struck the door again.

Now the screams were right outside the room, on the other side of the door. Rob jumped back and found the wall. Juli's hand found his leg. Rob reached down and took her hand in his as she stood beside him.

Suddenly, silence reigned. The only sound was the moan of the turbines and the rush of water. And that steady dripping that never ceased.

Something heavy and metal moved on the other side of the door. It sounded like a lock disengaging.

Rob's heart jackhammered in his chest. He gripped Juli's hand tighter.

The door opened on dry hinges. The sound of steel scraping concrete cut through the room like a serrated knife. Rob fully expected the small space to be flooded with darklings, claws and teeth going like buzz saws, but nothing happened. The door stayed open for a few seconds then shut again. All was quiet on the other side now.

Someone or something was in the room with them. Rob could sense its presence, and if he listened closely enough, he could just hear its breathing over the turbines. He imagined the big darkling standing there, sucking in air, licking its lips, waiting until they dropped their guard to pounce.

Metal tinked across the room.

Juli whispered something Rob couldn't make out.

Then, a light snapped on. An electric lantern hovered in the air, and behind it, illuminated by a soft white glow, was the dark-eyed man. Wax Man. He lowered the light to the floor.

As Rob's eyes adjusted to the light, he saw the room they were in. It was about the size he imagined with four concrete walls, a concrete floor, and ceiling. The ceiling was more than ten feet high, and there, in the far corner, at the top of the far wall, was the grated covering to an exhaust duct.

"You were fascinating to watch," Wax Man said. He was leaning against the far wall, arms folded at his chest, legs crossed at the ankles. His pale skin seemed to glow in the light of the lantern. His eyes looked like two rifle barrels pointed at Rob. A slight grin lifted the corners of his mouth. "I especially enjoyed watching you sleep."

A cold chill ran along Rob's nerves. He wanted to throw curses at the man, call him every name he could think of, but at the moment he could think of none. His mind was locked up.

"You don't have to be afraid of me," the man said. "Now them"—he tipped his head toward the door—"be afraid of them."

There was a moment of uneasy silence in the room. Wax

Man stared at Rob with those dark eyes like he was drilling holes in his soul. Then he said, "Are you afraid of me?"

"You need to spend more time in the sun," Juli said.

"Shut up!" Wax Man hollered. He pushed away from the wall and walked to the middle of the room. There he stopped and pointed a finger at Juli. His face twisted with hatred. "This doesn't concern you. It never did. You're just an added bonus."

Almost immediately his features softened, and he looked at Rob. "Are you afraid of me?"

Rob swallowed hard. No sense in lying. He was sure fear was written across his forehead in permanent marker. "Yes."

"So was dear Kelly."

The sound of Kelly's name passing over those thin lips and the way Wax Man said it sent a wave of anger through Rob's body. Juli must have felt it because she tightened her hold on his hand.

Wax Man walked back to the wall and leaned against it, assuming his previous posture. He ran a finger over his lips. "We had some good times, Kelly and I. She was quite the woman, Robert. Quite the catch."

Rob jerked his hand away from Juli and clenched his fists.

"Careful now, Robby. Watch that temper of yours." He glanced at the door. "One word from me and that door opens. And then all hell breaks loose. Literally."

Wax Man pushed away from the wall again and began to pace across the room. "You're not so much like Kelly, are you? She was polite, courteous, respectful. Do you hate me?"

Rob said nothing. Yes, he did hate him. He wanted to charge him and tear his pale body limb from limb. But he also feared him. And it was that fear that kept him silent.

The man continued his pacing. "Of course you do. And rightfully so. I took what was most precious to you. Kelly and James."

"No!" Rob could hold it in no longer. "Jimmy's alive. I know he is."

"Oh, hush, Robert. Really. If anyone would know, it would be me. I was there."

Rob fell quiet. It was lies. It had to be. He'd seen Jimmy with his own eyes. Heard him with his own ears. And the dreams. They felt so real. They *were* real.

The man laughed. "You know, the funny thing is, I never really even wanted them. They were simply a means of getting to you. Don't get me wrong; I enjoyed every minute I spent with them. They were lovely company. But you…" He stopped and faced Rob, chin propped by a fist. "Look at you. Like a scared mouse in a corner. You have no idea how much suffering you've caused me. I find that fascinating."

The words made no sense to Rob. He looked at Juli, who had her head bowed and eyes closed. Her lips moved silently.

"I've always found fear fascinating. Do you know why? It cripples. Even the most powerful of men, if ruled by fear, are worthless."

He paced some more, then said, "Hey, what say we turn this light out and let my friends in, shall we?"

He turned and reached for the lantern.

"Wait!" Rob said. "Tell me one thing. I have to know. Look me in the eyes and tell me Jimmy is dead."

Wax Man turned back toward Rob and smiled. His black,

lifeless eyes were two holes in his head. "I killed him with my own hands. Snapped his little neck like a dead branch."

Rob ground his molars. "You're lying. I can see it on your face."

Wax Man turned his palms upward. "If you say so." He reached again for the light.

From Rob's side, Juli said, "Light has come into the world—"

"Shut up!" The man spun around and faced Juli. His eyes seemed to grow darker, if that was possible.

"—but men loved darkness instead of light."

"Shut up *now.*"

Rob looked at Juli. Her head was up, eyes firmly fixed on Wax Man. "God, who said, 'Let light shine out of darkness—'"

"I'll tear your tongue out," the man yelled. His face was contorted with revulsion.

Juli turned her face toward Rob. Her eyes met his, and he found peace in them, not fear. "'—made His light shine in our hearts.' In *your* heart, Rob."

The man across the room spun around, screaming like an Indian warrior, snatched up the lantern, and threw it against the wall. The thing exploded in a spray of glass, and the light flashed and went out. The room was engulfed in darkness once again. Juli's hand found Rob's immediately, and she said, "He's in your heart, Rob. I know He is."

She was right, he knew. When he was a boy of five, he'd given his life to Jesus. The past twenty-two years had been ruled by fear, an irrational fear with no beginning. And that fear had paralyzed him. Like it did now.

He heard the man say, "Now, welcome the darkness," and the door scraped open.

Eighteen

AWAKENED FROM SLEEP, THE OLD WOMAN SAT ON the edge of her bed and combed the sleep cobwebs from her head. She'd gone to bed early, not feeling well. The spiritual battle that raged not far from her home (and heart) had taken its toll on her physically.

But now she was awake. She rubbed her eyes and folded a loose lock of hair behind her ear. Her fingers were stiff and sore. Slowly and with much effort, she stood and took those first few steps. If the soreness in her hands was bad, it was twice as bad in her knees. They felt like two dry gears trying to turn on one another, neither gaining any ground. Eventually the movement caused some lubrication in the joint, and things started moving a little easier.

The kitchen was dark when she arrived there. The fluorescent light above the sink was out. Odd, because she left it on all the time. She thought maybe the bulb just burned out but then remembered she'd had it changed just a few months ago. And it always lasted a lot longer than a few months.

Flipping the switch on the wall for the overhead light, she found it to be out too. And there was no time on the microwave. That explained it; the power had gone out.

But it was more than just a power outage. She sensed it.

Standing in the middle of her kitchen, surrounded on three sides by countertop and on the fourth side by a refrigerator, she felt it, the presence.

Tonight was the night. The night the man would have to make a choice: face his fear and step into the light, or surrender everything and lose it all.

Despite the malevolent presence, she felt the overwhelming need to pray, to intercede, to lift up the man and the child accompanying him.

She dropped where she was and knelt on the linoleum. Almost immediately she was assaulted by wicked thoughts, hateful emotions, vile images. From somewhere inside her these revolting things surfaced, brought to the forefront of her mind by the presence.

Falling prone she spread out her arms and legs and hugged the floor. "Abba!" she cried. "Set me free from this evil vice. Let me focus on You."

A great weight pressed down on her and spread over her back, pushing her into the floor and squeezing the air from her lungs. It felt like a man was standing on her back. "Rescue me, Abba. Save me, Jesus."

The weight lightened and then disappeared, and she was left alone on the floor breathing hard. Now she had to turn her attention to the man. This was his time, his moment.

"Show him Your light, Abba. Let him see it in his own heart so he may shine Your light."

The old woman rolled over and lay on her back. Usually, her back would be screaming now, protesting the hardness of the kitchen floor, but she felt nothing. She was in a trance of sorts, fully focused on the task at hand. Everything else seemed to be inconsequential or to not exist at all.

"Let him find Your light, Abba. Let him find Your light..." Over and over she said it in a tone that resembled a chant. This was the man's moment, and so much rested on it. No matter what he decided, he would never be the same again; his life would be changed forever.

Hours passed like minutes, and still the old woman prayed until at last she stopped and whispered the final "Amen." She had done all that was possible; the rest was up to the man and the child.

She rose from the floor, got dressed, and did the only thing left to do: go to Darlington.

A cold wind blew through the room, and the sound of footsteps and grunts and hisses drowned the hum of the turbines. Rob could feel the presence of the horde, as if they'd displaced the darkness, and it was now pressing in heavier on him.

Beside him, Juli said in a calm voice, "Let your light shine, Rob."

But Rob did nothing. What could he do? This was it. They were both going to die like Asher had.

"Let your light shine."

Footsteps approached them, and Rob could hear the thing breathing heavily, wheezing.

"Light up the darkness, Rob."

"I don't have a light."

From across the room, Wax Man started laughing.

The thing was beside him, inches from his face. He could feel its body against his, its hot breath against his neck.

"His light is in your heart."

Suddenly, pain shot up the back of Rob's leg, and he fell to his knees. The darkling grabbed his hair and yanked his head back.

Wax Man's voice was closer now. "It's time you know the truth, Robby."

Juli hollered, "Let your light shine, Rob."

A voice went off in Rob's head then. Jimmy's voice, saying one of his Bible verses. *I am the light of the world.*

Something sharp traced a line on Rob's neck.

"You and I," Wax Man said, "we have something very unique in common."

I am the light of the world.

"Light up the darkness."

"Shut your trap," Wax Man yelled, and Rob heard a sharp smacking sound.

The thing holding Rob's head hissed, and one of the other darklings across the room let out a scream.

"The light is in you—" Juli's voice was cut short by another smack.

At once, Rob got it. He *got* it. Everything clicked. The decision he'd made when he was five. *I am the light of the world. His light in our hearts. Let your light shine.*

Let your light shine. Light up the darkness.

"You took something from me." It was Wax Man again, but Rob could barely hear his voice. "You took everything from me, so I took something from you. Now I'm going to take the rest."

Rob relaxed himself and let the fear melt. It held no power over him. It had no place in his heart. He would fear the darkness no more.

Jesus...

The hand relaxed its grip on his hair.

...I surrender.

In a small, distant voice, Wax Man said, "You put me—"

Then, as if someone flipped a switch, a light exploded from

within Rob, shining outward like a thousand forks of lightning. Warmth poured over him like liquid.

The darklings cowered and screamed and writhed in agony, pressing against one another and clawing at their eyes. Wax Man hit the floor cursing wildly.

"Go," Juli yelled. And they both made a dash for the door.

Still glowing like a thousand-watt lightbulb, Rob hit the concrete corridor outside the room running. It was long and straight, and there was a stairwell at the far end. The sound of his sneakers slapping the concrete sounded like thunder claps. He looked at his hands, amazed. Light radiated from his palms and fingertips like high-powered spotlights.

"All stairs lead up and out," Juli yelled from behind him.

As they neared the stairwell, Rob's light began to dim. He looked back, but neither darkling nor dark-eyed man followed.

Up one flight of stairs they climbed, then two, and three. At the top of the third flight was a steel gray door with a small square window and crash bar. Rob didn't even slow down when he hit the bar. The door flew open, and he and Juli stood on top of the spillway, sucking in the cool night air. Rob stopped, bent at the waist, and pulled air into his lungs. His legs were rubber, barely holding him up. His light was out now, and he was just Rob again.

Juli walked to the edge of the spillway and looked at the water below. She didn't even appear to be out of breath.

"Would you mind explaining what happened back there?" Rob asked.

Juli turned and faced him, her hands on the railing. "Let your light shine," she said with a smile. "You found the light inside you."

"You're bleeding," Rob said. Her upper lip was swollen on the left side, and blood smeared across her cheek.

"It was worth it." She ran a sleeve over her cheek.

Rob stood erect and put his hands on his hips. "I wasn't afraid."

"And that was some light show you put on."

"Jimmy's out there. I have to go to him. I can feel the pull." He was referring to the invisible tether he'd felt the day before in the woods. It was there again, gently tugging him, leading him back into the woods. And the darkness. But this time, he felt no fear.

"You sure you want to trust that? Last time it was a trick."

"It's different this time. I know where he is. I have to go. Will you come with me?"

"Right by your side."

Rob looked back at the open door. "Will they come again? The darklings."

Juli shrugged. "They'll always be there, in the darkness. You just choose not to fear them." She smiled again. "And let your light shine."

"And what about the creep with the eyes?"

Juli shuddered. "He's that unwanted guest that just won't leave."

"He murdered Kelly." He said the words like the bad taste they were.

"I'm sorry," she said. "I'm sorry you had to hear all that. He's murdered before too. But justice will find him."

Rob felt Jimmy's pull even stronger now. He turned and

started walking across the spillway. "I have to go to Jimmy now."

They walked, then jogged across the length of the spillway and around the powerhouse with its large glass windows and power grid above. Inside, the massive turbines churned away, rotating the generators and producing electricity from the power of water.

When they stepped off the dam and onto asphalt again, Rob stopped and faced the woods. "Somewhere in there, there's a broken-down shack, and in that shack is my son." He looked at Juli. "I'm going to get my son."

"Let's close this matter once and for all."

PART SIX

The enemy is fear. We think it is hate; but it is fear.

—Mahatma Gandhi

Nineteen

VEN WITHOUT A FLASHLIGHT THE WOODS DIDN'T seem as dark as before, nor did they seem as menacing. Juli breathed in the scent of the wild, the smell of pine and bark and leaves. It brought back memories of hiking as a kid and camping with friends. A time when the woods were void of darklings and things that screamed in the night. When there was nothing there to fear but your own imagination. A time when nightmares were just dreams, restricted to the bony confines of your skull.

Back there, in that room with *him*, she'd never felt what she had experienced. It wasn't fear—no, not quite—but more like revulsion. She could feel the evil oozing from him; he was so immersed in it. But what surprised her and bothered her more was that she felt no pity for him, no compassion at all.

Reaching to her lip, Juli touched it tenderly. It throbbed only a little now and was more numb than sore and made her think of her mother and the punishment she had endured. How many fat lips had she nursed? But back in that room it was a small price to pay for what was accomplished. She was still having a difficult time believing what she saw, but she couldn't deny that it had happened.

Rob was just feet ahead of her, methodically picking his way through the woods. His glow was gone now, not even a spark remained. If she hadn't witnessed it with her own eyes, she would say it was the stuff of urban legends or modern myths. Man glows to drive off horde of demon creatures. But why was she so surprised? She knew God was capable of providing a way of escape. After all, isn't that what she had been praying for?

Stepping over a fallen tree, doing her best to keep pace with Rob, Juli prayed a silent petition for protection. She knew what happened back there in the dam was not the end. It wasn't over. Rob may have conquered his fear and found the light within, but there was still Darlington to deal with, and that place dripped with fear and darkness.

Darlington would have to make its own stand, but right now, she had to be there for Rob when he needed her most.

It was after midnight the next time Rob looked at his watch. He no longer counted the hours until sunrise. He had only one thing on his mind: finding the shack that held his son. He allowed himself to be pulled by the unseen tether, straight through the woods. It was slow going, what with navigating fallen trees, broken limbs, stands of honeysuckle, saplings, and tangles of kudzu, but progress was being made. As they grew closer to the final destination, the pull felt stronger, as if it were no longer just a pull anymore but a push as well.

Rob had told Juli about the pull early on, and she followed silently, only adding commentary or asking a question occasionally.

At one point, after ascending a steep incline, Rob stopped to sit on a fallen tree and catch his breath. His legs were tired, and his mouth and throat felt like he'd been eating sand.

Juli stood before him. "Does that GPS of yours have a destination arrival time?"

Rob shook his head. "No." He looked around. "It could be right here; it could be clear on the other side of the state."

He bent over and rested his elbows on his knees. Juli's hand rested on his head. "We'll keep walking until we find it. You need this."

He did need it, both the walk and finding Jimmy. After all that transpired the past few days and then coming off of whatever it was that happened in that room with the light, he needed some time to clear his head. And as long as they were making progress and getting closer to Jimmy, he was OK with it. His heart constantly urged him to run, but his mind reminded him that he had no idea how far he'd be traveling, and if he ran now, he may not have the stamina to finish the journey. Better to walk it now and run when he felt he should. And he was sure that when the time came and they were within running distance, the pull would trigger it.

Rob ran his fingers through his hair and rubbed his face with both hands. "Your father, did he do time for what he did to you and your mom?"

Juli was quiet for a few seconds. "He did time but not nearly enough. It would never be enough. He's one really bad dude."

"I'm sorry you live with that. It can't be easy."

"No, it can't be."

Standing again, Rob checked the time. Three forty. He looked around, but their surroundings looked the same as they had for the past three hours. Trees, shrubs, kudzu, leaves, all dusted with moonlight and dappled with shadows. A thought entered his mind then: What if they'd been walking in circles? How would he even know? What if the pull was just a trick of his mind, like so many of the hallucinations he'd suffered? What if he was no closer to Jimmy than he was when he stepped off the dam?

No. He pushed the doubts aside. The pull was real. He could feel it now, tugging like someone had attached a rope to his sternum. The pull was strong enough that he felt like he almost had to take a step forward to maintain his balance. And the more he focused on it, the more intense it got. Finally, he had to take a clumsy step forward or he would have fallen on his face.

Juli must have noticed. "You OK there?"

"The pull, the more I think about it, the stronger it gets." He took another awkward step forward. "It's like I have to keep moving."

Rob could feel Jimmy now too. Like his son was inside him and they were one. He knew his fear, his loneliness, his tears as if they were his own.

Clearing his throat and wiping at his eyes, Rob said, "Let's keep moving. I think we're close."

Huddled in the corner of the cabin, knees pulled up to his chin, the boy buries his face in his hands and cries, but he has no more tears. His eyes are dry. Dirt is dried on his palms and caked under his fingernails. Mommy would have a royal fit if she saw his hands this way. His shirt is ripped too. That upsets him more than his dirty hands. He lifts his head and looks around again. Not that he hasn't before, because he has. His eyes have adjusted to the darkness, and the little bit of moonlight that peeks in through the cracks in the roof is enough to lighten the place just enough. Like the nightlight in his bedroom at home.

He'd be lying like a dog if he said he wasn't scared, but that isn't why he's crying, or at least trying to cry. No, he's crying because he knows he'll never see his mommy and daddy again. There's no way anyone will ever find him out here in the woods, and the man will come back in the morning and take him even farther away. Then he'll be lost forever... or worse.

The inside of the cabin isn't much to look at. There's no furniture, no kitchen area, and no stove. Just four walls and a floor. A dirty, wavy floor that kind of sags when you walk on it. He's already tried the door a hundred times, but it won't open; it just jiggles like the change in Daddy's pocket. It must be locked from the outside.

He thinks of Mommy and the way she smiles at him in the morning and the times he's helped her make cookies for Daddy and her kisses at nighttime. He pictures her eyes and how they crinkle up when she laughs. Then he thinks of playing soccer in the backyard with Daddy and trying to get around his big legs and quick feet. He loves it when Daddy picks him up and takes him "high in the air" over his shoulder, turning him almost upside down. He laughs so hard his belly hurts. And then Daddy laughs so hard his face turns all red and his ears wiggle.

Thinking about them makes him cry again, but still, no tears come.

He stands and walks over to the door. Pushes on it. Bangs on it with his fist. Kicks at it. But it is still locked. He leans up against it and tries to pray, but the words just won't come. He doesn't understand this. It's as if someone's holding his tongue and not letting it say words. And every time he tries to pray he gets even more scared. He could swear someone is in the room with him, watching him. But, of course, he looks around and no one is there.

Going back to the corner he sits with knees pulled up again and wraps his arms around his legs. He wonders what his parents are doing right now. Are they looking for him? Are they scared too? Are they even OK? He closes his eyes and pictures their faces, smiling and happy, saying his name. Mommy is looking at him like she does when they snuggle together. Daddy is smiling like he does when he listens to the boy tell a funny story.

Thinking about Daddy now, he can almost feel him. Almost hear his voice.

Rob stopped in a small clearing and caught his breath. A half hour ago he felt the pull so strongly he had to start running to keep up with it. Now, he needed a rest. He was in fair shape but certainly no accomplished long-distance runner. His pulse tapped in his ears. He put his hands on his hips and looked around. "We're close."

Again, Juli's breathing seemed barely stressed by the running. And she hadn't even broken a sweat. "The pull is stronger?"

Rob nodded and ran his sleeve over his forehead. "I'm fighting hard to stand still here, but I need a breather for a second. Man, I could really use some water too."

"We could find a spring."

He looked at his watch. It would be sunrise in a little over an hour. "No. We have to keep moving. It can wait." Taking a deep breath, Rob listened to the woods. He kept expecting to hear a distant scream or the bark of a dog, but the forest remained noiseless and still. As always.

Breathing in deep and even, he shut his eyes and pictured Jimmy playing in the backyard. The boy loved soccer. Every chance he'd get he was dragging Rob out there to kick the ball around. But Rob didn't mind one bit. He was a soccer fanatic himself and got Jimmy interested in it as soon as he was old enough to walk and kick.

"You're thinking about him," Juli said.

"It makes the pull stronger."

"What's he doing?"

"We're playing soccer, kicking the ball around."

"Like Ronaldo?"

Rob shook his head. "No. Pelé. The greatest."

"Ah, old school."

"Definitely."

Rob opened his eyes and looked at Juli. "I hear him."

If the boy is very quiet and holds his breath so he doesn't even hear the sound of his lungs, he can hear his daddy calling his name.

He jumps up and runs for the door. "Daddy! Daddy!"

He pounds his fists on the door and kicks at it. He has to get Daddy's attention. If he passes the area without seeing the cabin or hearing the boy's voice, he may never come back again. The boy feels like a man stranded on a desert island seeing a ship pass by in the distance. He has to be heard.

He hollers louder. "Daddy!" So loud his throat hurts and he goes into a coughing fit.

Then he holds his breath and listens again.

Running full speed now, hurdling trees and ducking limbs, weaving around saplings and shrubs, Rob was in total surrender to the pull. It was in control now, not him. He was just moving his legs fast enough to keep up. He no longer knew or cared if Juli was behind him. He had to keep running.

"Jimmy!" He didn't stop to listen for a reply. He didn't have to. The shack was before him, close, just out of sight.

The boy hears Daddy's voice closer now. He's coming this way. He has to be close enough to see the cabin. He hollers again, "Daddy! Here, I'm here!"

Real tears come now. He's crying real tears again, but not because he's sad or scared. Because he's so happy.

Daddy is on his way.

Rob stopped so abruptly he almost toppled forward. The pull was gone, and his body suddenly felt fifty pounds heavier. There, up ahead, was the shack. The same one he saw in his dream. His heart stuttered in his chest.

Jimmy. He was so close. He could feel his son in his arms again.

He took off, tripped on a branch, got up, and dashed madly for the shack. Nothing mattered now but reaching his son. The woods around him vanished; the sound of his steps in the leaves fell silent. Even the steady thumping of his pulse in his ears was no more.

"Jimmy, I'm here, buddy. Daddy's here." Tears choked his words and tumbled down his cheeks.

The boy can now hear the sound of Daddy running in the leaves. He can hear Daddy saying his name, over and over again. It sounds like he's crying.

"Daddy, I'm here. I'm here!"

Twenty

ROB REACHED THE SHACK AND GRABBED THE DOOR handle. The metal was cold in his hand.

"Jimmy." His son's name spilled out of his mouth as he yanked open the door. It swung wide and Rob rushed in. "Jimmy."

His son was standing before him. Jimmy. His little buddy. Just as he imagined him—G.I. Joe shirt and camo shorts. "Jimmy." Rob choked out the name. His throat was in a vice. Finally, he was here. He took one large step toward Jimmy and took his son's tiny body in his arms. Sobs wracked Rob's chest and exploded from his throat.

He turned around, squeezing Jimmy tighter, not wanting to let go, but having a difficult time feeling his boy in his arms. It was as if…

…he wasn't there.

Rob's arms were empty.

Spinning around saying his son's name over and over, tears streaming from his eyes, blurring everything in the shack, the reality of the moment hit Rob like a shotgun blast to the chest.

The shack was empty. Jimmy wasn't there.

Suddenly, like a rush of raging water, the truth engulfed him.

He remembered.

This place. He knows it.

It was him.

He was the boy…

He was the boy in his dreams. Not Jimmy.

He was the boy in the cabin. The shack.

Rob collapsed to the floor and let the sobs come. He didn't know how long he lay there crying, but when he sat up again, morning had dawned and the woods were dusted with a soft light.

Juli stood in the doorway of the shack, leaning against the jamb, hands clasped behind her back.

"How long have you been standing there?" Rob asked.

Juli shrugged. "Long enough to watch you accept the truth."

"You knew all along."

"Would you have believed me?"

"No way." He climbed to his feet and ran his sleeve over his eyes. "Jimmy's dead." He knew he wasn't telling her anything new, for that was what she'd known all along, but he needed to hear himself say it. The sound of the words was like a judge's gavel. So final. So irrevocable. Jimmy was dead, and there wasn't a thing to be done about it. He was gone. The thought put a knot in Rob's throat, but he had no more tears to cry. "Jimmy's dead." He said it again for no good reason.

"In one way," Juli said. A slight smile tugged at her lips. "In every other way he's more alive than you could ever imagine. Kelly too."

Rob took one last look at the inside of the shack and turned away. Memories were flooding his mind now. It would take some time—lots of time—to sort through it all. He took Juli's hand in his and walked away from the shack and his hopes.

After a while, Rob said, "Didn't it bother you to keep it from me?"

"You have no idea, but you had a road to travel," Juli said. "I wasn't going to stand in your way."

"I'm glad it's over."

Juli paused and gave his hand a little squeeze. "Oh, it's far from over."

After walking a few minutes in silence, alone with his thoughts and memories, eyes still burning from all the crying, Rob said. "So how do we get out of here? You said there was only one way out."

Juli looked at him with those emerald eyes and smiled. "You already found it."

"The dam?"

"Not unless you want to go for a swim."

"Then what?"

Juli stopped walking and pointed at Rob's chest. "It's there. It's been there all along."

"My heart. The fear was keeping us here, not letting us out."

She started walking again. "You're pretty sharp."

"I don't understand." And he didn't. Not any of this. And he suspected he wouldn't for a long time.

"You don't have to. Just accept it. It's called faith."

"I think I need some more of that."

"Oh, don't say that."

Ahead, through the trees and underbrush and kudzu, sunlight hit the ground unhindered. The edge of the forest. Juli smiled at Rob and started running, hopping fallen branches and leaping small saplings. Rob took off after her.

Juli reached the edge first and stuck her hand into the sunlight. She laughed. "Boy, if you could bottle this stuff and sell it."

Rob arrived and did the same. "It'd be priceless. That's why it's free."

Stretching from the tree line out was an expanse of grass so green Rob thought it looked like something out of a story-book. And on the other side of the meadow sat the town of Darlington with its dilapidated homes and decaying church. But today, at this moment, bathed in brilliant morning sunlight, Darlington looked like a city of gold.

"C'mon," Juli said, taking Rob's hand.

Together they stepped from dead brown leaves to lush green grass, leaving the darkness of the woods behind. Never did being in the light feel so right.

Rob noticed his car was still parked in the church lot, but there was another car, an old Buick, parked alongside it.

"Someone's here," Rob said.

"A friend," Juli said, keeping her eyes on the car. "And so much more."

Stride for stride they walked until they'd crossed the field and stood on the gravel lot. Radiating off the white stones, the sunlight felt even warmer. Across the street, the door to a house opened, and an old woman stepped out. Rob shielded his eyes with one hand.

Juli said, "She came."

Standing there on the stoop, hands behind her back,

shoulders squared, wearing a shin-length plain brown dress was the last person Rob expected to see. Mary Jane.

When Mary Jane saw Robert and Julianne emerge from the woods and cross that field as if they were walking on a cushion of air, she felt like she was twenty again. Nothing about her felt like an old woman. Even her knees didn't hurt.

"Thank You, Abba," she said aloud, pulling away from the bay window and opening the door.

And when she stepped out into the morning light and felt the warmth of the sun against her skin, she may have even passed for a teenager. "Thank You, Abba," she said again.

Descending the steps one at a time (she may have felt years younger, but she still knew her limitations), she hurried across the front lawn and stopped on the sidewalk, hands to her mouth. Tears pooled in her eyes, and her nose started to run. Nothing a hanky couldn't take care of.

But her happiness was tempered with the reality that faced her. One, Robert would have questions—many of them. And she would do her best to answer them no matter how painful the truth was.

Two, Robert would still need much prayer. He may have beat back the fear that ruled his heart for so long, but in doing so he lost the hope that had sustained him these past three months. He would need time to grieve his son as he did his wife.

And finally, this was not the end for Robert. He'd surely face many more challenges in the days and months to come before confronting his greatest challenge of all, the reason he was given the gift.

"Wisdom, Abba. Give me Your wisdom."

Crossing the deserted asphalt that was once Darlington's Main Street, feeling a little less giddy but nonetheless confident, Mary Jane met Robert and Julianne in the tall grass and took them into her arms.

Sometimes a hug is just a hug, and sometimes a hug is much more than that. For Rob, standing in the middle of that field, grass tickling his legs, Mary Jane's was more than just a hug. She was one who had answers. And he had plenty of questions.

After a while, Mary Jane patted Rob on the back and pulled away, leaving her hand on his shoulder. "Come" —she nodded toward the church—"come sit and we'll talk."

Rob followed her to the front of the church and sat on the wooden steps. Juli sat beside him. Mary Jane stood at the foot of the stairs, back straight as usual, hands clasped in front.

Propping his elbows on his knees and holding his head in his hands, Rob said, "Jimmy's gone."

"You know that now," Mary Jane said.

Juli's hand found Rob's arm, and she squeezed.

"I know it, but I can't accept it yet."

"No one says you have to accept it right away. Give yourself time to grieve."

Rob was watching a large black ant on the ground, but

now he pulled his eyes away from the ant and looked directly into Mary Jane's eyes. "I was the boy in the shack."

She looked at him, her face a question mark.

"I've been having dreams about a boy being kidnapped and taken to a shack. Every night now for the past few nights. I thought for sure it was Jimmy, that God was telling me he was still alive."

"But it was you." She said it, not like a question, but like something she'd known all along and was only now confirming.

"You know about it."

Mary Jane's mouth drooped at the corners and sadness darkened her eyes. She dipped her head a little and nodded. "Yes. I've known. And I've known sooner or later you'd be drawn back to this place."

"Drawn back? What—?"

"In 1987. You were five?"

Rob nodded. His mouth was going dry, and his palms were getting sweaty.

"The apple harvest festival in Mayfield. You came with your mother and father and visited your great-aunt Wilda."

The memories were flooding back now. He helped rake leaves that morning. He hated it, but his dad made him help. Wilda was alone and shouldn't have to do it, his dad had said.

Mary Jane turned her head and looked back at the main street running through Darlington. "The crowds were always so big, so many people. Just before noon you and your mother went missing. About an hour later she showed up, beaten badly and in hysterics. Said you were taken. The festival ended early, and a search party was assembled to look for you. No one thought to look here in Darlington."

Rob didn't say anything; he was remembering it all just

as Mary Jane said it. They parked in the field alongside the church. He remembered going back to the car with his mom and a man coming to tell her something was wrong with his dad. The memories were fuzzy, like an old 8mm home movie without sound, but they were there, and they were coming back in a steady stream.

"Evening came, then darkness, and we still didn't find you."

"I was blindfolded and taken to a woman's house."

He remembered the attic, the box, the car ride, being in Darlington, and hearing the dogs attack Asher. He remembered it all now, right down to the texture of the vinyl seats in the car. He also remembered the shack and his dad coming to rescue him.

Mary Jane nodded. Rob saw her Adam's apple rise and fall. "The woman was Wilda."

"She was in on it?"

Again, a nod.

"Why?"

"She was forced into it. He—your abductor—threatened to kill her, you, and your parents if she didn't go along with it and help him. He told her you wouldn't be hurt, but it was lies. His intentions were vile and wicked, the stuff of someone so depraved"—she put a fist to her mouth and swallowed hard—"so depraved."

"And no one pressed charges against her? My parents? The feds?"

Mary Jane shook her head. "There were no charges to press. She was as much a victim as you were. She was operating out of fear."

"And Darlington was kept quiet with fear," Rob said.

Mary Jane looked at him, again a question on her face.

"In the woods"—he nodded his head toward the forest—"we met Asher Wiggins, and he told us all about the dark-eyed man and fear and how Darlington wound up like this."

Mary Jane's mouth curved into a slight smile. "How is Asher?"

"He's dead now," Rob said. The words tasted bitter coming out. "The...darklings got to him. But his death wasn't in vain. Not by any stretch."

"Oh, dear." Tears formed in Mary Jane's eyes. "I always liked Asher. He was a good man."

"So did Wilda ever talk about what happened?"

"Once. She testified against your abductor at his trial. Told everything. She was the one who helped your dad find you that day in the woods. She knew you were being taken to Darlington and...if it wasn't for her, I don't know if your dad would have found that cabin. For her, though, it wasn't enough. She lived the rest of her life drowning in guilt and shame. Upon her death she did the only thing she could to try to make amends, and that was leaving you everything she had. It's not much, I know, but it was everything to her." Mary Jane met his eyes with hers. There was kindness there and wisdom. "Wilda was a good person. Always found the best in everyone. She died a tormented woman."

A chill raced along Rob's spine. "Why me? Why was the dark-eyed man after me?"

Rob caught the glance between Mary Jane and Juli. "So you don't remember?"

"Remember what? Things are coming back, but they're still spotty."

"You and Wilda were the key witnesses. A month after you were found, the police picked your abductor up and charged him with all kinds of things. It was your and Wilda's testimonies that sealed his fate. He was sentenced to twenty-two years in prison with no chance of parole. His cohorts were never caught, though. And they've never returned to Darlington."

"And what about the townspeople. They didn't testify?"

Mary Jane shook her head. "They were too afraid. Not a one of them came forward."

"What about my parents?"

"That's something you'll have to take up with them. It was all the lawyers could do to get them to allow you to testify."

Rob buried his head in his hands. "How could I forget all that? The kidnapping, the trial?"

Mary Jane's eyes darkened. "Your parents must have decided not to talk about it, to act as if it never happened. They moved further north and started over. But running from evil, burying it, never works. Only facing up to it, shining a light on it, changes things. Otherwise the evil grows and festers and putrefies in the darkness."

Rob grimaced. "I can't believe they let him out of jail."

She paused and kept her eyes on Rob. "They had no more reason to keep him. He'd served his time. It was a hard twenty-two years for him, but not nearly hard enough, not long enough."

"So this was some kind of revenge thing?"

"Revenge is putting it nicely," Juli said.

Rob suddenly felt sick in his gut. "Kelly and Jimmy. He killed them to pay me back for his time in jail." He looked at Mary Jane, who had tears in her eyes, then at Juli, who was already crying. "Who is he?"

"He's one bad dude," Juli said.

"That doesn't help."

Another look passed between the two women, then Mary Jane said, "He's my son."

And Juli said, "And my father."

Rob's heart suddenly felt like a lead cannon ball in his chest. "One bad dude."

Juli nodded.

"But why me? I was only five."

Mary Jane crossed her arms. "You were random. Just some boy. An easy target. In his teen years, Mitchell—that's his name—got involved in toying around with the occult. His father and I knew nothing about it at the time. At twenty-one he married Nicole, a sweet gal with a tender heart. Apparently, she knew nothing of his dark side either. Until he started sacrificing small animals in their basement. She came to us and told us about it. She was so scared. We confronted Mitchell and got nowhere. His demeanor had changed dramatically, and he harbored such hatred.

"A month later Nicole was pregnant with Julianne. When Julianne was born, Nicole thought about running. We told her we would help, but she was too afraid. She kept saying he would find her and kill her. We called the police, but there was nothing they could do. There was never any evidence of any wrongdoing." She reached out her hand and took Juli's in hers. "Then the abuse started. Julianne was a little over one. Mitchell would beat Nicole and Julianne. But the physical cruelty was only part of it. The psychological and emotional abuse were so much worse. He drove Nicole mad, and she eventually took her life."

Juli smiled through her tears at Mary Jane. "If it wasn't for my grandmother, I would have been next."

"If it wasn't for your grandfather and me. We took Julianne from Mitchell and hid her," Mary Jane said. "He was so angry. He cursed his father and me, swore to kill us both, and left Mayfield. We didn't see him again until the trial."

"So he took me instead."

Mary Jane closed her eyes and nodded. "At the trial he was very arrogant about what his intentions were. He was going to sacrifice you. You were in that cabin alone because he was off gathering his coven. Before they took him out of the courtroom, Mitchell promised to finish what he'd started. That's why your parents moved you north."

Rob looked at Juli. "He's still out there."

"But we're no longer afraid of him."

"Will he come? Here?"

Juli said, "He won't stop coming."

PART SEVEN

To a child, darkness brings fear, but light drives back the darkness and, with it, the fear.
—THE BOOK OF LIGHT AND DARKNESS

Twenty-one

ANGER GNAWED AT HIM LIKE AN INFLAMED ULCER. Hatred festered like an open wound. His insides itched and burned until he wanted to just peel back his skin and relieve the rage. He picked up a broken piece of lumber and hit it against the wall, over and over, imagining he was pummeling Shields's head, until the board splintered and broke. Throwing the fractured wood aside, he threw back his head and let out a deep-throated scream.

The underlings hissed and snapped their jaws.

"Cowards!" he yelled, saliva spraying from his mouth. His breathing was labored, and sweat had broken out on his brow and chin. "You let them go."

Again, the horde responded with a chorus of hisses and an occasional scream.

That was good. He wanted them riled. The more incensed they got, the more vicious they would be. And vicious was good. Vicious was exactly what he wanted. The time for games was over. Shields had to die. It would be quick and strong and very painful. He would make him suffer like he'd never suffered before and then snuff out his useless life and toss him to the underlings and let them finish off his carcass. It wouldn't be as satisfying, but his thirst for vengeance would still be satisfied. Like the difference between tepid water and an ice-cold beer.

He turned to the throbbing horde of underlings. "First

dark we go to Darlington. Take the town. Take them all. Have your fill. We have no need for them anymore."

One by one, like zoo-kept animals emerging from their cages to bask in the morning sun and curiously inspect their habitat, the citizens of Darlington exited their homes and approached the church parking lot.

Some of the faces were immediately familiar to Rob. Nana was there, looking like a crane with her long, bony legs and baggy dress. The foursome whom they met before was there: rifle man (minus his rifle this time), the tall guy with the Adam's apple and hook nose, hatchet man, and the short, balding guy. Others streamed from their homes now and made their way down the street. There must have been forty or so, all appearing to be over the age of fifty.

Like geese to water, they were drawn to the gravel parking lot, not a word spoken between them. Every eye was fixed on Rob, Juli, and Mary Jane. When the crowd had gathered and formed a half circle around them, Rob noticed three more familiar faces in the back of the pack. There was Norm Tuckey and Rose and Carl. Rob's eyes met Norm's, and they exchanged a slight nod.

Rob glanced at his watch. It was a little after ten.

The gathered Darlingtonians watched with an eerie expectancy in their eyes.

From the back, Norm spoke up. "We told ya not to come back here." He looked at Mary Jane, then back at Rob.

Rob felt Juli's hand slip into his. Her eyes were wide and concerned. "Tell them," she said.

Swallowing hard, Rob scanned the crowd. A swarm of butterflies took flight in his stomach. Nana was teetering back and forth again, her hands covering the lower half of her mouth. Carl was swaying too, one large hand on Norm's shoulder. "They're coming," Rob said. "Tonight. When darkness falls."

"It's your fault," Norm hollered. Heads turned to look at him. Rose tugged on Norm's arm and said something that Rob couldn't hear.

Juli squeezed Rob's hand.

"You brought this on us. We were makin' it."

"You be quiet, Norm Tuckey." It was Nana, hands clasped at her chin, face twisted in a weird blend of sadness and anger. "We weren't makin' it. We were livin' in fear of the devil, of that vile trinity."

Now it was rifle man's turn. "Oh, shush, Nana. All your talk about the devil and that trinity of yours. I'm—"

"My talk? What have you ever done, Will? How many have we lost? How much blood is on our hands? Do you even know?" She looked around the crowd. Her hands fell to her side. "I say we put an end to it and fight back."

"With what?" a thin, older man with a wild bushy beard said. "We ain't got no weapons save a few rifles and some knives and such. That ain't gonna put up much of a fight."

"Weapons will do no good against this enemy," Mary Jane said. The crowd hushed, and all faces turned to look at her. She paused and blinked slowly. "For twenty-two years I've been your umbilical cord to the outside world. Today it stops. Today you must learn to stand on your own faith and use your light to push back the darkness."

"They'll destroy us," someone yelled out.

Then another, "I ain't ready to die."

"Not like that."

"We need more guns."

"I got a deer rifle," Will said.

"You ain't fired that thing in over twenty years."

"We should lock ourselves in our homes."

The assembly erupted into a cacophony of chatter that sounded like the disjointed muttering one hears when the radio tuner is spun.

Rob said to Juli, "They don't get it."

"Nope. And I thought you had a thick skull."

"They will," Mary Jane said. "But it'll be the hard way."

Juli frowned. "Hard for who?"

Mary Jane didn't say anything.

Mary Jane knelt near the front of the small sanctuary. The place hadn't heard a human heartbeat for over two decades, and a thick coating of undisturbed dust covered everything like the gray skin of a corpse.

Her lips moved silently as she engaged in conversation with her Father, taking to Him the imminent fate of so many.

Since their brief meeting this morning, the townsfolk had spent much of the day bickering, worrying, and scurrying about like mice in a maze. Their faith was as dead and lifeless as this old building. A few of the men had vowed to fight the darklings and walked up and down Main Street toting their weapons. Two, Norm and Will, had rifles; the rest had knives or hatchets, and big Perry Oliver ambled around with a sledgehammer slung over his shoulder. No matter how many times Mary Jane told them weapons of this world were useless against the darklings, they were as deaf as wood to her warnings. Finally, she had given up and retreated here to intercede on their behalf.

It was evening now, and nightfall would be here within the hour. A thin film of perspiration covered Mary Jane's face, and her hands trembled almost imperceptibly. She knew this would be a battle like no other. She also knew victory would be theirs…but it would come at a price.

She prayed for the folks of Darlington. They were good people, really. All of them. They were just so enslaved by fear that they knew nothing else. Faith was as foreign to them as escargot or tiramisu.

She prayed for Julianne, that she would have the courage to overcome her own demons, the ones she'd wrestled most of her life. The ones constantly sitting in the back of her mind, reminding her of the nightmare she'd barely escaped but never fully banished. And that she would complete her calling, no matter how difficult it was.

She prayed for Robert, that he would use the gift he'd been given and when the time came that he would do the only right thing, the thing that had to be done, regardless of the outcome. That he would give himself totally to the light, holding nothing back, and do that which *he* was called to do.

The front double doors creaked opened, and the small sanctuary filled with muted sunlight. Footsteps, light and even, paced down the aisle behind Mary Jane. She knew the rhythm of those steps, the sound of the cadence.

The footsteps stopped behind her. "Come," she said. "Kneel beside me, Julianne."

Julianne obeyed. She'd been a good granddaughter, and

Mary Jane prayed she'd been the grandmother the girl had needed and deserved.

"They're not ready," Julianne said. Her voice was flat and sad.

"They don't need to be. This isn't about them." Mary Jane paused and massaged her aching hands. "They'll learn a valuable lesson at a great price, but it isn't about them, not really."

"It's about Rob, our ace in the hole."

"And you." She could feel Julianne's eyes on her.

"Me?"

"There's one more thing you have to do. Your calling."

"The calling thing again."

Mary Jane looked at Julianne and placed a hand on her arm. "You know what it is."

Julianne turned her head away, and Mary Jane felt the girl's arm stiffen. "I can't. He doesn't deserve it."

"Neither did you."

Julianne was silent for a long time. Finally she said, "You're right, of course. Will I be free of this calling thing then? Or at least be able to trade it in for something like kitten rescuing?"

Mary Jane chuckled. "No way. Your calling is yours and yours alone. It's part of who you are."

Julianne put her hand over Mary Jane's and smiled. There were tears in her eyes. "I can do it." Then she stood and retreated up the aisle.

Mary Jane called after her, "Julianne."

Julianne stopped and turned her head. Her slender figure was silhouetted by the light seeping in from the open doors.

"Make sure you mean it."

"The sun's almost gone," Rob said. He was standing in the church lot with Juli, facing the setting sun in the west. It had just dipped below the tops of the trees and was leaving behind streaks of orange and pink. "It's amazing that something so beautiful can be so ominous."

"Like the calm before the big storm," she said.

"The eye of the storm. We've already been through part of it."

"And lived to talk about it."

Rob thought about their earlier encounter with the darklings. If the demon things were still on the hunt after all that, he wondered what good his "gift" would do them this time. Would it only delay the inevitable a little longer? Was the fate of Darlington sealed?

He thought of Jimmy and the hallucination back at the shack. It was so much more vivid than all the others. He had actually held his boy, felt his little shaking body in his arms. Smelled his sweat and tears. Jimmy was there, he swore it, if only for a brief moment. A gaping hole had been left in Rob, an emptiness that would not soon be filled. If ever. He'd lost his reasons for living in Kelly and Jimmy. They were gone, and he was left. Here. Alone.

He looked over at Juli. She'd been a good friend through this nightmare, better than a good friend. Without her he would have lost his sanity for sure. Through the brokenness of his heart, he smiled at her.

"What?"

"Thank you," he said.

"For what?"

"For forcing me to let you come. You did a lot more than tag along."

She faced the woods again. "It's not over yet. But when it is, you have a relationship to mend."

Rob knew she was talking about his relationship with God, the Father he'd ignored for the better part of his life. "I know. I'm ready to do it too."

Silence fell between them, and after a few moments Juli's hand found Rob's. There was nothing improper about her gesture, and Rob knew that. In fact, he found more than a little comfort in it.

"You ready?" she said.

"Do I have a choice?"

"You always have a choice."

"Then, yes, I think I am."

"You think?"

"I won't know for sure until the moment's here."

After a long pause, Rob added, "The people, they're not ready."

"No," Juli said, "they're not. Fear still rules in their heart. But this battle isn't theirs. Thankfully."

A gentle breeze moved across the town of Darlington, as if the forest was sighing, bringing with it the scent of night. Rob turned his face to the air and let the wind comb through his hair. "How will it all end?"

But before Juli could answer, from somewhere deep in the woods, a scream ripped the silence.

Twenty-two

I T'S TIME," ROB SAID. HE TURNED TO ROUSE THE PEOPLE of Darlington, but they were already making their way to the church lot. Half of the townsfolk assembled, mostly men except for Rose Tuckey toting a polished butcher knife. Only two had firearms, Norm with his vintage shotgun and Will with his deer rifle; the rest brought shovels, hatchets, knives, pitchforks, and other assorted tools for the home and garden.

Everyone carried an oil lamp or candlestick.

Mary Jane appeared on the front landing of the church. She scanned the crowd of about twenty, a look of sadness clouding her face. Meeting Rob's eyes, she said something through her look, as if she knew something he didn't and was trying to warn him, but he couldn't tell what it was. Then she slowly descended the stairs and stood next to Rose in the rear of the group.

All eyes turned to Rob and Juli. Fear was evident on every face.

Another scream sounded in the distance, then another. The bark of the dogs could be heard too.

The sun was almost gone by now, and the glow of the flames cast a weird orangey light across the gang of untested soldiers. The swollen mango moon was low in the sky, hovering just above the treetops.

"Now I know how George Washington felt," Rob said.

Juli nodded. "An army of farmers and carpenters and cobblers."

A series of screams erupted from the woods, closer than ever. The barking continued almost nonstop. They were near, almost to the tree line.

"Well, ain't ya gonna say anything?" a short, round man, whom Rob had learned earlier was Phil Holiday, said.

Rob looked over the group. Only Carl was younger than fifty. "Nothing to say that hasn't already been said. Your weapons won't do any good against the darklings."

"I'll be the judge of that," Norm said. He held up his shotgun. "I killed more Viet Cong in 'Nam than any man in my unit."

Rob started to protest when someone yelled, "There they are."

All heads turned toward the tree line on the other side of the meadow. Darkness obscured any clear view, but by the light of the moon a line of darklings stretching at least fifty yards wide stood just inside the woods. The dogs were there too, tugging on the ropes that held them and barking like demons.

Suddenly, a grizzled man in worn coveralls broke from the crowd and rushed Norm. His eyes were wide and wild, the look of a man insane. He lunged for the shotgun and grabbed it with both hands. Norm twisted and cursed and jammed an elbow at the man. "Back off! Let go."

But the man held on. "I ain't gonna die by those things."

The other townspeople watched in silent horror as the tug-of-war continued.

Norm kicked at the man. "Let go, Noel. You're crazy."

Noel finally lost his grip, fell back, and landed on his

backside. He was breathing heavily and wheezing with each breath.

Norm stood over him like a conquering gladiator, holding his shotgun with both hands. "What's wrong with you?" he shouted. "You nuts?"

Noel spit to the side. "I'd rather blow my own brains out than let those devils have at it."

Across the meadow the throng of darklings throbbed restlessly, hissing and screaming.

"Back off, you hear?" Norm said to Noel. "Ain't no brains gettin' blowed out tonight." Turning away from Noel, Norm hollered, "Now get ready," then moved to the front of the group, shotgun held shoulder high. Will stepped into place next to him.

Juli's hand found Rob's arm and tightened around it. "God be with us," she said.

Then just like that it began. The dogs broke loose from the darklings that held them and tore across the meadow, ears back, tails low, ropes lashing behind them like whips.

"I got 'em," Norm said. He leveled his gun on one of the dogs and squeezed off a shot. The gun bucked, and Norm brought both hands to his face and cursed wildly.

All four dogs were still streaking across the open ground.

A shot rang out, a sharp crack, the sound of a deer rifle, and one of the dogs lifted into the air with a yelp, twisted once, then landed in a heap. Rob looked over at Will and watched him do the bolt action, aim, and pull the trigger. Another shot, and another dog went down. Quickly, now, like he'd done it in his sleep a million times, Will chambered another round and took down dog number three, the thing writhing and squealing from a shot in the rear flank.

The final dog was almost there and closing in fast. Will

did his thing, steadied his hand, and aimed. He squeezed the trigger but nothing happened. Cursing, he threw the bolt back and forward again. Pulled the trigger. Still nothing. "It's jammed," he said.

And just as the words passed over his lips, the dog hit Larry Fuhrman square in the chest, knocking him back ten feet.

What unfolded next happened so fast it was almost as if it had been choreographed. The group gasped and took a collective reflexive step backward. The dog dug into Larry, snarling and tearing with its teeth and claws. Larry tried to fight back, flailing arms and legs and screaming like a banshee. From the crowd stepped Phil Holiday, hatchet raised high, eyes wild with fear and anger, face twisted into an awful grimace. He rushed the dog, lifted the hatchet higher, and then brought it down hard on the dog's head with a sickening thud. The dog made no sound at all but went limp and rolled to one side, the hatchet still stuck in its head.

Larry, bloodied and mangled, curled into a fetal position and moaned. Phil stood over him, arms hanging limp, breathing heavily.

An eerie silence settled over the town of Darlington. Across the meadow, not a darkling screamed or hissed.

The silence persisted for a minute or so until someone behind Rob said, "What are they waiting for? What's happening?"

Suddenly, a steady breeze moved across the meadow from the direction of the woods, bending the grass in a wavelike motion. As it neared, it picked up strength, and Rob could feel the group of Darlingtonians collectively brace themselves. Juli tightened her grip on his arm.

Just before reaching the assembly, the breeze became a

gust of wind and, with a whoosh and a moan, hit the group with enough force to rock Rob back on his heels. At once, every oil lamp globe shattered and every flame was extinguished. Darkness moved in, and the only light now was the reflected glow of the moon.

A chill spread over Rob's skin. Beside him, he felt Juli shiver.

Rob looked at the night sky. Dark clouds were moving in and silently sailing across the black sea like pirate ships in the night. One passed over the moon, partially obscuring its light.

Now the darklings started screaming again. A chorus of howls and yelps and hisses erupted from the woods.

"What's happening?" a man said.

"I think they're gonna charge," said another.

The meadow was washed in a strange bluish light, and it was nearly impossible to see beyond the line of trees.

"Maybe we should all go back in our homes," Rose Tuckey said.

But before anyone could answer or take her up on her suggestion, a dark mob stepped from the woods and into the meadow. The darklings. Someone behind Rob cursed, and he heard retreating footsteps. Gravel crunched as the folks of Darlington shifted nervously.

For a moment, the darklings fell silent; then, as if the order had been given, they screamed in unison and broke into a run.

Rob turned and looked at the group behind him. They

weren't warriors, neither physically nor spiritually. The fear on their faces was evident, even in the muted light. They would be slaughtered. He knew what he had to do. It was the only way. And just the thought of it brought a cold sweat to his forehead.

He thought of Jimmy then, and Kelly too. He saw their faces smiling at him. Jimmy broke into a happy laugh. They would be proud of him; he knew they would. He'd learned a priceless lesson: that living fearlessly was less about not having fear and more about overcoming the fear you did have. Overcoming it and doing the right thing. And what he was about to do was the right thing. It was the only thing.

Turning back around, he said a silent prayer and stepped away from Juli.

She gripped his arm with both hands. "Rob, no."

Rob stopped and looked back at Juli. The look on his face said it all. She knew what he was doing. She hated it, but she knew it.

"I have to," he said. "It's the only way."

He was right. It was the only way. She released her hold on him as tears pooled in her eyes and a knot settled in her throat.

Rob walked steadily toward the meadow and the charging horde of darklings. Upon seeing his advance they picked up speed, and their screams became more frenzied.

A murmur spread across the group of townsfolk.

Juli whipped her head around and found Mary Jane in the

back of the crowd. Their eyes locked, and Juli didn't miss the tears on her grandmother's cheeks.

"Look!" someone yelled.

Juli turned back to the meadow and saw Rob in a full run, head ducked, heading right for the advancing wall of darklings. Her heart jumped into her throat, and her palms immediately took to sweating. "God, please be with him."

Rob and the darklings were only yards away now. The group assembled behind Juli gasped as one. In the final yards, the darklings converged into a smaller, tighter group and hit Rob like a truck. His feet lifted off the ground, and he landed hard on his back. Juli heard the air escape his lungs. In an instant, he was covered with darklings, biting and clawing at him.

A man behind Juli began to cry. Another whimpered.

Then, as if the sun itself fell to the earth, blinding light exploded from beneath the horde of darklings. Juli turned her head and covered her eyes with her arm. The world around her was silent and bright, brighter than a cloudless day at high noon. No screams were heard, no crying, no gasps. Through squinted eyes she peered at her feet. The gravel, her shoes, her pants leg, it was all washed out by a light so pure and white it was like nothing this world could produce.

The light continued to shine for maybe thirty seconds then shut off as quickly as it had flashed on. Slowly, Juli removed her arm and looked around. The world was back to darkness with only the light of the moon to illuminate the town of Darlington. One by one, the people opened their eyes and turned back around.

Rob was lying in the middle of meadow, motionless. No darklings were to be found anywhere. They were gone. Banished by the light.

Tears sprang from Juli's eyes and ran down her cheeks. She started toward Rob when she was stopped by a movement across the meadow. A lone figure moved toward them, a man.

Her father.

He'd tear her limbs off and beat the old woman to death with them. Hatred filled him now. It was in control. Calling the shots. So Shields had thrown him a curveball and managed to drive off the underlings. Big deal. He didn't need them anyway. And besides, in doing so, Shields had managed to take his own life. It would have been more satisfying to extinguish Shields's existence himself, but what was done was done. The outcome was the same.

Now he'd have the pleasure of taking two more lives. And these would be with his bare hands.

The girl was walking toward him, shoulders back, head up. Trying to be brave. She looked so much like her mother it made him sick. He hated that woman. Enjoyed every moment of tormenting her.

The townspeople were huddling together like scared rabbits. They'd give him no trouble. Especially not after witnessing what he was about to do.

In the center of the clearing they met. Shields's lifeless corpse was to his left, no more than twenty feet away. The girl turned and looked at it, her cheeks wet with tears. How pathetic.

In one quick motion, he brought his right hand up and hit her along the side of the head. She lunged to the side but remained on her feet. Someone in the crowd of cowards began to cry. The girl hadn't even tried to block it or move out of the way. This was going to be fun.

The sound of someone being hit roused Rob to some form of consciousness. His body burned and throbbed, felt disjointed. His vision was blurred crimson with blood. He lifted his head from the ground and saw Juli and Wax Man facing off. He towered over her. Juli was bent to the right and held the side of her face. Wax Man said something, but Rob couldn't hear what it was. He was fading in and out. His head fell back to the ground, and pain burned along the nape of his neck. His eyes closed, and the outside world grew quiet.

Rob lifted his eyelids again. Juli was still there, standing her ground. He heard her say something but wasn't sure if his ears were working properly. It sounded like she said, "I forgive you."

Rob's eyes shut again; he was fading quickly. He heard Wax Man laugh.

Pulling his eyes open for an instant, he saw Wax Man raise an arm to strike Juli.

The side of Juli's face burned like fire where she had been struck. Her ear felt numb and dead. She'd said what she needed to say, that she forgave him, and meant it. The weight was lifted from her now. She no longer feared him, no longer bore that beastly burden.

The man who was once her father raised a fisted hand and cocked it, ready to strike again.

Juli braced herself. She would do nothing to deflect his hatred. Let what may come, come. She was ready.

But before he could release his arm and drive his fist into her face a gunshot boomed. Juli flinched.

The man's left shoulder jerked back as if he'd been punched, and he fell to the ground with a grunt.

Juli whipped her head around, looked past the assembled group of townsfolk, and found Nana on her front porch, rifle raised and resting along her cheek.

Movement in the meadow caught Juli's eye, and she turned back around. Rob. He was moving.

"Rob."

She took one step toward him when the man on the ground—the man who was once her father—moaned and turned to his side. Like a marionette with tangled strings he clambered to his feet in a series of awkward and painful movements. His left shoulder glistened with a dark fluid, and his arm hung like a broken tree limb.

Juli froze and looked into his eyes. There was nothing there but empty hatred.

With his right hand he wiped a string of saliva from his mouth and cursed loudly at Juli. His face twisted into an awful scowl, and he raised his right hand again.

Another shot cracked like thunder, and the man's head snapped back so violently Juli thought it had detached from the neck. He staggered back a few steps and righted himself. A hole about the size of a nickel, a few inches above his left eye, just below the hairline, seeped blood. He wavered, grinned, then fell to his left, landing in a loose heap.

Epilogue

One year later...

Rob Shields looked at himself in the mirror. He'd grown a beard to cover some of the scars, but the rest were impossible to hide. Five different surgeries with two different plastic surgeons had done wonders to restore his face, but he still thought he looked like a monster. Almost like a darkling. His nose leaned awkwardly to the right, his left eye was rimmed with shiny scar tissue, and his left ear was a mangled mess of cartilage. The rest of his body was covered with scars too, constant reminders of that night in Darlington.

They'd hailed him a hero, said he saved the town by sacrificing himself. But he didn't want to be a hero; he just wanted to be Rob Shields and get on with his life.

Juli snuck up behind him and wrapped her arms around his waist. "How'd you sleep last night?"

Rob rubbed his face with his hand. He still had dreams about Jimmy and Kelly almost every night, sometimes nightmares. "Not bad."

"Did you have any visitors?"

Rob nodded. "Jimmy. Do you think they'll ever stop?"

"Do you want them to stop?"

"Not really."

"Then probably not."

Rob turned around and held Juli in his arms. She'd been in the sun lately, helping the neighbors catch up on yard work, and her skin had turned a rosy pink. He leaned forward and kissed her.

"Have you called your parents lately?" she asked. Over the last year Rob and his parents had been slowly working through the past they shared. In many ways it was a painful experience, digging up the past and all the emotional baggage that went along with it, but it was also liberating to finally shine some light on the dark corners of the secrets they'd kept.

"Talked to them yesterday. They're doing fine."

"Good. I'm happy to see you getting close to them." She pointed back toward the kitchen. "I have some coffee for you," she said. "You can sit on the porch and watch the neighbors groom their yards."

"Ooh, now that's entertainment you can't get anywhere outside Darlington."

Rob kissed Juli again then walked through the house, picking up his coffee on the way, and headed out the front door. It was a nice morning, not too hot and low humidity. He sat in a wicker chair and propped his feet on a wooden stool. Across the street, Nana looked up from her garden and waved at him. He waved back. Down the street, Norm Tuckey was cruising around his front yard on his riding mower.

Darlington was a much different place now.

After finishing his coffee, Rob entered the house and found Juli in the kitchen. "When's your grandma coming over?"

"She said she'd be here about five."

"What are you making?"

"Roast beast and smashed potatoes and stewed carrots all

made the way my grandmother does it. She owns a restaurant, you know."

"So I've heard."

Rob set his mug in the sink. "I'm gonna go work on the house."

Following the incident a year ago, he'd spent two months recuperating from his wounds, both physically and emotionally, then another month regaining his strength. For the past nine months he'd been slowly repairing the house in Mayfield, Wilda's place, while renting a house in Darlington. He'd hoped to have it done by the time he and Juli were married, but that came and went a month ago, and the house still wasn't ready.

"What are you doing today?" Juli asked.

"The rain spouting. And if I have time, there's some boards on the back porch that need to be replaced. After that, it'll be ready."

"Ready to move in?"

"Ready to call our own."

Juli walked over to him and gave him a peck on the cheek. "Thank you for all your hard work. Be back in time for dinner."

He grabbed his car keys and kissed her back. "I'll follow the smell."

She patted his cheek. "Just don't let your smell follow you."

Rob laughed. "See ya, babe." Then he said the same thing they both said every time they parted ways: "Keep the light on."

Coming in 2011 from Mike Dellosso...

ONE

SAM TRAVIS AWOKE IN THE MIDDLE OF THE NIGHT, COLD and terrified.

The dream had come again. His brother. The shot.

You did what you had to do, son.

He sat up in bed and wiped the sweat from his brow.

Next to him, Molly stirred, grunted, and found his arm with her hand. "You OK, babe?"

"Yeah. I'm gonna go get some water."

"You sure?"

He found her forehead in the darkness and kissed it. "Yeah."

The house was as still and noiseless as a mausoleum. Sam made his way down the hall to Eva's room, floorboards popping quietly under his feet. He cracked the door and peeked in. The Tinker Bell night-light cast a soft purple hue over the darkened room, giving it almost a moonlit glow. Odd-shaped shadows blotted the ceiling like dark clouds against a darker sky. In her bed, Eva was curled into a tight ball, head off the pillow, blankets at her feet. Sam opened the door all the way, tiptoed to the bed, and pulled the covers to his daughter's shoulders. She didn't stir even the slightest. For a few hushed moments he stood there and listened to her low rhythmic breathing. The past six months had been hard on them all, but Eva had handled it surprisingly well. She was just a kid, barely seven, but displayed the maturity of someone much older. Sam never knew her faith, so much like her mother's, was so strong. His, on the other hand…

Outside her room he pulled the door closed, leaving it open a few inches.

Further down the hall he entered the bathroom where another night-light, this one a blue flower, reflected off the porcelain tub, sink, and toilet. He stood by the sink, turned on the water, and splashed some on his face. Remnants of the dream lingered and stuttered like a bad cell phone reception. Just images now, faces, twisted and warped. After toweling off, he studied himself in the mirror. In the muted light the scar running along the side of his head, just above his ear, didn't look so bad. His hair was growing back and covered most of it. Oddly, the new crop was coming in gray.

From downstairs Sam heard a voice say his name. A chill tightened his scalp along the arc of the scar.

He heard it again. His name. "Sammy." Not haunting or unnatural, but familiar, conversational. It was the voice of his brother. Tommy. He'd heard it a thousand times in his youth, a hundred ghostly times since the accident that had turned his brain to mush. The doctor called it an auditory hallucination.

Sam exited the bathroom and stood at the top of the staircase leading to the first floor. At the bottom was a foyer. Little light from the second floor spilled down the stairs, and the empty space below looked like a strange planet, distant and queer. Who knew what bizarre creatures inhabited that land and what malicious intentions they harbored? He shivered at the thought.

He heard the voice again—Tommy's—calling to him. "Sammy."

Descending the stairs, Sam suddenly felt something

dark, ominous, present in the house with him. He stopped and listened. Through the silence he could almost hear it breathing, and with each breath, each exhale, he could hear his name, now just a whisper.

He started down the stairs again, taking one at a time, holding the railing and trying his hardest to find the quiet places on the steps.

The voice was coming from the kitchen. At the bottom of the stairway he stared at the front door, half expecting it to fly open and Tommy to be standing there, half his head...

You did what you had to do, son.

He looked left into the dining room then right into the living room. Turning a one-eighty, he headed back down the hall toward the kitchen...and Tommy's casual voice. "Sammy."

At the doorway Sam stopped and listened again. Now he heard nothing. No breathing, no whispers, no Tommy. The kitchen held the aroma of the evening's meal— fettuccine Alfredo—like a distant memory.

"Tommy?" His voice sounded too loud and strangely hollow.

He had no idea why he said his brother's name. Tommy had been dead for—what?—twenty-one years. Thoughts of his death came to Sam's mind, images from the dream. And not just his death but how he died. A chill rushed over Sam, and he shuddered uncontrollably.

You did what you had to do, son.

Outside, way off in the distance, Sam heard a cannon blast. Living in Gettysburg, near the battlefields, the sound was common during the month of July when the reenactments were going on. But not in the middle of the night. And not in November. Another blast sounded, echoed across the fields, then the percussion of rifle shots followed by a volley of more cannons.

Sam walked back down the hall and opened the front door. He saw nothing but darkness beyond the light of the porch lamp, but the sounds were unmistakable. Guns popped and cracked in rapid succession, cannons boomed, men hollered and screamed, and horses whinnied and roared. The sounds of battle were all around him. He expected Eva and Molly to stir from their sleep and come tripping down the stairs at any moment, but it never happened. The house was as motionless and quiet as ever.

Crossing his arms over his chest, Sam stepped outside onto the porch. The air was cold and damp, the grass wet with dew. On the porch, three rotting jack-o'-lanterns grinned at him like a gaggle of toothless geezers. Thoughtlessly, he felt the bandage on his index finger. He'd slipped carving one of the pumpkins and gouged the side of his finger with the knife. Molly thought he should get stitches, but he'd refused. It was still tender but healing up well enough on its own. Here, outside, his finger throbbing only slightly now that he was paying attention to it, the loamy smell of dead, wet leaves surrounded him. Beyond the glow of the porch lamp the outside world was black and lonely. The sky was moonless.

Across the field and beyond the trees the battle continued but grew no louder. Sam gripped his head and held it with both hands. Was he going crazy? Had the accident triggered some weird psychosis? This couldn't be real. It had to be a concoction of his damaged brain. An auditory hallucination.

Suddenly the sounds ceased and silence ruled. Dead silence. Not the whisper of a gentle breeze. Not the skittering of dry leaves across the driveway. Not the creak of old, naked branches. Not even the hum of the power lines paralleling the road.

Sam went back inside and shut the door behind him. The deadbolt made a solid *thunk* as it slid into place. He didn't want to go back upstairs, didn't want to sleep in his own bed. What had just happened was very disturbing, and it scared him. Instead, he went into the living room, lay on the sofa, and clicked on the TV. The last thing he remembered before falling asleep was watching an old *Star Trek* rerun.

〓〓〓

Sam's eyes opened slowly and tried to adjust to the soft morning light that seeped in through the windows. He rolled to his side and felt something slide off his lap and fall to the floor with a papery flutter. He'd slept soundly on the sofa. Pushing himself to a sit, he looked out the window. The sun had not yet fully cleared the horizon, and the sky was a hundred shades of pink. The house felt cold and damp. The TV was off, and, leaning to his left, he saw that the front door was open. Maybe Molly was outside already this morning and didn't shut it behind her.

"Moll?" But there was no answer. "Eva?" The house was quiet.

Sam stood to see if Molly was outside and noticed a notebook on the floor, its pages splayed like the broken wings of a butterfly. Bending to pick it up, he recognized it as one of Eva's notebooks where she wrote her kid stories, tales of a dog named Max and horses with wings. Turning it over, he found a full page of writing. His writing. Before the accident, he'd often helped Eva with her stories, but he never wrote one himself. He'd thought about it many times but just never got around to doing it. There was always something more pressing, more important. Since his accident he'd had the time, home from work with nothing to do, but his brain just wasn't working that way. He couldn't focus, couldn't concentrate. His attention span was that of a three-year-old.

Sitting on the sofa he began to read the writing on the page, the writing of his own hand.

November 19, 1863

Captain Samuel Whiting, Pennsylvania Independent Light Artillery, Battery E

Now I am full of darkness. It has completely overshadowed me. My heart despairs; my soul swims in murky, colorless waters. I am not my own but a mere puppet on his hand. My intent is evil, and I loathe what the day will bring, what I will accomplish. But I must do it. My feet have been positioned, my course has been set, and I am compelled to follow. He is my commander now, Darkness.

I can already smell the blood on my hands, and it turns my stomach. But, strangely, it excites me as well. I know that is the darkness within me, bloodthirsty devil that it is. It desires death, his death (the Pres.), and I am beginning to understand why. He must die. He deserves nothing more than death. So much suffering has come from his words, his poLicies, his will. He speaks of freedom bUt has enslaved so many in this Cursed war.

See how the pen trembles in my hand. I move it not myself, but the darkness guides it as it guIdes my mind and will. Shadowy Figures encircle me. I can see them all about the room, spEcters moving as lightly as wisps of smoke. My hand trembles. I am oveRcome. I am their slave. His slave.

I am not my own.

I am not my own.
I am notnotnotnotnotnotnotno
    my own

Sam let the notebook slip from his hands and scrape across the hardwood floor. His skin puckered with goose-flesh. He thought of the battle sounds last night, of Tommy's voice and feeling the darkness around him—*the darkness*; he remembered the grinning jack-o'-lanterns, sliding the dead-bolt and hearing it click. He had no memory of turning off the TV, of opening the door, or of finding Eva's notebook and writing this nonsense.

What was happening to him?

He stood and went to the front door, barely aware of his feet moving under him, Eva's notebook, the one where she wrote her kid stories, still in his hand. At the door, one elbow resting on the jamb, he poked his head outside and scanned the front yard, listening. "Moll?" His voice was weak and broke mid-word.

There was no answer. If Molly was out there, she must have been around back.

Then, as if the ethereal battle from last night had landed in his front yard, a rifle shot split the morning air, and the window in the living room exploded in a spray of glass.

GET READY FOR MORE SPINE-TINGLING SUSPENSE!

If you liked *Darlington Woods*, you will love these...

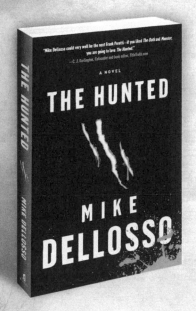

The Hunted

A killer is on the loose in Dark Hills. When his nephew disappears, Joe Saunders sets out on a search for the truth. Will he survive the final showdown?

978-1-59979-296-5 / $13.99

Scream

Eerie screams followed by untimely deaths catapult Mark Stone into a cat-and-mouse game with a killer in this fast-paced thriller.

978-1-59979-469-3 / $13.99

Visit your local bookstore. REALMS

FREE NEWSLETTERS
TO HELP EMPOWER YOUR LIFE

Why subscribe today?

☐ **DELIVERED DIRECTLY TO YOU.** All you have to do is open your inbox and read.

☐ **EXCLUSIVE CONTENT.** We cover the news overlooked by the mainstream press.

☐ **STAY CURRENT.** Find the latest court rulings, revivals, and cultural trends.

☐ **UPDATE OTHERS.** Easy to forward to friends and family with the click of your mouse.

CHOOSE THE E-NEWSLETTER THAT INTERESTS YOU MOST:

- Christian news
- Daily devotionals
- Spiritual empowerment
- And much, much more

SIGN UP AT: **http://freenewsletters.charismamag.com**

8178